secret

the agency
book one

offer

paige press

secret

the agency
book one

offer

STELLA GRAY

Paige Press
Leander, TX 78641

Ebook:
ISBN: 978-1-957647-68-5

Print:
ISBN: 978-1-957647-69-2

Editing: Amanda at Draft House Editorial Services
Proofing: Michele Ficht

The Charade Series: Books 1-3

The Bellanti Brothers

Unwilling Bride: A Bellanti Brothers Novella

Dante - Broken Series

Broken Bride

Broken Vow

Broken Trust

Broken Bride: The Complete Series

Marco - Forbidden Series

Forbidden Bride

Forbidden War

Forbidden Love

Forbidden Bride: The Complete Series

Armani - Captive Series

Captive Bride

Captive Rival

Captive Heart

Captive Bride: The Complete Series

The Agency Series

Secret Offer:

A Standalone Forbidden Romance

Cruel Offer:

A Standalone Fake Relationship Romance

(Coming April 2024)

ABOUT THIS BOOK

We'll marry her off to the highest bidder...but I'll pay the price.

The Agency is an open secret among men of a certain tax bracket.

You need a wife who understands your lifestyle? We'll hand-select options from the eligible daughters of men who'd love to cement a business alliance with you. Sometimes, the daughters don't even know they're being set up.

That's my specialty: I run a Caribbean resort so exclusive it doesn't even have a website, arranging meet-cutes between rich men and their future trophy wives.

I wasn't looking for love myself.

Blair found *me*, brooding on a beach the week before my next client showed up.

She made me break my rule about never going back for more. Over and over again. Our one-week stand was hotter than July on the island.

And then my client introduced me to the daughter who doesn't know he's signed her with the Agency. The woman I'm in charge of setting up with one of the men her father has chosen for her.

Blair.

PROLOGUE

SEBASTIAN

I SPEND HALF my time in a tropical paradise and the other half in NYC, but if you ask me which island I prefer? I'd go with Manhattan. Hands down. It isn't even close.

Here, everything is real. Grounded, gritty, and concrete —literally concrete. Sure, the city is a little short on palm trees and the standard dress code requires a few more layers than a bathing suit and flip-flops. But what New York lacks in laid back vibes, it more than makes up for in pure hustle, in sophisticated art and architecture, in culture, in world-class food and entertainment...need I go on? And most importantly, people here understand the intrinsic value of *time*. Monetary and otherwise.

Which is why I'm so on edge at the moment. I'm nursing a scotch at my usual table at Indigo, the members-only social club on the penthouse floor of The Regent Hotel where I was scheduled to meet with my three closest friends and business associates, oh, a good ten minutes ago. We hold our meetings here almost exclusively each month;

same time, same table. But those assholes are nowhere to be seen.

To be fair, Becker did manage to be his usual punctual self—as the brains of our business, he's always on top of every last detail, so naturally he was already here—but Nate and Theo are running late and neither had the decency to send so much as a text to give Becker or me a heads-up as to their ETA. Not that Beck wins all the brownie points; he's been on his phone ever since I arrived.

As we speak, he's pacing in front of the floor-to-ceiling windows, a frustrated hand working through his blond hair, so caught up in whatever's got him stressed that he isn't even appreciating the unparalleled view of the sunset over the Hudson River.

"Beck," I call out to him, tapping the face of my Girard-Perregaux watch with irritation.

Glancing over, he holds up his pointer finger and mouths *one minute*.

In response, I hold up my own finger. Not the pointer, either. Becker shakes his head, but I see him stifle a smirk as he turns his back to me again and paces farther away. Prick.

Don't get me wrong, I love the guy. Prick is a term of endearment in this case. And I'm sure that whatever he's got going on, whoever is on the other end of that phone call, it's related to something urgent. Not that I expect him to tell me anything about it once he hangs up.

I've known the guy for years, yet the man remains an enigma. He's the perfect business partner and an exceptional wingman, true, but the details of his past and anything too personal about him are virtually off limits. MBA from Yale, top of his class, fellow co-owner of The

Quattuor Group—the same Quattuor Group that owns this hotel, as it were—the man is literally a genius, and a visionary.

But has he ever bragged about anyone he's been to bed with? Do I know the first thing about his family? Or even what the guy does for fun? Not a clue. He's a closed book. Not that I have room to judge, but I wasn't always this reticent. Beck's been a mystery since day one.

The phone call that he's on is irritating me less and less by the second, though. Not because I no longer care that he's blowing off our meeting, but because I can see that something's seriously getting under his skin, and my interest is piqued. Becker is doing little to hide the emotions playing across his face—displeasure, annoyance, reluctant agreement—probably because he doesn't expect anyone to be watching him this intently.

Truthfully, I'm not sure why I'm observing him, except that his behavior is so out of character. Beck is usually the kind of guy who gives you his undivided attention when he's with you. The fact that he's so distracted by the call is telling.

Is he talking to a new contact? Is it agency business? Did a deal go south? Is it a woman?

My intuition has the hair on the back of my neck rising. Something is definitely up.

"Who's Beck on the phone with?"

Nate, our Chief Financial Officer and unofficial Deal Maker Extraordinaire, slides into the leather chair across from me, his dark hair slicked back and his suit impeccable. He waves at the cocktail waitress, signaling for what the entire staff already knows is his signature drink—a Negroni.

"How should I know?" I say. "You're late, by the way."

He checks his watch. "It's barely eight minutes after. Relax."

"This is a business meeting and you're tardy. It's a sign of disrespect," I point out.

"Disrespect? What are you, the mob, Sebastian?" He laughs. "Cut me some slack. I had to work late securing a new client—"

"By which you mean, you just finished a round of drinks with another investment banker."

"Not even gonna deny it, and you'll get on your knees and thank me when the ink on the contract is dry and I send her over to you. She's got twins, man. That's double the fee."

Before I can toss back a retort, the waitress materializes at his elbow with the Negroni. "Your drink, Mr. Windemere."

"Perfect timing," Nate says, flashing a winning smile at her.

"Like you know anything about that," I snark.

She returns his smile, leaning over just enough to put her perfume-scented cleavage on display as she places the drink in front of him. "Can I get either of you anything else?"

"Why don't you circle back in five," Nate says. "Appreciate you, Naomi. Don't work too hard."

The waitress—Naomi, apparently—sashays away, swinging her ass for Nate's benefit, but he isn't watching. That thing he just did wasn't flirting, see. The guy is just flat-out good at handling people, making them feel like he's interested in them from the get-go. He's charming, likeable, and he plays by his own rules. I swear he's got more connections than the bus terminal at Port Authority.

"How do you do it, man?" I ask.

"Do what?" Nate says, pushing up his glasses before he takes a long drink of his Negroni.

"You always remember names and faces and fucking drink orders, and which gallery you met someone at. Who's got a kid in Little League, who's looking at real estate in Cape Cod."

He shrugs. "Honestly? It's easy for me. I guess because I find other people interesting. They tell me their stories and I just...pay attention. It's a hell of a lot more fun than handling QG's financials, that's for sure."

"You ever wonder what his story is?" I tip my head toward Becker.

Just then, Theo rolls up to us with a drink already in hand. Tan and athletic, he tends to give off the vibe that he's dying to shed his bespoke suit and bolt into the first lifting gym or half-marathon he can find. Of the four of us, he's the youngest and most easygoing, yet he runs The Regent like a well-oiled machine, despite the fact that managing an elite luxury hotel in the heart of Lincoln Square is more or less an act of insanity. There are just too many goddamn logistics. Not to mention having to pamper and please hundreds of wealthy, finicky guests 24/7, wrangle employees, schedule maintenance. There are fucking floral arrangements to approve, financial what-have-yous to keep tabs on.

I guess it'd be more accurate to say Theo's easygoing until he's not. The man knows how to get shit done.

Theo's mouth quirks as he drops into a chair. "Becker? He's an asshole. That's all the story you need to know."

I shake my head and reach for my scotch. "Besides that."

Nate glances over at me with an assessing gaze. "Why are you asking? Getting tired of the skeletons in your own closet? Looking in other people's closets now?"

"Give him a break," Theo says around his drink. "Sebastian's just coming out of the off-season. The man's probably had way too much time to think."

"He doesn't have that kind of time anymore," Becker says as he walks up to the table, slipping his phone into the pocket of his blazer.

"How's that?" I ask.

Becker grins, but there's no humor in his icy blue eyes. "Because I have a very important job for you, Sebastian."

I don't like the look of that grin. Something tells me this isn't the kind of job I'm going to enjoy. I brace myself for the worst-case scenario as Beck eases into the last chair.

"I'm listening," I say, not bothering to lower my voice.

Under normal circumstances, I'd be more discreet. But Indigo is only open to clients we've worked with before, or those considering using our consulting services in the future. Not only that, but there's a strict NDA that goes along with the membership fee that these people have paid for the privilege of being here in the establishment. Every set of lips in here is sealed. Hence why the four of us so often meet here at the club when we have business to hash out.

Becker turns to me, but Naomi reappears with a scotch in hand. "Your Glenfiddich, Mr. Colburn."

He nods, and the rest of us decline a second round. We're here to talk shop, not get buzzed. As soon as the cocktail waitress retreats, all eyes are on Beck again.

"So what's the job?" I prompt. "Is this related to the call you were on?"

Becker frowns and says, "No. A ghost from my past just called. And she wants a favor. But you need not concern yourself with it."

I glance at Theo and Nate, lifting a brow. Skeleton, meet closet.

"Oh, really? What kind of ghost?" Nate prods.

"The kind I prefer not to discuss," Becker says shortly.

"Does she have something on you? Is she someone we should be worried about?" I ask, shamelessly fishing for information as my curiosity gets the best of me. "You seem pretty worked up."

Becker picks up his scotch and downs a generous swallow. "As I said, it's none of your concern, Sebastian. Just make it an early night and get your bags packed. You've got a flight to catch to the island in the morning."

This gets everyone's attention. No one is scheduled to go to the island until next week.

"But the Tisdale match isn't slotted for another eight days," Theo says, proving he's well apprised of the agency's schedule even though it doesn't fall under his purview. "Did it get moved up?"

I'm confused, too. The Tisdales are important clients, but they're no higher up on the VIP list than any of the other rich and influential families for whom The Quattuor Group plays matchmaker. Which is the specific kind of consulting we do. We mediate relationships. Marriages.

7

Arrangements, let's call them. And we're paid handsomely to do so. But it's a delicate task, one that relies on timing just as much as it does human connection, and as such, the agency's schedule is set in stone. There are too many moving parts for us to just shift potential matches around on a whim.

"This isn't for the Tisdales," Beck says, addressing me. "I need you to fly out early to train the new concierge. You'll need at least a week to show her the ropes. She's... unqualified, frankly."

"And you hired her why, exactly?" I say, annoyance tinging my voice.

"Her brother and I go way back," Beck says. "I'm doing him a solid. Plus, she's hot. I'm sure she'll be quite popular with the guests."

"Right. I'll handle it, then," I say, and the only reason I don't fight him on it like I want to is because I'm still chewing on the phrase 'go way back,' and thinking about how I can pump this new concierge for whatever info she has about her brother and Becker's past. Skeletons, I'm coming for you.

"Good," Becker says. "We're done here, then."

As if on cue, the lights dim, and a spotlight hits the baby grand on the corner stage. A woman with a swoop of dark hair over one eye and deep red lips begins to play an intro, something soulful and vaguely familiar, and it doesn't take long before I recognize the melody. It's a pop song from a few years ago, with gut wrenching lyrics that I know will be stuck in my head all night.

"They say that time's supposed to heal you..."

Nope. Not doing this. Time to go.

I push back from the table and get to my feet. Tossing back what's left of my drink, I give the others a nod.

"It's been a long day. I need to get home and pack," I say.

I can feel my heart pounding in my chest as I make my way out the door.

Maybe heading to the island a week early is exactly what I need.

1

BLAIR

"So what do you think our chances are at getting dibs on any of the college players from Florida State? Specifically Ty Jamieson, but honestly I'd even be happy with—"

"Ugh, Blair, must we?" Brooke peels a cucumber slice from one eye so she can squint a half-glare at me from the adjacent massage table.

"Must we what?" I ask my BFF innocently.

"Must we sit here and discuss boring business crap when we're on this luxurious vacation?"

I sit up like a shot, my seaweed body wrap rustling. "It's not business crap, it's the MLB Draft! This is our team's big chance to level up the roster. I'd hardly call that boring."

Though I've followed the draft every year since I was a kid, this will be the first time I'll have a chance to actively contribute to the club's wish list of potential rookies. I've been watching the up and comers all season, checking stats daily, following them on social media to learn their personalities as well as their professional abilities. While the team's general manager has the final say on all our picks,

11

the head coach and the owner carry a lot of weight as well, and I'm sure Dad will listen to what I have to say.

"It's still work-related. Don't pretend you're mulling picks purely because you love the game."

"I *do* love the game," I point out. "And who wouldn't be excited about Jamieson? His fastballs clock in at over ninety miles an hour, and his sliders—"

"Tell me what his butt looks like in baseball pants, and then we can talk," Brooke interrupts, popping the cucumber in her mouth and crunching on it.

"Okay, you want to talk baseball pants, I am all about the shortstop from ASU, because damn."

She laughs. "But seriously. Your family *owns* the New York Rockets. You're not excited about the team's potential new players, you're excited about the team's potential new dollar signs."

Laughing, I insist, "I can be excited about both! Besides, you know I'm not trying to look like some entitled nepo baby walking into this job without any real knowledge or passion for the game. My family's not that kind of team owner. And how lucky am I to be starting a career that's such a perfect mix of business and pleasure? Of course I can't stop yapping about it."

"I get that," she says, "but you're gonna have all the time in the world to talk at me about baseball stuff once you're working for your dad. For now, let's just enjoy our last summer of freedom before we're forced to put our shiny new business degrees to use. Look around you, boo. We. Are. In. Paradise."

Technically, we're in the resort's fancy spa, so there's not much to look around at besides the bamboo paneled walls of our private treatment room and the ceramic diffusers pumping lemongrass-scented mist into the air. But Brooke's right. We've been here for three days now, riding the high of our graduation from NYU Stern, and I haven't once stopped thinking about my future role with the franchise.

Not that I'm entirely certain what that role is going to be just yet. I still need to sit down with my father and hammer out the details. But even if I'm not sure *exactly* which department I'll get placed in, working to support the Rockets has been my dream for as long as I can remember, so no matter where I end up, whether it's operations or legal or public relations, I intend to shine. I've got to start somewhere if I'm going to work my way up and eventually take over as team owner whenever my dad retires.

"Why don't we get out of this seaweed and see about those mani-pedis you mentioned earlier?" I say, grabbing the cucumber off Brooke's other eye and taking a bite. "Then we can figure out what we're doing for lunch. Appetizers and daiquiris at the pool bar? Maybe grab something to go from one of the hotel restaurants and picnic on the beach? Or we could try someplace new in town; I heard there's a Japanese place that has sushi boats."

"Now you're talking," Brooke says, her mud-masked face lighting up with a grin.

I love Brooke like she's family. We've been friends forever, roommates since our first semester of college, and after four years of working our asses off, we're spending a whole week on our own at an all-inclusive resort to celebrate our hard-earned BS degrees in Business, Technology, and Entrepreneurship. But as much as I love her spontaneity and fun-loving nature, I'm also of the mindset that it's time to get focused and start acting like the badass, take-charge women we've been molding ourselves into. Brooke is chasing her own dreams, too. She's already accepted a job offer from a major fashion merchandiser with a mid-six-figure salary attached. Soon enough, that whole company is going to be eating out of her hand. Just you watch.

Forty minutes later, I'm admiring the polish on my nails as I rest my hands under the dryer.

"Cute red," Brooke says, nodding with approval. "It's like a cross between fire engine and cherry. Very va-voom."

It's not my usual choice—I prefer classic French tips—but today I felt like picking a strong color. I'm a woman of the world now, soon to step fully into my power, and I'm ready to be seen that way. By everyone, of course, but most especially by my parents. They arrive in a few days, and I'm hoping my dad will finally be amenable to discussing my next steps with the family business.

Originally, the plan was for me to fly to the island with Mom and Dad so we could spend seven days at some super high-end private resort that you have to be a member to even book in the first place. Which is the kind of graduation gift anyone would be grateful for, yes, but it wasn't quite what I had in mind. I'm sure the other members are all my parents' age, and they probably do nothing but talk about their investments and play golf.

However.

Before I accepted my parents' gift—which honestly sounded like it might be more of a vacation for them than for me—I negotiated an additional week beforehand, just for me and Brooke, at a nearby and much more famous resort on the island, Espadrilles. It was step one of my journey toward claiming my own personal power, and it took some convincing, but Mom and Dad finally agreed to my demands.

Which, thank God. So far, I've had a blast just doing touristy things and spending some R&R time with Brooke. Our first day here, we rode the minibus around town, drank countless Mai Tais, and danced in the street while local musicians worked the crowd into a frenzy. The next day, we joined one of Espadrilles' day trips so we could go swimming with dolphins. Then today, we had an early breakfast and went snorkeling at sunrise, before too many people showed up and scared the fish away. I'm not sure what's on the agenda for tonight, but I just know it's going to be amazing.

And the best part? Without my parents' watchful eyes on me, I can enjoy myself fully, do whatever I want, party all I want. This pre-vacation with Brooke is a wholly judgment-free zone. Once Mom and Dad get here, I'll have to be on my best, most responsible, most adult behavior.

Now that Brooke and I are properly seaweeded, mud masked, exfoliated, and polished, we discard our spa robes and head for the showers. Brooke always takes a few extra minutes to perfect her hair and makeup, so I'm already dressed and scrolling on my phone in the lobby when she runs up to me with her robe and spa slippers back on.

I do a double take. "Hey. Aren't we heading out for lunch?"

Her voice drops conspiratorially low. "Actually, it turns out that the superhot masseuse just had a last-minute cancellation, so I *may* have booked myself into that time slot. You don't mind, do you?"

"Would this just so happen to be the same superhot masseuse you were flirting with at the pool bar last night?" I tease.

"As a matter of fact, it is. Are you cool to find lunch on your own?"

"Definitely. Take all the time you need. I won't wait up."

"You're the best!" she squeals, her cheeks flushing. "I'll make it up to you, I promise. Maybe we can try that sushi boat place for dinner or something? I'll text you later." She darts away and all I can do is smile in her wake.

My stomach growls, reminding me that I haven't eaten since 7 a.m. As I wander outside into the bright sunshine, I consider where to eat solo. There is no lack of options on this island, from the five different restaurants inside this resort to the myriad of oceanside bars, cafés, and restaurants lining the beach. I decide to just start walking toward the beaches and see where my feet take me.

The sand is hot, but the air is cool, there's not a cloud in the perfect blue sky, and the salty breeze blows my sundress around my knees. I'm grateful for the floppy woven hat that Brooke made me buy at one of the boutiques yesterday, because my sunglasses are back in our hotel room. The scent of sunscreen mixes with the smell of fried seafood and Accra fritters, and fresh sliced mango and coconut. All the vendors I pass shout exuberantly about their edible wares. I feel like I've stepped right into a post-card. God, Sophie would have loved it here. The beach was always my older sister's favorite place to be.

As I weave through the crowd, overwhelmed by all my culinary choices, I see one person after another walking by with huge bowls of fresh conch salad—pronounced 'conk,' of course—a local Bahamian specialty. When I stop a couple to ask them where they got their food, they point me in the direction of a small corner restaurant with a bright blue awning, swearing the place serves the best conch on the island. That decides it for me; I've got to have it. Mouth watering, I get in line at the restaurant's to-go window, because the place is so packed that the wait for a table is almost an hour.

When I finally get my salad, fragrant with lime juice and peppers and cilantro, I can't believe how big the portion is. It's heavy in my hands and has two forks stuck in it. Oh well. I can eat for two.

I smile as I wander back onto the sand in search of the perfect picnic spot, past families sprawled on towels and parents chasing children in neon bathing suits, still other kids running around screaming and playing and kicking the sand. So much for R&R. Farther down the beach, I see a less populated stretch, and just beyond that there's a rocky cove that's practically deserted. Jackpot.

Making my way toward the cove, I pass more families, and couples who are clearly here on romantic vacations. Some frolic in the water together, some rub each other down with suntan lotion, others just kiss under the shade of their tasseled beach umbrellas. I'm not jealous, but maybe a little wistful. It would be nice to have someone to hold hands with on this beach, someone to nestle against after an exhilarating ocean swim when both of us are properly sunbaked and bone tired.

Sure, I dated in college, but those were just casual flings. My coursework kept me so busy that I didn't have time to engage in anything more serious, or at least that's what I told myself. Honestly, I probably would have been open to a real commitment if I had actually met the right person, but I never really fell for anybody. Dating in business school tends to be kind of...business-y. There's lots of flirting and lots of hookups, but it's basically transactional. You meet, you get a drink, you maybe fuck, and then you possibly exchange numbers in case you want to do it again sometime. That's about it. Anyone who wants to be in a serious relationship usually already is. In my experience, the single guys were way more interested in finding a shiny trophy than an actual partner.

Brooke, on the other hand, had no problem being a trophy girlfriend. Probably because she was just as proud to have her own trophy to show off. She was constantly getting involved in these epic, fiery entanglements with all the hottest guys in our program, which lasted anywhere from a few weeks to a few months at a time, and I've lost count of how many times she's told me that she's definitely met The One. But I kind of love that for her, and I don't mind living vicariously through her torrid affairs. One of us has to be having lots of hot, gossip-worthy sex, right?

Meanwhile, my parents made no secret of the fact that they hoped I'd find a good match in business school—that's where they met, after all, at Harvard. The two of them were convinced I'd come home for Thanksgiving break one year with a winner. A man with the potential to be as successful and wealthy as me, and intelligent enough to keep up as well.

Boy were they disappointed when I didn't bring home a single prospect. Honestly, I never understood why my parents were so invested in my relationship status, or lack thereof. Getting married and starting a family isn't even on my radar yet, but Mom loves to frequently remind me how fast the years go by and how I don't want to wake up single and childless at forty, when all the good men will be taken, and it'll be too late to freeze my eggs. Just what I want to think about when I'm barely twenty-two.

Luckily, Dad isn't as high-strung about the whole thing as Mom is. He knows I'm eager to work for the team and make my own way in the world. He's the one who encouraged that ambition, actually. Never once has he dissuaded me from it.

Mom has been more dismissive when I talk about my career dreams, but I think it's just because she still sees me as a younger version of herself; the kind of woman who has the brains and the drive to be successful but then realizes she's simply happier letting her husband take the reins— and all the responsibility that goes along with it—while she plays a supporting role instead. There's nothing wrong with that path, either. It's just not who I am. Not that I want to be alone forever, either.

Shaking my head, I realize that Brooke is right. I need to get out of my own head. Here I am, on one of the most beautiful beaches in the world, and I'm getting all broody about nothing. I should be enjoying the beauty all around me. Living in the now. I just need to find a nice, shady palm tree to stretch out under. Maybe sneak a peek at the socials of a few up-and-coming outfielders I've been following.

I squint into the distance and spot the perfect palm at

the other end of the cove, a whole grove of them, in fact. White sand stretches out ahead of me as I beeline toward the grove. By the time I reach the group of palms, the sound of the waves crashing in my ears, the breeze cooling the sweat that's starting to trickle down my lower back, I'm a little winded but exhilarated. I'm feeling more like my old self again. Someone who's ready to grab her future by the balls and has the bright red manicure to prove it.

As I step into the dappled shade, I realize there's a man sitting against the trunk of one of the palms. He's staring out at the ocean, his dark hair ruffling in the wind. I quickly note his incredible jawline and the way his T-shirt clings to his broad shoulders, but when he turns his head to look at me, it's his eyes—green, sharply intelligent, but far away, like he's lost in thought—that take my breath away.

"Hello," I say hesitantly.

He doesn't respond.

I try again, forcing more pep into my voice this time. "I, um, didn't think anyone was over here. Not that that's a problem or anything," I add, his hotness making me babble. "Ha—I mean, I was just coming over here to sit down and eat my lunch. Do you want to share?"

I hold out one of the forks to him and laugh out of sheer nervousness, trying to gauge how awkward I'm being by the expression on his face. But I can't read him.

His gaze sweeps me slowly and my smile wavers.

He's handsome, I think. *Really, really handsome. Hot damn.*

And I've just made a complete and utter fool of myself.

2

SEBASTIAN

THE TRANQUILITY of the turquoise Caribbean waters and pristine white sand stretched out before me should be giving me a dose of oxytocin, should be lowering my blood pressure, should be lifting the weight of the world right off my shoulders. But it's not. The beauty of the scenery doesn't have the power to affect me the way it used to. Not since Rachel died.

There's something just...flat-out offensive about being surrounded by this kind of paradise when she can't be here to enjoy it with me.

And sure, I've been promised by countless well-meaning friends and family members that she's enjoying her own kind of paradise now, but fuck that. Assurances that your dearly departed is having a great time in the after-life don't do shit to make the ones left behind feel any better. It's been three years now, and not a day goes by that I don't miss her so much it hurts.

People told me that time would heal my wounds, that I'd eventually be able to move on, but the loss feels just as fresh and raw as it did the day I got the call that ripped my life apart. I still wake up some mornings and forget that she's gone. And then it hits me all over again like a fucking sledgehammer to the gut when I roll over in bed and find nothing but cold, empty space.

I can still hear her laugh in my mind, full-throated and infectious. It takes zero effort to recall the feel of her hand in mine, or the absolute agony splitting my chest as I numbly listened to the tearful eulogies on the day of her memorial. No matter how irreversibly gone she is, she's always with me, and so is the reality that I'll never see her again.

I've learned to welcome moments of solitude, when I don't have to act like I'm fine and put on my brave face for the people around me. But whether I'm alone or with a group, what I've noticed is, the good times hurt the most. That's when her absence hits me hardest. When I'm reminded of the fact that I can't share this life with her. Thank God I've got my job to hide behind.

The Quattuor Group's matchmaking business has grown exponentially since we started, to the point where its revenue is about to surpass the millions we make on The Regent Hotel. We've got a steady stream of influential and wealthy clients lined up to utilize our "consulting" services. There are other matchmaking companies out there, of course, but our pool of matches—CEOs, real estate moguls, entrepreneurs, celebrities, tech giants, politicians, you name it—is truly exceptional. As is our reputation. Plus, everyone signs an ironclad nondisclosure agreement and we're unfailingly discreet, so clients know that their privacy is protected at all times, both before and after a match is made.

I'm the one who runs the resort where the magic happens, pulling all the strings required to play Cupid between the matches, and I take that role seriously. In my experience, successful matchmaking has more to do with data analysis than fairy dust, and I have an outstanding track record of arranging compatible matches between people with common interests, values, and life goals. Compatibility is the best way to facilitate a happy, long-lasting union. But what we do goes way beyond harmonious partnerships, because the whole *raison d'être* of the business is preserving legacies, ensuring that families with wealth and status are able to protect that wealth and status.

With few exceptions, our modus operandi is this: high-powered families come to us offering a marriageable bachelorette, and Nate facilitates the glad-handing and initial vetting and contracts. Once the girl is approved, I do my research and then select three to five potential matches and invite them to the island to meet her. After the meetings take place (separately, of course, and in a way that feels organic) and the sparks fly, an auction is set, and the interested matches bid against each other for the bachelorette. The agency and the bachelorette's family split the auction proceeds.

Between the consulting fees paid by bachelorettes' families, retainer fees paid by matches, and the final auction proceeds, The Quattuor Group's matchmaking business is swimming in revenue. We also vet mistresses, third parties for throuples, and more. All a client has to do is reach out and let us know what they're looking for, and we make it happen.

But no matter how much I try to bury myself in work, I'm not the man I used to be. My business partners know it, I know it. I'm sure Beck, Nate, and Theo are waiting for me to come back around, revert to my old self again, but I don't know if I ever will. In a lot of ways, that man died when Rachel did.

I wonder if I'll ever manage a smile that isn't forced again, if I'll ever laugh honestly again...

At the sound of footsteps approaching in the sand, I turn my head, getting ready to inform the intruder that this is my resort's private beach, which is clearly stated on multiple signs, only to find myself looking up at a startled girl in a sun hat and a gauzy yellow dress, carrying a takeout container.

Early twenties, blond, with a hesitant smile on her heart-shaped face. She's gorgeous, but the female tourists who come to this island tend to be. Pretty faces are a dime a dozen around here.

"Hello," she says.

When I don't respond, she doesn't take the hint to leave. Instead, she pulls her shoulders back, doubles down on the friendliness, and keeps talking. Something about wanting to eat her lunch under the shade, but I'm barely listening. My mind is still miles away.

Or at least, it is until she lets out a kind of exhilarated laugh, a little too loud, a little bit awkward, sounding so fucking much like Rachel in this moment that my heart skips a beat and all I can do is stare.

I realize she's holding out a fork to me, and that I still haven't said a single word to her.

"It's a cock salad," she informs me.

A smirk tugs at my lips as my inner fifth grader instantly comes out. "Pardon?"

"Conch salad? I was saying we could share?" she says, sounding less sure of herself, and I wonder if she realizes that the word 'cock' just came out of her mouth not two seconds ago. Stabbing the fork back into the bowl, she says, "You know what? I should just go. I'm clearly disturbing you."

"Actually, wait. Maybe you could tell me more about that salad," I say, unable to stop myself from teasing her.

Her sunny smile comes back, full force. "Oh, well, it's easy to find all over the island. It's like a ceviche. There's no shortage of the main ingredient around here!"

"I would have to agree with that statement," I say seriously.

She comes a little closer, and any hint of irritation I was feeling completely dissolves. There's just something so guileless and appealing about her, the exact opposite of the women I usually spend my time with. Not that I'm sizing her up for another meaningless one-night stand, of course, but still. She's got this wholesome quality that's...frankly, disarming. I can't possibly tell her to fuck off now.

Besides, my resort guests aren't due until next week anyway. She might as well take advantage of the private beach and enjoy it while she can.

"Do you want to try a bite?" she asks. "It's got a great mouth feel."

Scooping some onto the fork, she tries to hand it to me,

but I wave it away. "I'm sure the *cock salad* feels great in the mouth, but I actually just ate."

"Oh my God." Her eyes go wide, and a blush tints her high cheekbones. "I really said that before, didn't I? Cock salad. Jesus." She laughs again. "Brooke is never going to let me live this down."

"Brooke?"

"My best friend. She's actually on a date right now, which is why I'm having lunch by myself." She shakes her head. "Anyway! This was fun. I'm leaving now."

"Stay," I blurt without thinking, patting the sand next to me. "Have a seat and enjoy your not-cock salad."

"I...okay. Sure. I will," she says brightly.

Smoothing her skirt, she sits next to me, keeping a polite distance between us. When she digs into the food and takes a huge bite, I hear her quiet sigh of pleasure. Goosebumps rise on my arms, and despite the inches that separate us, I feel her proximity like a physical touch. It's a primal thing, nothing more.

"So what brings you and your friend to the island?" My tone comes out flat and uninterested, but that's my default setting. In reality, I wouldn't be asking if I wasn't curious.

"A very hard-earned vacation. We just graduated."

"High school?" I tease.

"Ha. No. NYU."

"Congrats. That's impressive," I say, meaning it.

"I know. And what better time to run away from real life and fly to some tropical dreamland to just beach out and relax, you know?"

I nod in agreement, even though being here is obviously more business than pleasure for me.

"I couldn't help but notice how serious you were looking before," she goes on. "Let me guess—you're not here for vacation."

"Work."

"Ah. That's why you're so scowly."

She shoots me another grin as she chews, and it takes any hint of insult out of her words.

"Well, I think you're lucky," she says. "I definitely wouldn't mind my office view looking out over the Caribbean every day."

"Fair point," I say. "Have you received any job offers with that shiny new degree yet?"

"As a matter of fact, I'm all set. I know exactly where I'm going."

I get the sense she doesn't want to elaborate, so I don't push. I'm trying really hard not to be the asshole that she doesn't seem to see me as, even though everyone else does. Because maybe I can just enjoy a few minutes today where I don't feel...broken. It's worth a shot, anyway. And it's not hard to appreciate the simple pleasure of sitting next to a beautiful woman like this. Taking in the sounds of the waves, the gulls, the palm fronds rattling softly in the breeze.

"Sure you don't want a bite?" she asks. "It's almost gone. Last chance to take me up on this amazing offer for some authentic cock salad." She wiggles a forkful in front of me.

Relenting, I lean slightly toward her and open my mouth. Our eyes catch as she brings the utensil to my lips, and I accept her offering.

"Mmm," I groan. The chopped vegetables and conch

meat are well seasoned with a spicy-sweet dressing that surprises me. "You're right, it does have a good mouth feel."

She laughs and sets the empty bowl on the sand. Gazing out at the water, we sit in amicable silence, just soaking up the atmosphere. After a few minutes, I subtly glance over at her and notice her fingers drawing figure eights in the sand, her nails a glossy red. My cock gives an involuntary twitch. Nothing screams sex, power, and confidence in a woman more than the color red.

I force myself to look away and get my animal instincts under control. Maybe I'll walk into town after work later and see if I can find somebody to bring back to my suite. I've clearly got some unchecked testosterone that needs to be released.

"You must be thinking about work, Mr. Scowl. You've got that serious look on your face again."

"Work is the farthest thing from my mind, actually."

Our eyes lock again, and this time the flare of heat between us is undeniable.

She licks her lips, and then takes a breath. "I—"

A cell phone rings, breaking the tension, and she mumbles a flustered apology as she digs the phone out of her pocket.

"Hey, you. I'm just sitting on the beach having my lunch," she says, sounding a little breathless. "Happy hour? Yeah, I'll come over. Sounds good. See you in a bit. Bye."

She ends the call and tucks the phone away. "Sorry. My friend says there's quite the party going on at Hurricane Sammy's. I'm gonna go meet her there."

I force myself not to cringe. Hurricane Sammy's is a dumb famous tourist bar, a loud and obnoxious place that locals avoid and that I wouldn't be caught dead in. But I tamp down my inner caveman that wants to tell her she shouldn't go, that I've got some better ideas for how she could spend her evening. She's young, she's on vacation, and she should enjoy her time here however she pleases.

"Have fun," I say. "It's good you're going early, by the way. The place is standing room only by nine every night. It can get a little wild once the dueling pianos get going."

She arches a brow. "You sound like you know the place well. Would you like to join us?"

"Not my scene. But thanks for the invite."

"Yeah. Of course."

Digging a hand into her pocket again, she pulls out a tube of lip gloss and then tears off an edge of the takeout container. I watch, amused, as she carefully writes her number on the thick cardboard with the gloss and then hands it to me.

"That's so you can text me if you change your mind about the bar," she says.

"Will do."

She stands up, collecting her trash and shaking sand off her dress. "Well. Off I go. It was nice to meet you, Scowl."

"You too, Sunshine."

"Sunshine?" She laughs. "I like that. Hope I see you around."

I nod, unable to keep myself from watching her walk away.

3

BLAIR

"So how was lunch?" Brooke asks.

"Good. More than good. I got the best conch salad from this great restaurant by the beach..."

I'm about to blurt out the whole story about meeting Scowl, but something stops me. I'm not sure what it is. Maybe I just like having a secret for now. Plus, I know the second I start going over all the details with Brooke, I'll be overanalyzing every look and line of conversation. I'd rather just let the butterflies I have last as long as possible without worrying that I only imagined the spark I felt.

"How about you? Good massage?" I ask, steering the focus back to her. "You've definitely got a glow about you."

She sighs. "I mean, the massage was fine and all, but he wouldn't take my number. Says it's against company policy for employees to date guests. So lame."

"Maybe it's for the best," I say. "You're more into the rule-breaker type anyway."

"I know! It's whatever. Plenty of fish, right?"

"Totally."

She leans her elbow on the bar, eyes roaming the crowd in search of her next potential conquest. Meanwhile, she's completely ignoring the Frooty Fishbowl drink that we ordered to share, which the bartender served us in a round, one-gallon fishbowl filled with some boozy concoction that tastes more like Kool-Aid than alcohol. Even for a themed drink, it's seriously over the top. Fish-shaped gummy candies float around in the bright blue liquid, and it's garnished with a maraschino cherry, a pineapple slice, and a few lime wedges. There are also a handful of paper umbrellas, and two straws that look like fishing poles. But Brooke is so busy casing the room that she hasn't even touched the drink yet, and I've barely sipped it either.

I bravely suck down a few swallows and then slide the bowl closer to Brooke.

"It's your turn," I tell her, still grimacing at the melted popsicle taste.

She takes a drink, but she's clearly distracted by someone on the dance floor already. Tracking her gaze, I find a silver fox of a man in a finely tailored linen shirt looking right at her. He's got to be in his late forties at least, with a sexy layer of stubble on his square jaw, gray hair at his temples, and deep lines in his forehead. The way he holds himself screams confidence. Exactly Brooke's speed.

"Looks like hot daddy is checking you out," I tease. "You gonna make a move?"

"Hell yes. I'm going to climb him like a tree. If you hear the ambulance come, it's because he got a head injury from breaking the bed, I gave him a heart attack, or both."

It might be funnier if I thought she was kidding.

"Please don't make me relive our senior year in college when the paramedics showed up at two a.m. because your boyfriend had an anaphylactic reaction to your edible underwear."

Brooke shrugs, still entirely focused on hot daddy. "That wasn't my fault. He never said he was allergic to strawberries."

Taking another sip of the ridiculous drink, I let my eyes roam the patrons of the packed bar, looking for a pair of soulful green eyes. But of course Scowl isn't here. Boo.

I've never been drawn to moody guys, but this was different. He wasn't just having a bad day. He seemed like he was carrying something heavy on his shoulders. Something real. Something dark. Which I know all too much about, ever since...well. I won't think about that right now. But I can't stop wondering what happened to him.

Unless I'm just projecting my own feelings onto the guy, reading too far into that look on his face. I don't think I am, though. The way he was sitting there all alone, gazing off into the ocean, totally lost in his head even after I started talking to him, it was like he was...haunted. That's the word.

Maybe it sounds weird, but I like that he didn't put up a front for me. That he let his scowl be seen, that he was just unapologetically *himself*. It felt intimate, somehow. Honest. Real. And it made me more comfortable, knowing that he wasn't trying to act like everything was fine when it so obviously wasn't. I have to say, I can't remember the last time a guy I met gave me butterflies like that.

Of course, it didn't hurt that he was freaking gorgeous. Those striking eyes, the dark hair, the olive skin, and yes, I couldn't help noticing his body. From what I could see, the man looked shredded.

"—is that cool?"

I whip my head toward Brooke guiltily. "Sorry, what?"

She laughs. "I knew you weren't listening. Probably daydreaming about baseball stats again. I said I'm going to hit the dance floor, is that cool?"

"Yeah, of course. Good luck with the silver fox."

"Come with me," she says, hopping off the bar stool and holding out her hand. "We can dance with each other and make all the guys sweat."

"I'm good here. Maybe in a bit. Besides, someone has to finish this drink, right?"

With that, I take a huge slurp of the blue drink and flash her a thumbs up. Seeming satisfied that I'm not going to sit here feeling sorry for myself, Brooke swans away from the bar and starts dancing with some random cute guy, like it's the easiest thing in the world. She whispers something in his ear, laughs, and then makes a point to lead him deeper into the crowd—conveniently close to the older man, giving her true target a clear view of her dancing with someone else.

I wonder if Brooke's attempt to make hot daddy jealous will work as well as it usually does on guys our age. I'd think someone older, with more experience, wouldn't take the bait. But as I watch him lock his gaze onto my best friend and the dude she's grinding on, I start to wonder if Brooke's method is worth a little more consideration. Maybe men don't like it if you're too direct, too friendly, too open. Maybe you really do have to play the game to get a guy interested.

Which means I went about my lunch not-date all wrong. Which means I probably won't hear from Scowl ever again. Pulling the fishbowl closer, I make another brave attempt at sucking down the beverage. The ice is starting to melt, which means it's going to take even longer to drink all the liquid. I'm also seriously questioning if it even has any alcohol in it. I should feel at least a tiny buzz by now.

And then my phone vibrates with a text.

My adrenaline spikes as I see the unfamiliar area code in the sender's number.

Enjoying happy hour?

I feel a flutter of excitement in my chest. This has to be him.

Well, well, if it isn't Scowl himself.

It's going okay so far. Looking forward to those dueling pianos you mentioned.

Just okay? Sounds a little disappointing.

He's not wrong.

It was. But now that you're texting me...

There's a pause, and then he replies,

> Are you going to finish that sentence? I'm intrigued.

Laughing out loud, I type,

> I'd say happy hour is getting a lot happier now that you're texting me. Brooke's having fun, but this isn't quite my kind of crowd.

> Oh no? I assumed you'd be swarmed by male attention by now.

I smile.

> I'm much too intimidating for most men.

My cheeks flush. I'm acting way more sassy than my normal self. Brooke would be proud.

> Any man who can't handle your confidence isn't worthy of you.

A wave of pleasure rolls over me at the compliment.

> You're making me blush.

I reply, and it's 100% the truth.

> So what is your kind of crowd if it's not the clientele at Hurricane Sammy's?

Biting my lip, I debate whether to keep up the banter or give him a real answer.

> Not the crowd type in general. I'll take a quiet night out with a few friends at a whiskey bar any day of the week.

I see ellipses pop up and then disappear, and then finally he texts back,

> What kind of whiskey?

Is this a test? I'm no expert on whiskey if he wants to get into the nitty-gritty, but I do know what I like.

> Connemara. But I'm still a newbie tbh.

> I'm guessing since you chose a peated whiskey, you're into the earthy smokiness.

> Nailed it.

> Connemara's a decent mid-shelf, but there's a whole world of better whiskeys out there. Just saying.

With a grin, I type back,

> I'd be interested in hearing your recommendations sometime.

The second I send the text, my heart starts beating faster. I've basically just flashed a neon sign at the guy that says, "Please ask me out now." When he doesn't immediately text back, I start to second-guess myself. Scrolling back through our conversation, I try to figure out if I came on too strong, or not strong enough, or if I should follow up my last text with some kind of invitation. I'm a modern woman, after all. I can ask him out, can't I?

"Hey!" Brooke says, sidling up to me with another random guy at her side. "This is Chase. He just graduated, like us! From Texas A&M."

"Congratulations," I say to the guy, dropping my cell into my lap.

"Thank you. Congrats to both of you, too." He smiles, and it's a good one. He's blond and athletic, kind of a surfer type, with a little bit of a sunburn on his nose.

"He majored in *Exercise Science*," Brooke adds, waggling her brows pervily at me. "And he's staying at Espadrilles, too. Isn't that *so* funny?"

"So funny," I say, watching her take an impressive number of gulps from the fishbowl. "It's nice to meet you, Chase."

"Likewise," he says.

Pretending to fiddle with my hair, I block the side of my face from Chase and silently mouth, *Where's the silver fox?* to Brooke. She grins around the straw and then mouths back, *Who cares?*

We order a pizza topped with grilled pineapple and something called "island fries" off the happy hour menu, but the music is so loud that we don't get to talk much while we're eating. I listen to Chase explain how he wants to be a physical therapist for professional athletes, and then a live band comes in and the lights go even dimmer. Brooke seems to take this as some kind of cue.

"So," she says, sliding off her stool and leaning her head on Chase's shoulder, "I think we're gonna head back to the hotel to check out Chase's room. It's number 4413. Chase, let her take a picture of your face to be safe."

I pull out my phone again and snap a photo, making sure I get a clear shot.

"Let's meet back up for breakfast in the morning," Brooke adds, bouncing on her toes excitedly. "I have the FindMe app turned on if you need to check on me. Oh, and I'll Venmo you for the drink."

"Don't worry about the drink. Go have fun," I say. "And be careful. See you at breakfast."

Brooke gives me a quick hug and then practically drags Chase out the door. I watch them leave with a smile on my face. Maybe I'll go back to the room and watch a movie. Order room service if I feel like it, or go for a dip in one of the hotel's fancy hot tubs.

As I start to dig some cash out of my pocket so I can settle the bill and get out of here, I feel a buzz again in my lap. Dammit, I told Brooke not to bother with the Venmo. But when I pick up my phone and look at the screen, it's not a notification from the payment app. It's another text from Scowl.

> So should we get out of here, too?

He's here right now? Breath catching, I look around and spot Mr. Scowl himself at the other end of the bar, gesturing at me as he hands a credit card to the bartender. The bartender nods, and I realize that Scowl is paying my tab. Shaking my head, I slide off my stool and walk over to him.

The hotel room is all mine tonight, this man is fine as

hell, and my nails are just bright red enough to give me the confidence I need to make my move.

Leaning in close, I whisper in his ear, "Yes. I think we should definitely get out of here."

The whole walk back to the resort, we hold hands. Neither of us even asks, we just fall into it naturally, like we aren't perfect strangers. And honestly? It's nice. More than nice. The heat of our palms pressed together has my whole body tingling, and I swear I can feel my pulse throbbing between my legs.

At first there are so many other people around us, so much laughter interspersed with loud voices and louder music spilling from cafés and clubs on the street, that all I'm focused on is getting through the noise and the bright lights. But the closer we get to Espadrilles, the more the chaos fades, and soon Scowl is giving me a lesson in Whiskey 101. He talks about the classes of grains used in mash, different types of aging barrels, the nuances of Japanese versus Scottish versus Canadian whiskeys.

I have questions, and he has answers. So many answers, in fact, that I blurt, "How do you know so much about whiskey, anyway? Do you work for a distillery?"

He laughs. "I do not. One of my best friends runs a bar, though."

"Is it here on the island?" I ask, as if I'm interested in going, even though I'm really just trying to see if Scowl will mention the city he lives in.

"No," is all he says, not giving me any further information.

Once we get through the hotel lobby, I tug him toward the bank of elevators and push the call button. When the first set of steel doors slides open, I'm pleased to see we have the car all to ourselves.

"I have a very fancy room," I tell him as we step inside and I punch the high number for my floor.

My parents booked a two-bedroom luxury suite for me and Brooke, and I've been enjoying every second of it. Rolling around in my huge king size bed, wrapping myself in the fluffy monogrammed bathrobe after taking a ridiculously long shower every morning, ordering ice cream from room service at midnight. It beats my NYU freshman-year dorm by a long shot, believe me.

Thinking back to the way Scowl was staring out at the ocean today, I add, "There's a balcony with a view of the water, too. I think you'll really—"

My sentence is cut off as he presses me against the wall, dipping his head toward mine. I lift my chin, eyes on his mouth, licking my lips in anticipation of the kiss, but instead he leans in close to my ear and says, "I only care about the bed."

I inhale sharply as he nips the top of my ear, biting down gently, and then pulls away. But the damage is already done. That nibble sent a searing-hot line of electricity straight to my clit. No guy has ever done that to me before. I had no idea ears were so erogenous. I'm giddy with lust.

I'm about to wrap my arms around his neck to pull him down for the kiss I was initially expecting, but the elevator doors open with a soft chime and then we're stepping out into the hallway, hands clasped again as I lead the way to my room.

My heart is in my throat, my breaths coming fast and shallow. If this is what the man does to me after barely using his mouth on my ear, I can't wait to find out what else he can do.

4

BLAIR

PULLING to a stop outside the door of my suite, I fumble for the key card and tap it against the electronic reader. The light on it blinks red, and I almost yelp in frustration. I try again, my eyes fluttering as Scowl slides my hair away from the back of my neck and drops his lips to my nape. A shiver races down my spine, my toes curling in my sandals. The light on the reader flashes green, and the lock clicks softly.

I push the door open.

He follows me into the suite, his hands sliding down my sides and over my hips to trace my curves. My whole body lights up as he spins me around, and then he kisses me.

And oh. My. God.

His tongue strokes against mine, slow and searching, and my knees instantly go weak.

This isn't the rushed kiss of a frat boy acting out what he's seen in porn because he doesn't know what a woman actually wants. Or the tentative, inexperienced tonguing of a guy without much experience. This is the kind of kiss that blows your mind, that fires up every nerve ending, that sweeps you off your feet. Literally, because now he's lifting me up and carrying me toward one of the bedrooms.

"Mine's the other one," I break away from his lips just long enough to say.

His mouth closes over mine again. God, his tongue. He's assertive but unhurried, as if he's showing me exactly what his cock is about to do to me. It's intoxicating.

A little sigh escapes me as he lays me out on the bed, then steps back. I realize I left the windows open, because I can hear the pounding of the surf from the beach down below, and the warm night breeze ghosting over my skin carries with it the sweet scent of tropical flowers and ocean salt. There's just enough light coming in from the hotel's pool area to make this man glow like a god as he pulls his T-shirt off over his head.

"Wow," I murmur. His six-pack is even better than I imagined.

His lips quirk in amusement and heat rushes up my neck as I realize I just said that out loud. But he must not mind me ogling him, because the deep green of his eyes darkens as his intense gaze rakes down my body and then back up to my lips. The outline of his cock is visible through his shorts, and it makes the ache between my thighs pulse even harder. I've never felt so wanted, so desirable.

He drops onto the bed and climbs over me, and then his mouth is on mine again, his kiss deliciously aggressive and crushing now. Hard enough to bruise but sweet with the promise of redemption. Wrapping my thighs around him, I moan as his hips press into me, the ridge of his dick hard against my inner thighs. Threading my fingers into his hair, I push his face gently away, turn my head, and present him with my ear. I'm dying for him to kiss me there again.

"I want you to..."

"I know what you want, baby," he murmurs.

And then his lips are cruising the curve of my ear, his tongue tracing the outer edge.

"Yes," I whisper, lifting my hips to meet his and holding myself against his thick bulge.

I turn my head again so he can kiss my other ear. He gently bites the lobe before sucking it into his mouth and groaning softly. The sound does something to me and suddenly I can't hold back, shamelessly grinding against the monster in his pants, my hands tracing down his back to grip his ass and pull him as close to me as possible. I swear I could come like this.

"Slow down," he says, sounding amused. "We've got all the time in the world."

"But I want you now," I tell him breathlessly, trying not to sound like a child begging for candy.

He gives my ear one last nip and then moves his mouth down my neck, kissing over my collarbone and then the tops of my breasts as he works the straps of my dress down. I sit up to unhook my strapless bra, flinging it across the room before I lie back again.

His mouth never leaves my body as he peels the dress off me, sliding it over my hips, my thighs, leaving me in nothing but my white cotton underwear. My breath hitches in my chest as he sits up on his heels to look down at me, his eyes studying every inch of me. Suddenly, I'm insecure about my small breasts, the birthmark over my left hip, the fact that he's so flawless while I'm just—

"You're a goddamned work of art, Sunshine," he says.

A nervous laugh flies out of me, my palm settling over my pounding heart. "Oh, please. I bet you say that to all the girls."

Despite my playfulness, his tone is serious. "I don't."

I notice his gaze is on my chest, so I move my hand over one breast, squeezing it as he watches me. Another low groan escapes him, the sound making me shiver. The need in his eyes is unmistakable, and I relish the power I have right now. *I'm* doing this to him. He's literally on his knees for me. I circle my tingling nipple with my fingernail, letting my eyes close as my other hand reaches between my legs. When I squeeze my pussy through the fabric of my underwear, he curses under his breath.

"Work. Of. Art," he repeats.

With a grin, I open my eyes and reach for him, but he's already climbing over me. He lowers his mouth to suckle my left nipple, hard enough to make me gasp, and then moves to the right one. The sensations give me instant pleasure-brain-fog, and my eyes close again.

He tortures me like this, licking and sucking and nipping until I feel like I'm losing my mind. Each time he switches his mouth to the alternate nipple, the air feels ice cold on the one he just stopped sucking, the pleasure building even higher when his hot mouth returns. I can't stop moaning beneath him, louder and louder, and I'm relieved that the suite is all mine tonight. This is ecstasy.

My pussy gives a few involuntary squeezes, and I realize just how close I am. Fuck.

"I think I'm going to come," I pant helplessly.

"Already?"

"You do good work," I tell him.

When he laughs, I can feel the vibration against my nipple, which has me squirming even more.

"But you haven't seen my best work yet," he says.

Before I can ask, he tugs off my underwear and moves down the bed, pushing my thighs wide apart, stretching the muscles there as he lowers his mouth toward my opening. I can feel how wet I am as his breath tickles my lips, and he must notice too, because a little growl escapes him. It's nothing compared to the sound of my wail as he glides his tongue in one long, slow lap from my ass to my clit.

I know there's no way in hell I'm going to be able to hold back, so I just go with it, tilting my head back and letting the moans spill out of me one after another. Usually, I'm too self-conscious to have an orgasm from oral sex, but this feels completely different. He's different.

Fingers tangling in his hair, I tighten my thighs around his head and start bucking against his tongue. His strong, thick tongue, pumping into my hole, circling my clit, tasting every drop of my juices.

I'm on fire from my scalp to my feet.

"Fuck," I pant, the hot sparks at my core signaling that I'm about to fly over the edge.

"Mmm," he groans, and the rumble coming out of him is my undoing.

My orgasm doesn't so much hit me as it radiates from my center in deep, gushing shockwaves that have me crying out and cursing at the same time. When he finally pulls away, we're both panting for air. I should be spent, but all I want is for him to do that to me all over again. With his cock this time.

"Do you have a condom? I do, but it's in my suitcase. I can get it," I say, lunging toward him, my hands fumbling with his zipper.

He laughs, and I look up with a pout. "What's so funny?"

"You."

"What about me?" I sass, narrowing my eyes.

"You don't want to take a breather? There's no rush. We'll get to round two eventually."

"But I want you *now*," I tell him, realizing I probably sound exactly like that bratty girl from *Charlie and the Chocolate Factory*, but I'm too horny to be mortified about it. "I'm on *vacation*."

Laughing again, he shakes his head. "That you are. I'm at your service, then."

Moving off the bed just long enough to unzip his shorts, he digs a foil packet out of his pocket and drops the shorts on the floor. He's not wearing underwear, and good lord. Obviously I've seen naked guys before, but I'm suddenly realizing that those were mere boys. As for Scowl? He's all man. The broad shoulders, the tight abs, the dusting of hair across his chest that leads straight down to his thick, perfect cock. Every inch of him is taut and toned, power coiled in each muscle.

Mouth dry, I manage to croak out, "Put it on. Hurry."

He rips open the package and gets the job done, purposely teasing me, doing it slowly, one freaking micro-millimeter at a time, until the condom finally unrolls at the thick root.

Positioning himself between my legs, he takes my wrists in one of his hands and pins them over my head. Then he lines himself up against my entrance, still slick and ready for him. Our eyes lock. He lowers his head and kisses me, flooding me with my own taste as he glides smoothly into me, burying himself deep, stretching me to the max until he can't go anymore.

"Ahh," I moan, tightening my pussy around him to give him a squeeze.

"Easy, girl," he says, shuddering a little.

Lifting my hips, I meet him thrust for thrust, trying to take more and more.

"Greedy, aren't you, Sunshine?"

Raking my nails over the muscles on his back, I can't form words as he pounds into me. Soon enough we find a rhythm, each glorious pump of his cock taking both our breaths away. We're caught up in the pleasure of it, moaning in tandem, and just when I think the crest that's been building won't actually amount to anything—which I'm absolutely okay with, because no guy has ever gotten me off twice in a row—he shifts his hips and angles his cock just right and suddenly I'm coming all over again.

"Oh my God yes, yes, *yes*," I moan, eyes shut tight, colors exploding behind my lids.

With a groan, his lips crash against mine, and he jack-hammers into me, releasing in a hot burst, his cock slamming into me hard enough to bruise. I hope it does.

His chest moves with harsh, shallow breaths as he rolls over to lie beside me, and I turn onto my side and rest my head on his bicep. The last thing I remember is him pulling the sheet over us as I drift into a blissful slumber.

I'm woken up the next morning by the insistent buzz of a text from Brooke: *Don't hate me, but Chase wants to take me out for breakfast on a catamaran! Can we do dinner instead?*

There's already a smile on my face as I tap back an affirmative, because now I don't have to ask her for a raincheck on breakfast like I'd planned. Scowl is still passed out next to me, and I wouldn't mind sleeping in. Maybe when he wakes up, he'll be ready for round three.

It's a nice surprise that he's still here. I fully expected him to tiptoe out in the middle of the night, as most one-nighters do. His arm goes immediately around me as I settle back under the covers.

The next thing I know, he's kissing me awake, his lips cruising over my back and shoulders as the sun streams in through the windows.

"What time is it?" I mumble drowsily.

"Almost eleven."

I sit up like a shot, and that's when I realize that he's just gotten out of the shower, a towel wrapped around his waist and his hair still damp. He looks good enough to eat. Except that I'm starving, and I literally need to eat, preferably as soon as humanly possible.

"Eleven? How'd that happen? Do you think it's too late for breakfast?"

"It's never too late for breakfast," he says seriously.

"Do you want to hit the buffet?" I ask. "It comes with the room. It's all-inclusive."

He smiles and says, "I've got a better idea."

His better idea is him calling in an order at a café by the beach while I'm in the shower. Once I'm dressed and ready to go, we stroll down to pick it up and end up taking it back to the cove where we met yesterday. That's when I find out that it's actually a *private* beach. No wonder it was empty yesterday.

"We should go," I say, pointing at the No Trespassing signs.

But Scowl just takes my hand and keeps tugging me along. "A members-only resort owns this cove," he says. "But I'm friends with the owners. Trust me, we're welcome here."

"Okay," I say, happy to let him lead me toward the shady palm grove.

It turns out that the food he ordered is far better than anything I've had at the Espadrilles buffet. As we watch the waves lap in and out, I gorge myself on sliced papaya and mango, shrimp and grits, and coconut pancakes. We also share a rum-roasted coffee, which I've never had before. It's excellent.

In between bites, I chatter about how excited I am to start working for my family's business, and though I don't mention the phrase "New York Rockets" or "Tisdale Corporation," I make it clear that the company is a Very Big Deal and that I'm looking forward to climbing the corporate ladder and someday taking over. For once, I'm not embarrassed to nerd out about my career aspirations in front of a guy, because Scowl seems content to lie back and listen to me talk, nodding along so I know he's following.

"You're barely eating," I point out as I push my to-go container away, gesturing at his still-loaded plate. "Not hungry?"

"I'm not much of a breakfast person."

"So this was all for me, then," I tease. "Well, thank you. I feel so spoiled."

"You should," he says. "I usually just have a protein shake on my way out the door."

"What's your favorite food, then?" I ask, taking one last bite of pancake.

He thinks about it and then says, "Steak. Or really anything with grill marks on it."

"Ha! So basically, char is your favorite food."

"Definitely," he says, taking my razzing with good humor. "I'm a connoisseur of char."

As we start to pack up the leftovers, I can't help asking, "What are your plans for the day?"

Because yes, I'm kind of hoping he'll invite me along.

"I have to work," he says. "I've been training a new employee. It's been...challenging so far."

"Ah. Should we get going, then?" I ask, trying to sound cool and aloof even though my hopes have just been dashed. What if I never see him again?

Except that's the whole point of a one-night stand, isn't it? And I knew that going into this. There's no reason for me to be feeling so attached. Which I'm totally not. I just had a really good time.

Getting up, he reaches for my hand and pulls me to my feet. Then he cups my face and leans in to give me a slow, sweet, knee-weakening kiss. A goodbye kiss, I'm sure of it.

"So we're going?" I say, once we finally break away.

"Yes," he says. "We're going to check out the tidepools by those rocks over there."

A stupid smile pulls up the corners of my mouth. "But you have to work."

"I have every intention of putting in my hours today."

He leads me down the beach until the waves are lapping around our bare feet. The tidepools are shallow, warm as bath water, filled with an incredible array of life. Scowl points each sea creature out to me, naming them one by one. Spiny sea urchins, hermit crabs, brightly colored starfish, and anemones in shades of blue and green and orange and pink.

"So beautiful," I say, crouching down to get a better look.

He lets out a little laugh, and when I look up at him, he just shakes his head.

"What?" I ask.

"Nothing. I just...didn't know it could be this easy."

I don't ask him what "it" is. I think I know. Just being together like this, enjoying each other, with no expectations. I haven't even seen his trademark scowl once today. I don't push him to explain what he means, either, because I know that if he wanted to talk, he'd talk. Instead, I just tease him.

"Are you calling me easy?"

He pulls back, a horrified look on his face. "No. That's not what I meant."

I make a horrified face of my own and say, "But I'm trying so hard to get laid again!"

It takes a second before a smile cracks on his lips, and then he's lifting me up and pushing me against a smooth boulder, the two of us kissing in the privacy of a half-circle of tall rocks. No one on this beach could see us even if they did ignore all the No Trespassing signs and walk by, which is good, because I'm already tugging his shorts off and stroking him in my fist, my other hand digging for the condom I slipped into my pocket just in case.

By the time he pulls my panties down and starts fucking me against the warm, smooth rock, I know that it might already be too late.

I might already be too attached.

5

SEBASTIAN

IT'S BEEN days since I last saw Sunshine, but I can't get her out of my head. Her tight little body, that laugh, the smell of the sandalwood perfume behind her earlobes. The sweet glide of her pussy. How the hell did everything between us feel so easy? There was nothing complicated about it.

The complicated part is the aftermath.

Because it's so out of character for me to dwell on a one-night stand that I don't know how to reconcile it in my mind. I wake up every morning with a raging hard-on for her; at work I'm taunted by flashbacks of her on the beach, at the bar, in her hotel room. I beat myself raw in the shower at night trying to release the tension enough to fall asleep. Still, the memories linger.

And meanwhile, attempting to train the new client concierge has been a living nightmare. It was sheer idiocy on my part to take that half a day's vacation on the beach with Sunshine after we slept together, because letting my concierge trainee do anything on her own without me standing over her shoulder to supervise has been nothing short of a disaster.

I'd left her with a very simple task the day I was at the beach, which was to update the resort's database of local bar and restaurant recommendations to ensure we have the correct operating hours, directions, phone numbers, that kind of thing. We also need to delete any businesses that have closed permanently and add any new establishments that have popped up. So what did Daisy do for five hours?

She read restaurant reviews on Yelp. For five whole hours. That is all she managed to do.

Did she update a single line in the spreadsheet? Did she call any of the restaurants to confirm their business hours? Maybe gather some information about the new sushi spot in town? No, no, and no.

What she did do was give me a ten-minute explanation of how Café Caribe prepares their piranha dish, because apparently the carnivorous fish is not actually toxic to eat, although it doesn't taste the best, which is why they marinate it in some lime-infused whatever the fuck, and by the time she was done yapping about the whole thing, I had a headache.

When I'd reminded her about the spreadsheet, her eyes had gotten big and she'd immediately started apologizing. And yes, she'd then worked overtime in order to get the spreadsheet taken care of. But ever since then, I've had to watch her every move. Which isn't my preferred management style, to be frank, but since the busy season starts this week, I couldn't take the risk of leaving her to her own devices and having things blow up in my face once the agency's new clients start checking in. We're known for a high level of service here, and I can't let anything jeopardize our reputation.

This is all Becker's fault.

I still can't quite figure out if Daisy is incredibly ditzy, doesn't give a shit about this job, or is flat out trying to sabotage us. She's a courtesy hire for Becker's friend, however, so I'm assuming it's not the latter. And since she's a courtesy hire, she's also not getting fired...yet.

Besides, I still need to find out what she knows about Becker's past. Daisy has to have heard *something* from her brother. It doesn't even need to be anything spicy; just knowing Beck was in Boy Scouts or Yale's chess club would constitute good intel. I mean, it's just not possible that the man has no past. Nate and I have wondered for years if Beck is in witness protection or worked in black ops, or if he's trying to hide a childhood that was somehow sordid or tragic. Inquiring minds want to know.

I take the private elevator from my set of rooms down to the lobby at 8 a.m. Margo, who handles reservations and works at the front desk, waves me over as I'm on my way to the management offices.

"Good morning, Mr. Argos," she says. "Your guests' arrival for later this morning has been confirmed. Their plane took off as scheduled from Miami and they'll be landing in about ninety minutes. We already sent a limo to wait for them."

"Perfect. And their suites are all ready? Pillows fluffed, flowers arranged, et cetera?"

"Yes, and the rooms are located at opposite ends of the third floor, as you requested."

"Thank you, Margo."

She holds out a sheet of paper. "The family also sent a shopping list of personal items that they'd like delivered to their room before they get here. Shall I get started on this, sir?"

Ah, Margo. So professional, so efficient. "I appreciate it, but as you know, it's the concierge's job." I take the list. "Daisy will make sure it's taken care of."

But when I get to my office, I find Daisy sitting at my desk, staring dreamily off into space.

"I appreciate your improved punctuality today, Daisy, but what exactly are you doing?"

"Oh!" She pops up from the chair and smooths her skirt. "The, um, internet browser was restricted on my computer, so I thought I'd use yours. Only it's password protected."

"It is. What do you need the internet browser for?"

She tugs the end of her ponytail, looking nervous. "I wanted to do some research for an itinerary...for a guest?"

This piques my interest. "Which guest? Did someone put in a request?"

Her cheeks go pink. "Um, no. This would be for a future guest. Not a guest we have yet. Just in case they wanted someone to plan a day in paradise for them. I was thinking parasailing?"

Pinching the bridge of my nose, I take a deep, calming breath. "It's a good idea, Daisy, but I have more pressing matters for you to address. Building itineraries is something we do upon request, and we tailor them to each specific guest, per their interests. You're just making more work for yourself, when what I need you to do is handle the work that I give you. Sound good?"

"Yes, Mr. Argos. Absolutely."

She nods, her brunette ponytail bouncing, and I'm struck once again by how young she is. How inexperienced. No matter how clearly I try to give her direction, she always ends up sidetracked somehow. I still can't believe Becker saddled me with her, and for what? A favor for an old friend of his?

"I have to make a few phone calls. Go back to your desk and take care of this list."

I hand over the list that Margo made.

"Okay. Sure." She glances down, her brow furrowing. "Wait. What is this for?"

Forcing a smile, I say, "This is a list of personal items that we need to obtain for the guests arriving later this morning. Their names and room numbers are at the top of the page. Remember when we talked about making special accommodations for guests?"

"Yes. But...I forgot—what do I do now? Should I Uber to town and buy all this stuff?"

"We have personal shoppers to do this," I remind her. "Make some calls."

"Okay, but...I forgot—where do we keep their contact info?"

Reaching deep inside my soul for one last shred of patience, I tell her, "On the computer. In our management system. Under vendors. Remember how we went over vendors a few days ago?"

"Right. Sorry. I'm still figuring out the whole business software thing. I've never had a desk job before. I *told* my brother I might not be the best fit for this gig." She giggles.

"Tell me something, Daisy," I say with a sigh. "Did you

actually want this job? Or did your brother force you into it? Does he control your trust fund or something?"

She frowns. "Well...not exactly. I mean, I do have a trust fund, but I won't have access to it until I'm twenty-five. That means I have five more years to make my own way first. But I tried that already, and it wasn't going great, so my brother said he'd figure something out for me. And now I'm here."

"What do you want to be doing with your life? Just out of curiosity. Because I don't get the impression that this is it."

To my surprise, her face lights up. "Oh! So like, honestly? I always wanted to work on one of those big, fancy cruise ships. Like...be the person who plans day trips and organizes the onboard entertainment and just, you know, makes sure everyone's having a blast at all times. But after I graduated high school I tried to apply to all these cruise ship jobs and I got nowhere, because they want you to have experience in hospitality first, so I kind of gave up. But then my brother hooked me up with Becker to see if he could give me a job that would look good on my resume, and so...here I am."

"I see." It's all making sense now. This actually *is* the perfect job for Daisy. We're her training wheels. Except she hasn't exactly impressed me so far. "And what did you do for work before this?"

"Cocktail waitress on private yachts. Which sounds fun, but it kinda isn't. I wanted to do something funner. Something where I can make everybody happy, not just rich old men who want to play grab-ass while you serve them alcohol. Because ew. And also, I want to see the world. So yeah. A cruise ship sounds like the right place for me. I know I can quit when I get access to my trust fund, but maybe I won't. Maybe I'll keep working because I want to."

For a moment, I don't even reply. I'm still processing everything she just said.

"You're more than meets the eye, Daisy," I finally tell her.

Her smile falters. "I'm not dumb, Mr. Argos. I might not be a rocket scientist or whatever, but I'm pretty good at taking care of people. And I like to have fun and live life, and is that so bad?"

"No. Not at all. And I think you've got potential. We just have to work on your focus, okay?"

She nods. "I really want to be good at this job. I'll look up the personal shoppers now."

I sit down behind my computer and gesture for Daisy to do the same. Both of us get to work.

Unfortunately, my short-lived sense of peace doesn't last long. Because the potential matches I intended to have quick courtesy calls with today have all emailed me, telling me they haven't yet received their itineraries for the week they're here. As I'm reading over the second email, which asks if canceling the trip is necessary, my head starts to pound. Fucking Daisy.

There's no time to ream her out, though. Right now, I have fires to put out.

Quickly getting on the phone, I call each of the matches to apologize for the fuck-up and explain that there was a logistical issue with the scheduling, giving them all my personal guarantee that I'm already handling it. I keep my tone relaxed and courteous, assuring the clients of my competency, but by the time I hang up with the third match, Daisy is watching me from her desk with wide, scared eyes.

"They...they didn't get the itineraries?" she asks.

"No," I say evenly. "They did not. Daisy, this task was the first thing I put on your to-do list when you started on Monday. In fact, I recall telling you it was your top priority. Why wasn't it done?"

"It *was* done! I mean...I thought it was." She looks at her computer and starts clicking the mouse frantically. "OMG. I totally forgot to send the emails. They're still in my drafts. I'm *so* sorry."

Long, deep, calming breaths.

"I need you to send those emails right away, with your sincerest apologies," I tell her finally. "Then I need you to get a personal shopper booked to take care of that list in your hand."

"Yes, Mr. Argos," she says somberly.

"I'm leaving now to go prepare for a meeting with the clients we have flying in today, so I won't be able to supervise you for the next several hours. Do not—I repeat, *do not* —get sidetracked. When you're done with the tasks I've just given you, go ask Margo what you can do to make her life easier, because she's been covering for you all week."

"Okay."

"Stay focused," I tell her. "And remember, you are the face of client services for this resort. When you have a task to complete, you need to follow through. Our clients are extremely powerful people with very tight schedules, so timing is everything. If we say they'll receive photos or information or a specific brand of fucking champagne, we absolutely must provide what we've promised, otherwise we risk losing those clients, and then our entire business model collapses. Understood?"

"Yes," she says meekly.

My whole body is tense as I turn off my computer and stand. I'm back to the old me again, it seems. So much for being calm with my new employee. I'm going to have to find Sunshine and fuck her brains out just to get through this client meeting without exploding.

This will be a first for me. A duplicate one-night stand. Does that make it a two-night stand?

Not that it matters. This doesn't mean anything, it's just sex. Sex with a very hot, very entertaining blonde who very much enjoyed the orgasms I gave her a few days ago and who very clearly seemed open to a repeat performance. Which I'm more than happy to give her. One last time.

And after that, I'm going to get my head on straight, put my nose to the grindstone, and pretend I won't miss the fun, laid-back guy I pretend to be when I'm with her.

6

BLAIR

"I'm GOING to miss you, Blair! Thanks for an amazing time."

Brooke hugs me tightly. I can't believe our week together is already over and she has to head back to New York, where her new job awaits.

"I'm so glad we got to do this," I tell her. "I'll text you as soon as I'm back in the city."

"Definitely. We'll do a girls' night."

I give Brooke one last squeeze and then she grabs the handle of her rolling suitcase and scurries toward the glass doors of the small airport. As I duck back into the cab, I watch her go with a sigh. I wish she could have stayed to be the buffer between me and my parents.

They're arriving today, and that means I have to pack up all my things and move to the members-only resort where they've booked us rooms for the next seven days. I'm supposed to meet up with them later. I'd be perfectly happy staying at Espadrilles, of course, but it would never meet my mother's standards. The place she and my dad picked is going to be ritzy and luxurious, I'm sure, but I'm also sure I'll be the only person there under the age of forty. There probably won't be a 24-hour buffet, either.

My heart suddenly feels heavy. I'm glad that I took this time for myself, but now it's back to reality. Unfortunately.

Staring out the window on the drive back to my hotel, I think back over the last week and can't help but smile. Snorkeling, Mai Tais, souvenir shopping, beach days, nights out dancing. Brooke and I had *so* much fun. Especially Brooke—particularly in the hot guy department. She claimed this was her last hurrah before she has to buckle down at work and stop chasing men, but I'll believe it when I see it.

Although I can't say I didn't have my own perfect summer fling. I haven't heard from Scowl since that day we had sex on the beach, but I have no regrets about the time I spent with him. Nobody has ever made me come like that before. I'll probably be touching myself to those memories for the rest of my life. Who cares if I didn't meet any other guys on this trip? I'm more into quality than quantity anyway.

I still haven't told Brooke. Not because I'm ashamed or anything. I'm sure she'll 100% approve. The fact that I didn't get his name is probably a gold star in her book. But I guess the secret just feels sweeter when I get to keep it to myself. Plus, gossiping about Scowl and turning him into a spicy little anecdote doesn't appeal to me. What we did meant more than that. I felt like we connected in some unspoken way. Or maybe I'm just romanticizing the whole thing.

The cab pulls up outside Espadrilles and I pay the

driver in cash and hop out. It's hot today, the breeze tossing my long hair every which way and blowing my skirt against my legs. Check out isn't for another few hours, so that means I can take my time packing my suitcase. Maybe order one last round of room service before I have to go. The hotel's lobster mac and cheese is to die for.

I'm just finishing zipping up my makeup bag and texting Brooke about the contact lens case she left behind when I get an incoming message on my phone.

> I need to see you again. One last time, before the real world eats my soul.

Heat instantly floods my core, my heart starting to race, and my legs go out from under me. Luckily, my ass lands on the bed. I don't even have to think about how to respond.

Yes.

He must be leaving the island today. Maybe that's for the best. My mom already texted to say she and Dad had landed and to remind me about our early dinner reservations this evening—as if I needed another reminder—and I had planned to make my way to their hotel once I checked out of Espadrilles this afternoon. I'm not going to be able to sneak off for beach sex whenever I feel like it anymore.

But I still have a few hours before my parents will be expecting me. More than enough time for a final farewell fuck with my mystery man.

> I'm free right now.

> I'm in my room.

I reply, hoping he knows exactly what I plan to do with him when he gets here.

On my way.

A shiver of excitement races through me, and I rush to finish up my packing and straighten the bed. Urgency fills me as I dig out my toiletry kit and frantically brush my teeth, imagining him sprawled out naked in my sheets with his cock hard and ready for me. We're going to destroy this room.

Wow, Brooke really has rubbed off on me.

Giving myself a once-over, I hurriedly touch up my lip gloss and then smooth down a few flyaway hairs, my heart leaping in my chest as a knock sounds at the door. He's here. And I'm ready for him. God, am I ready. My whole body is buzzing.

I pull open the door and find him standing there in gray slacks and a cream linen button-down that pops against the golden tan of his olive skin. He looks positively mouthwatering. Being this close to him makes my brain malfunction, and I can't get a single word out. Not that I need to.

Stepping into the room, he cups my face and draws me up for a dizzying kiss. His fingers move through my hair, wrapping it around his fist, and when he tugs hard enough to make my scalp tingle, I let out a low moan. I start to unbutton his shirt, but he gently pushes my hands away.

"What are we waiting for?" I ask breathlessly.

He laughs. "How much time do you have?"

I'm so caught up in the sensations caused by his grip on my hair that it takes a moment to answer. "A couple hours."

Taking my hand, he pulls me toward the door. "We'll be back in plenty of time. I have something planned for you."

My heart leaps. I'm curious, but I don't ask questions. I want to be surprised.

He leads me out of the hotel, behind the resort, and down a narrow, sandy path along the beach that meanders through palm trees and flowering bushes. The trees get closer together, the sounds of tourists on the beach fading, until we reach a cast iron gate. On either side of us is a beautiful stone privacy wall, dripping with climbing vines and purple flowers. He taps what looks like a fitness watch against the sensor beside the gate and it slowly opens.

"Okay, this is not what I was expecting," I say, shaking my head. "What is this place?"

"You'll see," he says.

We pass through the gate and into a private courtyard, and I stop short. I feel like I've walked into a dream.

A small pool sits beneath a splashing waterfall, surrounded by tropical foliage and limestone statuaries that look like modern art. There are two lounge chairs under a thatched umbrella and a small table holding a few towels, a bottle of sunscreen, two champagne flutes, and a bottle of champagne wedged into a bucket of ice. Gold and turquoise tiles on the bottom of the pool glimmer beneath the water, sparkling in the sun. The ten-foot walls and masses of flowering vines create an exquisite private area, and as Scowl begins stripping out of his shirt and pants, any apprehension I was feeling quickly fades. We're alone back here, completely hidden from prying eyes.

"Take off your clothes, Sunshine. I want to feel your naked body pressed against mine."

He doesn't need to ask twice.

I pull my dress over my head and shimmy out of my lacy pink bra and matching underwear.

Fully naked now too, he stands there admiring me, then lowers himself into the pool and holds his arms out in an invitation. Water glistens as it streams off his shoulders and down his chest, making me lick my lips. My eyes follow the line of hair trailing between his abs and disappearing beneath the water, which is so clear that I can see every last inch of him. His cock is rigid and ready. It's a beautiful sight.

I can't get into the pool fast enough. The water is almost as warm as a hot tub and feels like silk against my body, but it can't compare to his smooth, bare skin caressing mine as he pulls me against him.

Our eyes catch, and my nipples turn into tight, aching buds against his pecs as heat pools in my lower belly.

"This is better than anything I could have imagined," I tell him.

His cock twitches against my thigh. Reaching down to wrap my hand around his length, I trace my opening with his tip, up and down, over and over, until we're both breathing hard, his gaze never leaving mine. Yet as much as I'm ready for him to hitch me up and take me against the side of this pool, he seems to be in no hurry.

When he dips his head down to kiss me, I close my eyes and block out everything except the sensation of his lips against my own. This is what I want to remember forever. The feel of being completely swept away by this man.

As we kiss, his hands circle my waist and then slide lower to skim over the curves of my hips, my ass, the backs of my thighs. Then he trails his fingers up my back, making me shiver with pleasure. He palms my breasts and my ribcage, bringing his thumbs back up to brush my nipples. It seems like he wants to explore every last inch of me, one gentle caress at a time.

"I could touch you for hours," he whispers in between kisses.

"Don't stop," I moan, digging my fingers into his hair.

He doesn't, until I have to pull my swollen lips away from his. I'm breathless and squirming and the water is suddenly much too hot. He must feel the same, because he lifts me in his arms and carries me under the waterfall, both of us gasping as the cool water pours over us.

We come back out, laughing and sputtering and brushing wet hair out of our eyes. I feel exhilarated. Free. Alive. I haven't felt like this in longer than I can remember.

Ever since my sister died, my life has been a shadow of what it used to be. I've gone through the motions of school and social events and holidays, but there's been an emptiness to it all. A dark cloud hanging over me, wishing Sophie could be there, knowing that she's gone forever. It isn't just my own grief that has weighed on me, either, but my parents' as well. None of us have really worked through the loss in a healthy way. Mom won't even talk about it; she just spends all her time worrying and trying to micromanage my life because she thinks controlling me will somehow keep her from losing me. And as for Dad, he's buried himself in work, but that distant, pained look in his eyes is always there.

Maybe I haven't allowed myself to put that weight down, all these years. Maybe the weight was a comfort because it was familiar. A weight I carried because it proved that I loved her.

Maybe the universe is making it up to me right now.

He lifts me from the pool and sets me on the edge, then jumps out to join me. Water sluices from my hair and down my back, sending a chill down my spine despite the hot sun. Taking my hand, he pulls me to my feet and walks me backward to sit on one of the lounge chairs. The canvas fabric is soft when I lie back, heart pounding as I await his next move.

The playfulness I was feeling a moment ago is suddenly replaced by undeniable sexual tension. He puts one knee between my legs on the chaise and nudges my thighs apart. Then he lowers himself onto the chair and dips his face down to where my pussy is on display for him. Threading my fingers into his hair, I hold on to the breath that sticks in my throat as his tongue parts my center and begins a deep, thorough exploration.

He feasts on me beneath the island breeze, drawing louder and longer moans out of me, letting me rock against his tongue until I come helplessly in his mouth. The intense, toe-curling orgasm has me gripping the sides of the lounge chair, my head thrown back, eyes open wide to take in the perfection of the bright blue sky. A satisfied smile curves his lips when he finally sits up.

"Roll onto your stomach for me."

His command fills me with delicious anticipation. I'm aching to have him inside me again, and my brain goes wild thinking of him taking me from behind. He lowers the chair's back rest and I lie flat with my chin on my crossed arms. But when I look over my shoulder at him, he isn't grabbing a condom. Instead, he's flipping open the lid on the sunscreen.

"What are you doing?" I ask.

"Can't have you getting burned, can we? Face down. Spread your legs."

I obey, letting out a sigh as his palms streak down my legs and my back with the warm, wet touch of lotion slicking over my skin. The scent of coconut fills my nose as he massages my shoulders and lower back, drawing more soft moans out of me. The man is an expert with his hands. They cup and knead my ass, then slide down to my thighs and my calves. Still relaxed from the orgasm, his strong hands on my body amplify it by a hundred until I'm nearly asleep.

"No sleeping, Sunshine," he whispers in my ear. "I'm not done with you yet."

"Good. I was beginning to wonder when you were going to have your way with me."

"As soon as we have a little champagne."

Turning onto my back, I sit up and watch him expertly pop the cork. He pours us two glasses, and I accept the flute he offers. The champagne is bubbly and cool on my tongue as I sip it while taking in the work of art that is his perfect, naked body.

I never want this to end.

I wish my parents hadn't flown in to meet me, and that I was still here alone to spend the rest of my vacation with this man. The phantom tick of the clock taints my enjoyment as our time together dwindles, second by second.

But the two of us are in a world of our own right now, and I'm determined to take every advantage of it.

Which is why I'd rather just...not say goodbye. Not officially. Because when I get back home and I have to work fourteen-hour days while I try to learn how to eventually take over running the team, all so my parents can retire someday and maybe properly mourn my sister, well...a big, sad goodbye with my summer fling isn't going to be the memory I want to sustain myself with.

And I'm not going to embarrass myself by asking if he thinks we could work out something long distance, either. Even if he agreed to try, we'd both be lying to ourselves pretending it wouldn't fail. Part of the reason this feels so good is because we know it's fleeting. A fire that's meant to burn bright and hot and wild for only a brief time, which is why it's so damn beautiful.

Draining my glass, I set it on the table and get up, pulling on my clothes quickly. Extending my hand to him, I thread my fingers through his and smile.

"Finish your champagne and get dressed. You and I have a hotel room to destroy."

7

BLAIR

WE DON'T GO BACK to the hotel right away. Instead, I'm led down yet another path lined with palms and cedars and fragrant frangipani bushes which opens into a lush botanical garden with a stone fountain splashing at its center. Perched at the edge of the courtyard is a small snack hut painted in shades of yellow, pink, and bright green. A woman with multi-colored braids serves coffee and cold drinks and delicious looking pastries to the people waiting in line. To my surprise, it's a mix of tourists and locals. Whatever this woman is serving, it must be pretty spectacular.

"Can I interest you in a switcha?" Scowl asks.

As much as I want to get back to the room, I can't turn down an island limeade. "Sure."

The line moves quickly, and when we get to the counter, he chats with the woman as if they see each other frequently. A minute later, we're walking away with cups of icy cold switcha and a paper plate of sliced duff, the national dessert. It's similar to a jelly roll cake, except a million times better. The light, spongy cake has spirals of guava in it, and the slices are covered with a rich rum butter sauce.

"I've had plenty of duff on this trip already, so it's going to take a lot to impress me," I warn Scowl teasingly.

"Trust me, Sunshine, this duff is going to put all those other duffs to shame," he says. "This is the real reason I brought you here."

Taking the treats to a nearby table, he pulls a chair out for me and then sits. He must sense my urgency to get back to the room and have my way with him because he lightly takes my hand and says, "I know you're dying to get back to that room so I can fuck you senseless, but one bite of that duff and you won't blame me, I promise."

How can I be frustrated at such a delightful gesture? He scoops up a forkful of the dessert and hands it to me. "Cheers," he says, and then I take a bite. The burst of sweet guava, cinnamon, and rum in my mouth makes my entire face tingle.

"Oh my *God*."

"I told you."

I quickly take another huge bite, moaning as the flavors hit my tongue again.

"Why is this so much better than any other duff I've tasted?" I ask incredulously.

He smiles. "She adds a layer of cream cheese to the guava, and the cinnamon goes in the rum sauce instead of the fruit. It makes all the difference in the world. There's mango duff there, too. Try it."

We don't speak again as we finish off the treat, washing it down with sips of the crisp, refreshing limeade. Sweet aromas from the flower garden surround us and ocean waves roll and crash in the near distance. The breeze cools my hot skin and tosses my hair in my face. This is a perfect moment in time.

Scowl stretches his legs out in front of him while he sips his drink. As I watch his lips wrap around the straw and his throat move as he swallows, the flicker of desire at my core reminds me of our reason for meeting today. Goodbye sex, or something very much like it.

Kicking off a sandal, I run my foot up the side of his leg. His dark gaze meets mine.

"Almost done with that?" He nods to my paper cup.

"I can be," I say coyly.

He finishes his drink and tosses the cup in a trash can. "Let's go."

As soon as we disappear onto the wooded path again, he stops to take me in his arms and drag me up for a kiss that tastes like sweet rum and cinnamon. His tongue sweeps my mouth, and the kiss deepens until I'm about ready to let him take me right here and now. I sigh as his hands stroke up and down my sides and then move to cup my ass. Lifting me onto his hips, he holds me tightly against him. My thighs clamp around his waist, and I kiss him with everything I have. I feel drunk on the taste of him, and the way he's devouring my mouth, I think the feeling is mutual.

The sound of approaching footsteps prompts him to dart into the trees and hide us behind a thick tree trunk. Pressing my back to the smooth bark, he nudges my head to the side and lightly bites the sensitive skin along my neck, making me gasp as a handful of people walk past, oblivious. His mouth moves down the center of my chest, and then he starts to suck the top of my breast. Holding back a moan, I clamp my legs more tightly around him as the rise of his erection presses against my core. I slip a little in his arms and the movement makes us perfectly aligned. Grinding against him, pulling his lips back up to mine, it takes no time before I could easily come from the friction.

He pulls back slightly, and I let out a frustrated whimper.

"We should go," he whispers against my lips.

"Definitely," I agree before pressing my hungry mouth to his again.

The kiss quickly turns frantic, and we lose track of time. My lips feel bruised and swollen, but I'm not ready to stop drinking him in. It's not until we hear another group of people coming down the path that he finally pulls back and sets me on my feet.

Both of us are breathless, our eyes glazed with desire. I've never experienced anything like the wild abandon we have for each other and the carefree way we go about our tryst on this island. It would be so easy to lose myself in this man, forget I have a life back home. But before my mind can wander too far along that train of thought, I take his hand and nudge him back onto the path. He leads because I'm not quite sure which way to go, and soon we're back to the gates that lead to my hotel.

I can't get my keycard out of my pocket quickly enough when we reach my room. He swings me into his arms the moment we cross the threshold, closes the door with a nudge of his elbow and takes me to the bed. I'm naked faster than I can blink. His clothes pile on the floor. Palming his chest, I imagine him as he was earlier by the pool, gloriously naked, tan skin gleaming in the sunlight. Kneeling on the bed, I run my hands over him as he stands. The thick mattress is the perfect height...

Urging him to back up a little, I lie on my back with my head hanging slightly off the mattress. His cock is right above me, giving me a nice lateral view.

Grasping it, I bring him closer and suck the fat tip into my mouth. From this angle, he can slide in easily, pump back and forth against my tongue at his own pace. Sucking on him until he's slick, I relax and take him all the way in. The tip bumps the back of my throat and then goes farther with each thrust, a little at a time. Harder, faster. I can tell he's starting to lose control, and it makes me feel powerful. He groans and palms the sides of my head. He must be getting close.

Emboldened, I reach up to grab his hips and drive him even deeper into my throat, again and again until the root of his cock rests against my lips. And then I swallow, and I swear he almost loses it.

"Sunshine, fuck, that's beautiful, that's fucking beautiful," he whispers harshly.

Breathing hard, he slows his thrusts, as if he doesn't trust himself not to turn into a crazed animal that wants nothing more than to ram his cock into my throat until he comes. Considering how much he swells in my mouth, I'm sure I could easily push him over the edge. But suddenly he withdraws and moves onto the bed.

"Get on your hands and knees," he commands.

I follow his orders, jutting out my ass toward him. A shiver of anticipation races down my spine as I wait for him to enter me, but first he rakes his fingernails down my back, giving me goosebumps. A hard smack on my ass has me crying out with a mix of pleasure and pain, and then I wait as he unwraps a condom and rolls it on, the hot pulse of need between my thighs growing more insistent by the second.

Once he's ready, he lines himself up against me. God. I want him so bad I can't stand it.

"Fuck me. Please," I beg. I don't know where my nerve comes from. I've never talked dirty in bed before, but hearing the need in my own voice turns me on even more. "Fuck me, fuck me, fuck me."

"Jesus," he groans, spearing into me so hard we both gasp.

I start to move first, impaling myself on his dick, finding my own rhythm as I take what I need from him. He lets me use him like this until he can't hold back anymore, and then he starts meeting me thrust for thrust, matching my pace, giving me exactly what I need.

"That's so good. You feel so good," I moan, almost senseless with pleasure. "So good."

He wraps my hair around his hand and tugs my head back, every taut strand sending delicious tingles of pleasure through my scalp. And then he starts to take control, pumping faster, slapping my ass again. A lick of wickedness courses through me, my moans pitching higher. I love this.

The feeling of him pounding into me with such control threatens to unravel my brain. One hand gripping my hip, the other fisting my hair, he begins to space out his thrusts, alternating between shallow and deep so I never know what's coming next.

"More, please, more," I beg.

He rides me until I can't think, his thighs slapping into mine, his grip tightening on my hair. The sound of my voice is dull to my ears, as if I'm moaning and pleading from somewhere far away. I don't know how he's doing this to me. Teasing the pleasure out like this, driving me right to the edge and somehow pinning me there, on the brink of an orgasm but never quite reaching the pinnacle. It's torture. It's bliss. It's both.

Without warning, he pulls away and flips me onto my back. His hands push my thighs wide apart as he dives back into me. Lifting my hips, I find that spot inside me so perfectly primed that the slightest touch has it going off.

"Yes, yes, yes," I moan, the climax sending shockwaves through me.

"Good girl," he growls.

Slipping a hand between us, he strokes my clit as he thrusts into my clenching pussy, setting off more sparks that light the entire length of my body. He releases inside me as I'm still coming. His mouth covers mine and we kiss and groan and whisper to each other as we ride out the sensations together.

It's not until I feel him shift his body off of mine that I realize we must have dozed off. My body is still slick with sex, our skin damp with sweat. The sheets are hanging halfway off the bed and somehow a pillow ended up on top of the window curtain. I have no memory of getting that wild, but then again, I was too consumed by the things he did to me to pay much attention.

I try to sit up, but he pulls me back down.

"I can't fall asleep here," I tell him mournfully. "I have somewhere to be soon."

"Just a little longer."

"You're procrastinating," I accuse him, unable to suppress a smile.

Looking up, he runs his finger down my cheek.

"I don't think we destroyed this room nearly enough, Sunshine. I've got a few ideas for how we can procrastinate some more."

I loop my arms around his neck as he moves between my thighs. "Show me."

8

SEBASTIAN

I'M LYING in bed with Sunshine tucked against my body, my arm around her waist, her ass tantalizingly close to my groin. We've exhausted ourselves fucking creatively on every suitable surface in this hotel room: I bent her over the couch, I lifted her onto the vanity in the bathroom and spread her wide, I had her ride me in reverse cowgirl in an upholstered club chair that I dragged over to face the closet's full-length mirror so we could both watch her tits bounce. And now it's all over.

The clock is ticking. Time to go.

I shouldn't still be in her room, to tell the truth. I'm not even sure why I am, or why I chose to see her again in the first place. My eyes stray to a lacy scrap of fabric on the floor that has to be her panties, no doubt soaked with the scent of her arousal, and my dick twitches. I know exactly what she looks like in those panties, and exactly what she looks like out of them.

She's a hot piece of ass, I remind myself. Nothing more. But even as I think it, I know it's not a reasonable excuse for my behavior. I've slept with plenty of beautiful women, and I've never felt the urge to get a second taste. There's something about *this* woman, though. She's an itch I can't stop scratching. And the scratching feels so fucking good.

That's all she is. An itch. A compulsion. An addiction, maybe—a rush of dopamine that I keep going back to get another hit of. She's young and fresh and carefree, an escape from reality wrapped up in a perky set of tits and a smile. No wonder I wanted more. She lights up the reward centers in my brain.

It's the only explanation for why I'm hit with a wave of anxiety when I think about her leaving the island. I just got a new toy, and now it's being taken away from me. That makes sense, doesn't it?

I watch the slow rise and fall of her shoulders as she breathes, the anxiety rising up in me again. Pulling my gaze from her, I search the floor for my clothes. This needs to end right now. I can't sit here trying to deal with a bunch of random, senseless brooding just because my testosterone is raging. I need to get the hell out of this hotel room and put this woman out of my mind for good. Shake her off and get back to my old self. Predictable, routine, and always in control of my actions.

It's the best thing for both of us. The last thing either of us needs is for Sunshine to get attached and start thinking this thing between us means more than it does. It's just a vacation fling. Hot sex with a time limit. We're consenting adults, and this is the deal we willingly signed up for. A good old-fashioned hit it and quit it.

I'm not just saying that to convince myself I'm not a villain, either. We knew what this was going into it. She's never acted shy about what we're doing or expressed any second thoughts. She hasn't tried to play games or ask for anything more. Not that there's even a remote possibility we could have more.

Unless...

Christ, why am I even thinking this way?

Yet the thought has been intruding on my mind all morning. The thought that maybe we could try to do something long distance. Not a relationship, nothing like that, just a kind of...arrangement. Where every so often we meet up again and screw each other's brains out and then we go back to our normal lives and there's nothing complicated about it. As long as it's mutually beneficial for both parties, I don't see a problem with it.

I think it over some more. We could meet once or twice a month on the weekends, jet setting from one hotel to the next, until we have the time to take a longer vacation. Maybe she's the kind of person who enjoys her independence and has no desire to deal with a partner whose very presence demands massive quantities of her time and attention, demands that she consider them first before making any life choices of her own. That's something I can understand.

On the other hand, I know next to nothing about her. Not her name, where she's from, what she's about to start doing for work. Maybe this kind of arrangement doesn't fit with the life she's going back to. Maybe she's only comfortable with this no-strings-attached sex *because* she's on vacation. Sunshine might be a completely different person at home.

Shit, she might even have a boyfriend waiting for her. I

never directly asked, and she didn't volunteer the information. They might have an open relationship, and do I want to be one more guy out of many guys that she's fucking? A spike of jealousy turns my stomach, even as I dismiss the thought. If she does have a boyfriend, it's none of my business. I have no right to feel possessive.

Silently, I scoff at myself. Who the hell am I? It seems like I barely recognize myself since meeting her. Those icy walls I've put up the last few years have begun to thaw. My body feels lighter, my mind less filled with destructive thoughts. Even at work, dealing with Daisy's frustrating lack of competence over the last few days, I haven't felt my usual levels of stress or annoyance. It's like the tiniest sliver of Sunshine's sunny personality has rubbed off on me.

Fuck. This isn't at all what I intended...or expected. But it might be what I need.

I circle back to the idea of a long distance situationship. Nothing too serious, of course, but some kind of regularly scheduled interaction—not even exclusively sexual in nature—with Sunshine. Someone who lifts the dark clouds off me for a little while. Who makes me laugh and forget all the shit that I'm dealing with on a daily basis. It could be a kind of therapy, except it would be much more effective than the psychiatrist I forced myself to see a few times after Rachel died, not that it did me any good.

Rachel.

Instantly, my mood deflates. I can't believe I just sat here spinning out all these ridiculous fantasies for myself. As if Sunshine is somehow going to be the gigantic Band-Aid that fixes me and my entire broken life. Yeah. Brilliant plan, Argos. You selfish asshole. Like that would even work.

She's a great fuck, we had a nice time together, end of story. I need to stop trying to drag things out longer and walk away before I get tangled up in something that could destroy both of us.

Easing my arm off of her and climbing out of bed as quietly as I can so I don't wake her up, I gather up my clothes and get dressed. My chest is aching, and the weight on my shoulders suddenly ten times heavier than usual— because the tides of grief that had receded while I was off in fantasy land with Sunshine have now turned into a tidal wave. A tidal wave that's crushing me.

This is my reality, I remind myself. My fiancée is dead, I'm a workaholic with no soul, and all I can do is try to live my life with as little outside interference—and pain—as possible.

But once I'm standing at the door, I hesitate. From here, I can see through the bedroom door, see Sunshine curled up in the bed with the afternoon light pouring over her, turning her to gold. Her golden hair splays across the pillow in a tumble, her ripe lips slightly parted, the sheet pulled up over her but not quite high enough to cover the pink flash of her areolas. She looks like something out of a dream.

I don't know how it happened, but the woman's got a hold on me. It's messing with how I see myself. Making me believe I could be more than the hard ass who people move out of the way for when they see me coming. That I could be the guy who teases and laughs, who shows up for happy hour, who arranges a midday skinny dip complete with champagne on ice and dessert afterward.

Except that's not the real me. Sunshine doesn't know it, but I sure as hell do.

Who am I kidding? I know I wouldn't be good for her. I can't be what she needs. I can't even be what I need. I'm broken, cold, detached from the rest of the world, even if I might sometimes be able to act otherwise. Deep inside me is a barren landscape. I gave everything I had to Rachel, heart and soul, and now I have nothing left to give.

Darkness and anger descend on me, and my hands clench into fists. I grab the knob and pull the door open, stalking out of the room and down the hall as fast as I can. I don't bother making sure the door closes softly. All I care about is reaching the elevator and getting the fuck out of here. The farther I get from this woman and the lies I tell myself when I'm with her, the better I'll feel. I'm sure of it.

I'm halfway back to The Quattuor Club when my phone chimes with an appointment reminder and I'm suddenly hit with the realization that I won't have time to shower before my dinner meeting with the new clients who just arrived. I'm going to show up smelling like sex.

Too bad I can't muster up the energy to care.

9

BLAIR

A PHONE RINGS shrilly on the nightstand, jolting me from my nap, and my eyes fly open.

Sitting up in a panic, I fumble the receiver off the cradle.

"Hello?"

"This is the front desk, just reminding you that your late checkout is in fifteen minutes."

"Oh! Yes, um, thank you. I'm just on my way out."

Thank God I packed up earlier.

Hanging up the phone, I check the time on the digital clock and my stomach drops. Shit. There's no way I'm going to be able to meet my parents on time.

I glance around the room, but I don't see Scowl. I quickly slide out of bed and pop my head into the bathroom, the sitting room, and the other bedroom, but they're all empty. He's gone already.

He left without saying goodbye.

Why didn't he wake me up before he left?

Disappointment washes over me, but then I start to

wonder if he felt the same way I do—wanting to keep only good memories of our time together and not end things on a sad note. The thought of us both holding onto the blissful moments, knowing we'll never see each other again, is so romantic that I almost text him to say as much, but then I mentally kick myself. I can't text him. That's not how vacation romances work. I have to let him go.

Starting now.

Acutely aware that I'm only making myself more late by the second, I burst out of bed and rush to the bathroom to take the world's fastest shower. When I get out, I grab my phone and see several missed text messages from my mother. She's going to be worried sick when I don't show up on schedule. I need to come up with a good excuse.

An excuse that isn't "I was having sex with a hot stranger I met on the beach." That'd give Mom a heart attack for sure.

My relationship with my mother is complicated. She doted on me and my sister when we were growing up, but once Sophie hit her teen years, something changed. Mom changed. She still loved us, of course, but once she and Sophie started butting heads all the time, Mom became very passive aggressive. She started working later, going out to social events and fundraisers with Dad more, leaving notes around the house or texting me and my sister instead of just talking to us. Looking back, I can see that it was probably because Mom would rather avoid us than get into arguments, but at the time it felt like she wanted nothing to do with her daughters. Which only made Sophie push back harder, get even more confrontational whenever Mom *was* home.

Then, after Sophie died, Mom did a complete one-eighty. She wanted to know exactly where I was and who I was with at all times, she barely left the house, she insisted on checking in with me every day after school and before bed. I hated it at the time, but as I've gotten older, I've realized that the reason she holds onto me so tightly is because she's scared of losing me, too. Which is why, as hard as she is to take a lot of the time, I try to remind myself that her being so overprotective is just proof that she cares.

Scrambling to assemble an outfit, my hair still dripping wet, I have a lightbulb moment. I'll just tell my parents that my final spa appointment at Espadrilles ran late. Thank God for all the overpriced but heavenly scented spa products that Brooke and I bought there. My bright red manicure still looks perfect so I can pretend I was getting my nails done too.

I unzip my toiletries case and start slathering myself in lemongrass scented lotion and scrunching my hair with rosemary-lavender oil. Once my mother gets a whiff of me, she'll have no reason not to buy my story. After slipping into a pair of palazzo pants and a sleeveless mock neck top, I give my hair a quick towel-dry, put on some gold hoops, and reapply my lip gloss. Dashing out the door and down the hall, I call the front desk on my cell and confirm my checkout, hanging up just as the elevator arrives.

It's only a short Uber to the members-only resort my parents are staying at. In fact, it's in the same direction that Scowl and I went this morning for a dip in the private pool. The back of my neck prickles. What are the chances that I might be going to the same resort now? It's hard to tell. The hotel properties here tend to run into each other, with tropical flowers and overlapping groves of palm trees and poincianas in the spaces between. I didn't pay much attention to exactly where we were anyway. I was too caught up in the moment.

Instantly, I flash back to him laying me out on the lounge chair, his hands and mouth everywhere, the sweet taste of champagne on my tongue. Heat flushes me from my head to my toes and I can't help thinking that someday, when I take over running the team from my parents, I'll be able set my own schedule. Maybe then I could fly out to Chicago or L.A. or wherever Scowl is and see if he's interested in meeting up again. Implausible, maybe, but not impossible. It's an effort to shove all my memories of him aside and snap back to the present as the Uber pulls up at my parents' hotel, The Quattuor Club.

Wow. This place is even fancier than I imagined. The architecture is clean and modern and harmonious, with almost a Japanese influence. There are lots of glass walls and manicured foliage indoors and out. The path leading up to the entry doors is lined with thick stands of bamboo, and I walk over a little wooden bridge with clear, koi-filled waters flowing beneath it. The second I walk inside, I'm greeted by name by a smiling staff member and I catch the subtle scents of aloe, cucumber, and ocean breeze. I actually let out a sigh, feeling my shoulders relax. This is so much nicer than Espadrilles.

The lobby is gorgeous. Cream sofas, plush boucle armchairs, dark stone floors, soothing charcoal walls and brushed brass light fixtures everywhere. The space is huge and yet gives off a cozy vibe.

"Shall we check you in?" the staff member asks.

"Um, actually, I'm running late to meet my parents for dinner and I don't know my room number yet," I say.

She nods. "Of course, Miss Tisdale. The bell desk will handle everything."

Another staff member appears at my elbow to whisk my bags away and then I'm escorted directly to the restaurant. By the time I get there, I actually feel calmer. I'm late, yes, but only by about twenty minutes.

As I walk into the restaurant, however, my anxiety reappears full force—because the first thing I see is a sign that reads *Closed for Private Event*. Of course it is. Why do they have to act like this? Who cares if other equally rich people eat near them? Booking out the entire restaurant is so unnecessary.

It's something they've done on occasion since I was a child, purchasing a few rows of seats for our family at the opera or the theater, renting an entire museum for the afternoon, buying out all the tickets for the botanical garden. But over the last few years, their desire for solitude has extended beyond special outings. It's gotten so much worse. Ever since Sophie died. As if they're afraid other people will see their grief and ask questions or offer sympathies.

While I can understand wanting to sequester themselves from the world, I think they're taking it too far. At least after they retire, they can spend all the hermit time they want. Maybe they'll start to feel a bit more social again once they've had enough quiet time to themselves.

"Miss Tisdale."

I whip my head toward the voice and see an elegant woman standing behind an onyx podium.

"Yes?"

"This way, please," the hostess says, leading me into the dining room.

Following her, I see that there are no other guests here, thanks to my parents reserving the entire place just for us. The room is empty and echoing, devoid of any signs of life save for Mom and Dad taking up a massive table by the picture windows that look out at the ocean. They both have wine glasses in front of them, as well as a basket of bread that I'm sure my mother hasn't touched.

I glance around in the desperate hope that I might spy one other person, just one, anyone who can act as a buffer. But the only other people I see are two servers and a bartender behind an extravagant mahogany and hammered brass bar with his back turned to us.

As I walk up to the table, I notice my mother is nervously twisting a cloth napkin in her lap, her brows knitted, but my father immediately rises from his seat to give me a hug and a kiss on the cheek.

"Darling, you look beautiful."

"Thanks, Dad."

He pulls a chair out for me across from him, clears his throat at my mother, and then sits back down. Mom just gives me a tight, fake smile.

"You should have called," she says. "Your hotel said you'd checked out already, but you weren't here, and I couldn't stop thinking that something had happened—"

"Victoria, please," my dad admonishes. "She's just on island time, that's all."

"No, Mom's right. I'm sorry," I say. "My spa appointment ran late, and I left my phone in my room, and then I had to rush to get here."

I fluff my damp hair a little in an effort to waft the rosemary oil in my mom's direction.

"So. How have you been spending your time on the island?" Mom asks.

Oh, wouldn't she be scandalized to know. "Relaxing. Snorkeling. Swimming, trying local foods. A little shopping. And many spa appointments. Brooke and I needed all the R and R we could get."

"Glad to hear it," Dad says. "You've earned it, college grad."

I lean over the table and slide my hands toward my mom.

"Speaking of which. Like my nails? I just had them done."

Her blue eyes meet mine. They soften for a fraction of a second. "I'm not sure I would have chosen that shade, sweetheart."

"Brooke liked it," I say breezily.

Mom's about to reply—probably with some version of, "If Brooke jumped off a cliff, would you?"—when a server comes by and pours us all champagne. Thank God.

"Blair," my mother scolds. "Slow down on the alcohol."

Glancing at my flute, I realize it's already empty.

"Sorry," I say. "I guess I was thirsty."

I turn to my father. I'm about to change the subject and ask him if he's given any more consideration to what position I might be taking on at the Tisdale Corporation. I need to remind him that I'm ready to prove myself. That this is what I've studied for, worked myself into exhaustion for.

The words are on the tip of my tongue when Dad says, "Well, you aren't the only late one." Pushing back his chair, he rises to his feet. "Here's one of the owners of the place, who's personally taking care of us."

Turning in my chair, I look over my shoulder, following his gaze. Chills race down my spine and my jaw falls open as I take in the man heading toward us.

No. Freaking. Way.

10

SEBASTIAN

Sunshine is sitting with my new clients, her expression frozen and inscrutable as her eyes meet mine.

I can do nothing but stride toward the table as my brain races to make sense of what I'm seeing.

But there's only one explanation: Sunshine is the fucking match.

Her parents are Mr. and Mrs. Tisdale, who have signed their daughter up with The Quattuor Group to be wined and dined by a succession of three wealthy men, who will then bid handsomely for her hand in marriage at an online auction. An online auction which she'll know nothing about, because only the parents and the bachelors are ever aware that the agency has orchestrated the whole thing.

Of course Sunshine is the match. Thinking back to the day we first met on the beach, when I wondered if I'd ever laugh honestly again, I suddenly realize that meeting her—and having the chance to laugh with her—was clearly God's way of playing a cruel joke on me.

She's not just some incredible woman who serendipitously ran into me. She's *Blair Tisdale*, daughter of Walter and Veronica Tisdale, financial moguls, and owners of the New York Rockets pro baseball team—one of the wealthiest power couples in the United States.

And there's nothing I can do now but grit my teeth and make nice with her parents.

"Mr. and Mrs. Tisdale, welcome," I say cordially as I approach the table.

Swiveling my gaze in Sunshine's—*Blair's*—direction, I give a cursory shake of my head, hoping she can read my mind. *You don't know me.* Because I'm sure as hell going to pretend that I don't know her. She blinks, lips still parted in shock, but thankfully she doesn't speak.

Aware that her parents are looking at me expectantly, I smooth my tie and plaster on a smile.

"My sincere apologies for being late," I go on. "My last meeting ran over."

Walter shakes my hand with a vice-like grip and a smile on his face, while Veronica shakes perfunctorily, her cool blue eyes seeming to judge me. I wonder if she smells the sex I didn't have time to wash off.

"And you must be Blair," I say. I keep my hands to myself this time.

"So nice to meet you," she says. "Mr...."

"Argos. Sebastian Argos."

Forcing myself not to stare at her, I take the open chair and sit, keeping my bearing as casual and in command as possible. Being so close to the woman I was buried to the hilt in not even an hour ago makes it difficult. I still can't believe the universe dropped the one woman I can't have right into my lap.

I can't even imagine how bad it would look if anyone found out I'd been messing around with one of the agency's bachelorettes. The degree of unprofessionalism is staggering. Not to mention, three men with very deep pockets will be vying for her attention soon enough, each of them tossing cash into the ring until one comes out on top. If any of them knew that I'd slept with their prize...

"Mr. Argos," Mrs. Tisdale says, "Have our personal requests been taken care of?"

I think of my new concierge, still failing to meet the demands of her position. I can only hope that she's handled everything, or that Margo has stepped in if necessary. There are a few things, however, that I had to take charge of myself.

"Yes, ma'am," I answer smoothly. "You'll have the resort almost entirely to yourselves, as you asked. The only other guests are those of high status who had prior reservations that I was obliged to honor. Regardless, no one should bother you. The private beach is yours. The chef will prepare a daily menu according to your dietary specifications. And the spa has been fully staffed to meet all your needs.

"As you know, once the Junkanoo Festival gets going next week, the resort will be at full capacity. I do hope you'll enjoy every moment of your stay here."

I glance at Blair's glossy red fingernails. They dug so nicely into my back while I fucked her.

"Thank you," Mrs. Tisdale says.

"Although," I add, "it looks like Blair won't be needing a manicure. That is a lovely shade of red, might I add."

Almost as lovely as the color rising in her cheeks as I compliment her. "I hope they indulged all your needs."

"Oh, they indulged my needs *very well*," Blair says, tilting her head as she smiles at me.

Oblivious to the friction between me and her daughter, Mrs. Tisdale waves down the waiter for a refill of her champagne. Blair pushes her glass across the table for a top-up as well, but her mother blocks her with a hand.

"You've already had enough, Blair. Control yourself." To the waiter, she adds, "She'll just have sparkling water."

Sunshine tightens her lips into a hard line but doesn't respond. I don't appreciate Mrs. Tisdale's tone, but I can see that there's something deeper going on here than an overbearing mother's rebuke over how much alcohol her daughter is drinking. Because the tension between them doesn't flare brightly; instead, it simmers. This is something long running.

And Papa Tisdale remains mum as well, letting out a barely audible sigh rather than intervening on his daughter's behalf. It only lends credence to my theory that Blair and her mother have a complicated relationship, one that Walter prefers not to involve himself in. Or maybe Mrs. Tisdale simply has trouble accepting that her child is a grown woman who can make her own choices about alcohol...and everything else. I've seen my fair share of overprotective parents in this line of work.

Witnessing this family conflict isn't what's bothering me, however.

The real thorn in my side is the fact that this gorgeous, driven, extremely sexy young woman sitting across from me has no idea that she's here at the resort to be courted by three different suitors. She'll think the introductions are random, when in reality, each meeting will have been carefully arranged for her by me, after choosing the potential matches who most seamlessly align with Blair's values, interests, and passions. The kind of matches she won't be able to stop herself from having instant chemistry with. And in the end, the choice will be out of her hands. The man she ends up with will come down to who has the most money to win her.

The thought turns my stomach.

Even though the agency's matchmaking business has always been run this way, I've never thought twice about the fact that the women involved don't realize what's happening. Because the matches we make support the greater good. The eligible bachelorette gets an attractive, wealthy partner who is as well-suited to her as possible, and our track record proves that Quattuor marriages tend to last.

But now...it's oddly unsettling to think of Blair in this position. To bear the responsibility of arranging her future. A future that, only hours ago, I was contemplating involving myself in, if only for an occasional fuck. What the hell was I thinking? And thank God I didn't broach the subject with her. Now that I know her true identity, I realize that I dodged a bullet. Blair Tisdale is off limits to me for good.

The waiter arrives with the appetizer—seared ahi with ponzu sauce served over sliced cucumbers with edible flowers for garnish—and everyone seems grateful for the interruption. It's usually a dish I enjoy, particularly as prepared by our chef, but the food tastes like ash in my mouth.

Turning to Walter, I attempt to steer the conversation back into neutral territory. "Mr. Tisdale, you informed us that you'd need a private workspace for the upcoming MLB draft, so I arranged a conference room for you in the business center."

Blair looks sharply at her father, her eyes taking on an eager gleam that is all too familiar to me by now. Whatever she's thinking about excites her.

"The room is soundproof," I go on, "and a private phone line has been set up for you. Of course, no one will be allowed inside the room save for yourself and a staff member to assist you."

"Wait a second." Blair blinks and a divot appears between her brows. "Dad, *I'm* supposed to be with you tomorrow. We talked about this."

Walter smiles at her and shakes his head slightly. "Well, sweetie, it's just..."

That's when it hits me: *this* is the family business Blair had talked about so excitedly. The business she's so passionate about, so convinced she'll one day be in charge of. The Tisdale Corporation. The same Tisdale Corporation that owns the New York Rockets. My chest goes tight when I see the crestfallen expression on Blair's face.

"Dad, I've been preparing for the draft for a year. I can tell you anything you'd want to know about all the up-and-comers, their stats, their social followings, what kind of career goals they have. I've been diligent. Let me help."

"Blair, we'll discuss this further in private," her mother says.

But Blair continues as if she didn't hear her. "I have put hours, weeks, months of my life into researching these players. I know the game, I have a business degree from Stern, and I'm telling you, I'm ready to step up. Please don't take this away from me."

Walter's voice drops pleadingly low. "Like your mother said, we'll discuss it in private, Blair. That's the end of it now, okay?"

But it's not okay. Not according to the look on Blair's face. She's devastated, and the hopeful light in her eyes has completely died.

The worst part isn't even that her father is cutting her off from taking an active role in the team's draft picks. It's that Blair is still convinced she's going to eventually be in charge of the Tisdale Corporation—when I know that nothing could be further from the truth. There's so much more at play here than she realizes.

She pushes her chair back from the table and straightens her spine. "You always say we'll talk later, and then we don't. Talk to me right now. I'm sitting here in front of you, and I have a right to know what you're planning for my future."

An uncomfortable silence descends over the table.

Nobody is going to tell her that her future includes being married off to the highest bidder—a man she will not choose for herself. A man who will not only gain a stunning wife and the daughter of one of the richest families in America...but also an extremely attractive bonus. Because he's also going to be groomed to inherit ownership of the baseball team. Not Blair. Never Blair.

And she has no idea.

Walter quickly changes the subject by asking me about the weather forecast for the next few days, if any boat charters might be available for a day of deep-sea fishing, and if I have any recommendations for the best places his wife can lay out and tan while still having access to an attendant to wait on her? Blair silently observes the conversation for a few minutes, and then rises from her chair.

"If you'll excuse me, I've lost my appetite. I'm going to go get settled into my room."

"Blair!" her mother snaps. "Sit down."

But Blair simply smiles tightly, her gaze bouncing off me as she quietly pushes in her chair and walks away.

Mrs. Tisdale drums her fingernails on the table before giving me a charming smile.

"Blair has always been an impetuous child. A temper like you wouldn't believe. Unappreciative for what she has. Sadly, I imagine you see a lot of that with the clientele who can afford to stay at this establishment, don't you?"

I very nearly say that I don't agree with any part of that description of her daughter. But of course it's my job to smile sympathetically at her and use my very best placating voice. "I could share some stories. Believe me."

She laughs a little. "Oh, I bet you could. Now, why don't we put all this fuss behind us and you can tell us all about the itinerary you've built for the trip."

"Of course."

But as I shift into full-on resort host mode, I can't get the image of Blair's face out of my mind.

If her parents think she has a temper now, I can't imagine what they'll think when the truth finally comes out.

11

BLAIR

I'M so livid at my parents that I'm about to explode by the time I reach my new hotel room, but I'm relieved to see that my luggage has been delivered. At least I have something to do with my hands now.

I put my things away with harsh, angry motions, stuffing clothes into dresser drawers, stabbing hangers through the straps of my dresses, slapping my toiletries onto the bathroom vanity. It's hard to say if I'm more disappointed at my dad's sudden refusal to let me help with the draft, furious at him and my mother for refusing to discuss the career that I've been planning to build my life around, or humiliated that Scowl was sitting at our table to witness the entire debacle. But one bright, shiny fact keeps circling in my mind: Scowl—no, Sebastian Argos—is one of the owners of this resort.

How interesting. How...fun.

How *naughty*.

Apparently my parents have paid him a hefty sum to cater to them and provide all the personal attention they desire. But that might just work out to my benefit. Because now that Sebastian is on the clock and I'm technically one of his VIP hotel guests...well, we could easily come up with all sorts of clandestine ways to continue this fling a little longer. He can come and go anywhere on the property, after all. And I can excuse any disappearances by saying that Sebastian was just showing me around.

He hadn't mentioned he was a resort owner. Granted, we never got to know each other that well. Leaving out the personal details of our lives had been intentional, and I get that. But he seemed so down to earth, I never suspected he was a secret millionaire. And there I was, feeling so pleased because for once I was seeing a guy who was interested in me for who I am, who didn't know how rich my family is, who wasn't just trying to get a foot in the door at the Tisdale Corporation like the guys I dated at NYU.

Is it possible that Sebastian knew who I was all along? But no. The look on his face when he walked up to my parents' table said it all. He was just as shocked as I was to be crossing paths again, and so soon after we said our not-goodbyes.

I flop onto the bed and heave a sigh. I still can't believe that my dad is purposely cutting me out of assisting with the draft. It doesn't make any sense. We've been discussing potential picks for a year, and never once has he let on that he had no intention of allowing me to sit in on the proceedings with him. He knows how much I care about the game, about our team, about proving myself. What changed? Why now? Why didn't he say anything before?

There's something else niggling at me, too. I can't put my finger on it, but I know something is up with my parents. I keep getting the sense that this family vacation is more than just a vacation, that they're going to spring some other horrible news on me. Maybe they're getting divorced, or worse, maybe one of them is sick. They are getting older, and Dad's such a workaholic. And Mom...she hasn't taken care of herself properly since Sophie died, either. All of her focus has been on me. My stomach churns.

I'm overthinking this. Maybe it's nothing to do with their personal lives. Maybe they've finally decided to sell off some of the family business. Mom's always saying the corporation is getting too big and unwieldy, and Dad has talked about slowing down someday. *Please, let them both be healthy*, I think to myself. *And if they do have to sell off some of the business, let it not be the baseball team.*

"I need a drink," I say out loud. And I need to stop pouting in my room like a bratty teenager. I'm a confident, competent woman of the world. Time to start acting like one.

Sitting up, I go over to the closet and pull out a sheer floral coverup. Then I dig out my skimpiest string bikini and high-heeled sandals. My plan is to find the beach bar closest to the resort and lay out with a drink for a few hours, in the hopes that a little sun (and alcohol) will improve my mood enough for me to face my parents again. Maybe then I can take my father aside and ask him to reconsider letting me assist him during the draft. He's always more reasonable when my mother isn't there nagging him.

As I change, I can't help hoping that Sebastian will show up at the beach too, nursing a drink of his own after dealing with my parents. If he does, we can talk, maybe clear the air and make each other privy to a few more personal details. After that...I certainly wouldn't mind a private tour of the resort's more exclusive areas. We could even go back to the hidden pool with the waterfall—which must be tucked away somewhere around here, after all—or maybe he'll surprise me again.

There's no better way I can think of to work off my current frustration than in his arms.

The beach bar is packed when I arrive. Since the venue isn't on the resort's property, it's open to the public, and it's full of enthusiastic tourists and hard-partying college kids. Music thumps through the air, and a crowd of dancing bodies moves in an undulating circle on the beach. The tiki bar has a huge line, but I manage to find one of the smaller drink carts and order myself a Sky Juice, which I sip slowly as I wander through the crowd.

I didn't actually expect to bump into Sebastian here— he's at work, obviously—but I'm more and more disappointed as I circle the entire perimeter and don't see him. I scan under umbrellas, in lawn chairs and lounge chairs, even the wooden benches around the fire pit. Every open spot seems to be occupied, but not by him.

Resisting the urge to text him, I lose myself in the throng and end up finishing my drink much quicker than expected. I grab another one and am looking around for a place to sit when, to my good fortune, I spot an empty chaise longue positioned on the edge of the dance floor.

I dash over to the chair and practically dive onto it, then take off my coverup and arrange myself as sexily as I can. Back arched, bikini top adjusted, legs folded to one side. If Sebastian does show up, I need to make sure he notices me. But the minutes pass, the sun dips lower in the sky, and still no Sebastian. Feeling dejected, I end up downing my second drink. I'm about to ask the frat boy next to me if he'll watch my chaise while I get a refill when a waiter stops by and hands me another Sky Juice.

"Thank you so much," I say, reaching for the cash in my clutch.

The waiter waves off my money. "Courtesy of the gentleman at the bar."

He makes a motion behind him at some random group of men, not pointing out anyone in particular before walking away. Studying the men, I sip the gin drink slowly, trying to figure out which one of them is my benefactor. None of them are looking my way, though. In fact—

A shadow falls over me, and my pulse instantly picks up, my skin zinging as I get a whiff of masculine cologne. I grin. He's here. With a sassy smile, I glance up...

And do a double take. It's not Sebastian Argos, but I recognize this face instantly. I've seen him on television more times than I can count. I've studied everything about him, from his early beginnings playing baseball in high school a decade ago to his performance during his college years, to his impressive professional stats, to the way his body moves when he throws a killer pitch. I whip my sunglasses off and sit up straight, hardly believing my eyes.

"Enjoying the drink?" the guy asks, adjusting his baseball hat.

"Ted Polansky!" I blurt. "I always thought we'd meet under different circumstances."

I'm not starstruck, per se, just flustered—because I literally thought I'd meet him when he became the owner of a rival MLB team someday, or maybe when our club made him an offer he couldn't refuse to ditch the Miami Marlins and be a star pitcher for the Rockets instead.

He raises a brow. "Blair Tisdale wanted to meet me?"

It's a question, not a statement, which means he isn't doing the kind of off-puttingly arrogant flirting that I've come to expect from the guys in my usual social circle. Admittedly, the question mark at the end of his sentence is kind of endearing. Like somehow, the multimillion-dollar price tag on him hasn't given him the grossly inflated ego of most pro athletes.

"I...yeah," I say, still taken aback. "What are you doing here? Is this a work trip? You're not leaving the MLB for one of the national teams here, are you? I thought Miami was treating you well."

"Nothing like that," he says, laughing. "I flew out to the island for a weekend off. But this is wild, running into you like this."

"How do you even know who I am?" I can't help asking.

"Everyone knows the owners of the New York Rockets," he says. "You and your dad go to almost every game together. Not a lot of owners are that dedicated. It's obvious you love the sport."

I can feel myself blushing. "I really do."

It's not just his attention that has me flushed. He's objectively handsome. With his muscular build, his shaggy, dark blond hair, cleft chin, and warm brown eyes, he's got an All-American charm that's pretty undeniable. I'm sure Brooke would kill to be in my shoes right now.

"Do you mind if I join you?"

He moves his long, athletic body as if to sit on the sand

beside my chair. Without really thinking, I scoot over on the chaise.

"Oh, don't sit on the sand. It's too hot. I can share." I pat the seat next to me. "Please, sit."

He looks genuinely pleased and I can't help but wonder if he doesn't realize that he could literally take home any woman, or multiple women, on this beach tonight. Anyone but me.

Because as he sits, all I can think is that he's not Sebastian. But Ted is a big deal in the industry, and it can't hurt to show him just how friendly the Rockets franchise can be, so I'll make nice.

And yet, as we get to chatting about how the first half of baseball season is going, I find that I'm really enjoying myself. He has a smooth, deep voice that's easy to listen to. We discuss the upcoming MLB draft and which players are looking the most desirable, then we quiz each other on who we'd pick for a fantasy baseball team. He talks about his flight here being delayed because somebody tried to sneak a goldfish in a tiny bottle of water onto the plane. As we banter, we finish our drinks and then more magically appear. I'm shocked when I check my phone and find that a few hours have passed.

"I'm really glad I ran into you," he says. "You know, the Junkanoo festival is this week. Are you going? I've never been, but it's supposed to be like a cross between Mardi Gras and the Fourth of July. Or maybe more like one of those big luaus they have in Hawaii."

"I might check it out. Sounds like it could be a blast."

"It's supposed to be a really big deal at this resort. The concierge said that guests from all the other hotels on the beach come here to participate, too. There's live music, costumes, a parade..."

"I'm sure there's great food, too," I muse. "Have you had fried conch yet?"

"Not yet."

"You've got to try it," I tell him, realizing I'm slurring my words a little. "Anything with conch, really. You can't vacation in the islands without eating your fill. Or 'conching out,' as I like to say."

Ted laughs at my dumb joke, but suddenly all I'm thinking about is that first day I met Sebastian on the beach and offered him my conch salad. My mood deflates a little. Yes, I'm enjoying my time with Ted, and there's nothing wrong with that, but I can't help wishing he was someone else.

Not that I can fault Sebastian for not being here. He didn't know I was coming to the beach bar. Neither of us reached out to the other after I abandoned him with my parents at the hotel restaurant, and maybe it's better that way. Maybe it's best to let our brief affair fade into memory already.

But as I look over at Ted and find him smiling warmly at me, I get the urge to be done with this flirtation. I don't want him to get the impression that we're going back to one of our rooms together, and honestly, I don't think I can stand to be on this hot, crowded beach for one more minute.

"I think I'm gonna call it a night," I say with a rueful smile.

To my relief, he doesn't try to talk me into staying longer. He just stands and helps me up from the chair. I bend over to grab my coverup and as I struggle to get my arms into it, I waver a bit on my feet.

"My heels clearly aren't made for the sand," I say with a laugh, toeing them off, and he's gentlemanly enough to pick them up and hand them to me.

"You going to be okay getting back to your room?"

"Oh, of course. I'll be fine."

"Cool. Well, it was really nice to meet you, Blair. I hope we run into each other again."

"You too, Ted. Have a good night."

As I walk away in my bare feet as steadily as possible, I realize he mentioned the Junkanoo but didn't invite me to go with him. He didn't ask for my number, either. I feel equally jilted and relieved.

12

SEBASTIAN

TODAY HAS FELT like the longest fucking workday I've ever experienced. Between the high of my sexcapades with Sunshine—*Blair*, I remind myself—and the visceral shock of seeing her at the hotel restaurant with the Tisdales afterward, not to mention my incredibly frustrating efforts to train Daisy properly for the concierge position, I'm ready to go to my residential suite and crash out in front of the big-screen TV for the night, maybe with an order of pad thai or some sushi. I could use a reward.

I'm still reeling with the knowledge that I've fucked one of the agency's bachelorettes. It's not just unprofessional, it's forbidden. Unfortunately, the fact that Blair is off-limits is only making my craving for her even more powerful. The more I try to convince myself I'll never touch her again, the more my balls ache, the more I'm haunted by the memory of her pussy clenching around my cock, the taste of her sweet juice on my tongue. I need to get it together. Shake her off.

But as I stride through one of the back corridors of the

resort, responding to one last work email on my phone, a door swings open down the hall, and the familiar scent of sandalwood hits my nose.

My head whips up and I take in a pair of blue eyes, a mass of blond waves, and the easy smile that's had me hooked since the first day I met her. Sunshine. Blair. No—Miss Tisdale. That's all she is to me now. And she's walking toward me in the tiniest string bikini I've ever seen, her coverup flaring out to her sides, her tits bouncing with each high-heeled step. Fuck.

"Good evening, Miss Tisdale," I say in my most professional tone. "Can I help you with something?"

She stops in front of me, just out of arm's reach. "Actually, maybe you can."

I catch the faint scent of masculine cologne and gin mixed with her perfume, and a surge of jealousy has me seeing red. I try to shove the feeling of possessiveness away. The ill-advised fling I had with Blair Tisdale is over. It's no concern of mine what she's been getting up to, nor with whom.

Locking her gaze onto mine, she suddenly sways a little on her heels, and that's when all reason flies out the window and my protective instincts go into overdrive.

"Did something happen? Did someone...take advantage?" I ask, my skin crawling at the thought of another man touching her without her consent.

"No," she says, cocking a hip at me as her smile widens. "Not yet anyway."

I don't miss the fact that she's flirting, daring me to make a move, giving me those come-hither eyes. But even if I hadn't just sworn her off, there's no denying the fact that she's drunk. And even if I can be a wolf sometimes, when it comes to intoxicated women, I am nothing if not a perfect gentleman.

"Whoa, there," I say, holding her up gently as she tilts to the side again. "You okay?"

"Mmm," she says, and the sound of her half-moan makes the hair on the back of my neck rise. "Too many Sky Juices. They were strong."

Our bodies are so close that I can feel the heat of her skin radiating into me. Perfume, gin, sunscreen, that foreign cologne, and I swear I detect a hint of pussy—the combination has my senses overloaded, and the wolf comes out. I'm almost dizzy with lust, with the primal urge to take her right here against the wall. It would be so easy, pulling the stretchy fabric of her bikini to the side, ramming into that sweet cunt as I bury my face in her neck.

Christ, I should walk away right now. Or show her to her room first, make sure she's tucked in for the night, and then walk away. I shouldn't act on all the dirty thoughts that have been in my head since seeing her in the restaurant. I shouldn't feel satisfied that I never washed her off of me from earlier today.

"I'm about to call it a night, but I can help you get to your suite," I tell her coolly, with no hint of inuendo. "Have room service sent up for you, if you'd like."

"I should eat something. But I don't want to go back to my room yet. Got any ideas?"

Her mouth quirks up, and she doesn't look like a woman in distress. She looks like a woman who's fully aware of the effect she's having on me and enjoying it.

"I know where to get the best conch fritters on the

island," I hear myself saying, utterly disregarding all the reasons why this is a really, really bad idea.

"Really?"

"Really. You want to get out of here?"

Instead of answering, she grabs my hand and leads me out the door. Once we're outside, I can hear a live band on the beach playing music that reverberates through the air. The temperature has cooled since earlier, but the breeze is still balmy and sweet. Blair ties her coverup tighter so it looks more like a dress, and I notice her steps becoming steadier as we walk. Maybe the fresh air is helping her sober up.

"I can't believe my parents booked us a family vacation at your resort," she says, glancing at me sidelong. "Almost seems like fate."

"Just a coincidence," I reply brusquely. "I run the most exclusive resort on the island, and your parents are very much in the demographic of our typical clientele. Hardly sounds like fate to me."

"That's fair," she says, but I can tell I haven't changed her mind.

Before she can start asking questions about the resort or what I do here, I deftly steer the conversation toward more neutral topics. Blair catches me up on what she's been up to the last few days—more of the usual tourist activities, as expected—and bemoans the departure of her best friend, who apparently flew back home early this morning. I find myself sharing a few stories about my new concierge trainee, though I don't mention Daisy by name, and Blair's laughter helps ease the stress I've been feeling over the whole thing.

We reach the street corner I've been drawing us toward, and Blair gives me a dubious look as I tug her to a stop outside a dilapidated little shack with a hand-painted sign that simply says, 'Mo's.'

"What?" I ask.

"This is the best place in town? I was expecting, I don't know, a Michelin star."

I shrug. "We can go somewhere else if you'd prefer."

"Hell no." She grins broadly. "I'm always down to check out what's off the beaten path. Especially when it comes to food. Besides, I like to live dangerously."

Don't I know it.

She tucks her arm around mine as we head inside, and I let her.

The place is busy and boisterous, as it usually is. We manage to find a table on the back patio, and I leave Blair to hold our place while I go up to the counter to order. I can barely carry all the food containers back to the table. We're going to share the conch fritters and a lobster roll with coleslaw, peas and rice, baked mac and cheese, plantains, and yucca fries. I also got us two Cokes to wash it all down.

"You ordered the entire menu!" she says, clearly pleased. "This barely fits on the table."

"Figured you should try a little bit of everything since it's your first time here."

"I like your style, Argos," she says, leaning forward.

"I like your style, too," I say, and even though I meant it to sound casual, our eyes get caught when they meet, and neither of us looks away.

Clearing my throat, I force myself to grab the plate of fritters and aioli and push it toward her.

"Here. Eat," I tell her.

We dig into the food, and I'm glad for the distraction. Two bites into the crispy, golden-fried fritters, Blair starts nodding, then lets out a huff of breath and grabs her Coke.

"Too spicy?" I ask as she drinks.

"Never," she says breathlessly, setting the bottle down, but her cheeks are flushed with the heat and she immediately takes another long drink of soda. "What is this pepper I'm tasting?"

"*Piment antillais*," I tell her. "Habanero. It's in the batter. They're generous with it sometimes."

"As they should be."

With that, she grabs another fritter and swipes it through the sauce before popping it into her mouth, followed by a big bite of creamy coleslaw to ease the burn.

"So, what's the verdict?" I ask. "Michelin worthy?"

"Best cock I've ever had," she says with a grin, calling back to our joke on the day we met, though I can't pretend I don't know that she's also complimenting my dick.

"Glad to hear it," I reply. "Try the lobster roll next. No habaneros in that one."

Blair digs into the lobster roll without hesitation. And when she makes an appreciative sound for the food deep in her throat, my cock twitches so hard I have to shift in my seat.

Fuck.

I switch my focus back to the food, spearing a couple fried plantains with my fork and shoveling them into my mouth even though they're hot enough to burn my tongue. She's so focused on her meal that I don't think she notices my sudden discomfort. That's when my phone vibrates with an incoming text from Becker.

> How did the Tisdale meeting go?
> Everything on track?

Fuck you very much for reminding me why I have to behave, sir. I slip the phone into my pocket without texting him back.

Blair sets down the lobster roll and clears her throat. "I, um, feel like I should apologize for not telling you who I was or who my parents are."

I wave her away. "You don't need to apologize for anything."

"I know. But this whole thing...with us...it's not something I've done before. I mean, I'm not in the habit of hooking up with strangers on vacation and hiding my identity." She forces a laugh. "I guess I'm just so used to everyone knowing who my parents are and how much money they have that a little anonymity felt sort of nice."

"I get it," I tell her. "No explanation necessary. In fact, we don't need to talk about it at all. Water under the bridge."

"Right. Cool." She hesitates and then goes on, "But I was thinking, Sebastian..." She says my name as if she's trying it out on her tongue. "This doesn't have to be over. I'm here for another week, and I'm staying at your hotel..."

But of course it has to be over. Her parents are my clients, and Blair is the commodity. Soon, she'll be walking down the aisle with a man who can provide for her in every way that counts. I need to shut her down before she convinces me to make even more bad decisions that I'll have to regret later.

Not that I regret anything I've done. I should, though. I know that.

"Let's just enjoy right now," I say.

"Yeah. Of course. I just meant—"

A small shadow falls over the edge of our table, rescuing me from the direction this conversation is heading in. Glancing over, I find an island boy maybe six or seven years old, with an arm full of colorful woven bracelets. Each bracelet has a one-cent coin in the center that has been smoothed flat so most of the markings are removed, stamped with a letter of the alphabet.

The little boy turns his huge brown eyes on Blair, and she visibly melts. Before I can warn her of how quickly children around here can guilt trip you into emptying your wallet, she's ruffling through the bracelets on the child's arm to find her letter.

"What letter?" he asks.

"B."

"I got you." Flashing a megawatt smile, he immediately finds the correct letter and removes the other bracelets to get to it. Gesturing for her arm, he slips the bracelet over her hand and onto her wrist, pulling the ties so it fits snugly.

Blair oohs and ahhs and the child turns his eyes to me.

"Twenty dollars. Special price."

It takes an effort to hold my tongue. I could get ten of these bracelets for that price at any of the kitschy souvenir shops along the beach. But knowing that I'm caught hook, line, and sinker, I dig a twenty out and hand it to the kid.

He bounces away happily while Blair appreciates her new bauble.

"I think 'right now' is the best place I've ever vacationed," she jokes, her face lit up with that contagious smile.

And I just can't help myself. I smile right back.

13

BLAIR

I WAKE up with a killer headache, but the second I roll over and see the bracelet Sebastian bought me last night, the residual effects of all the Sky Juices I drank seem to instantly fade.

It's tied to my left wrist, woven out of threads in bright magenta, turquoise blue, lime green, and yellow with the shiny penny in the middle sporting a rudimentary hand-stamped B. I know it's a cheap touristy item, but I honestly love it. It reminds me of this beautiful island, the heavenly flowers, and the amazing food, and, of course, the time I've spent with Sebastian. It's a memento I'll never part with.

Working the string, I loosen the knot and slip the bracelet off so I can put it in the zippered compartment of one of my suitcases. I'm meeting my parents for another early dinner, and I'd rather not answer any questions about my new accessory. The dreamy smile on my face would no doubt give away any lies I might attempt, and then Mom would start drilling me about the guy I met and getting her hopes up that he's marriage material.

Which, no. This Sebastian thing is nice, but it's anything but serious. Both of us are in agreement about that. And honestly, given the way he acted last night—standoffish, distant, avoiding any conversation related to whatever "we" are—I'm not even sure if we'll see each other again.

I really hope I'm wrong about that, though. It's not just the sex. I like simply *being* with him. It feels...easy. In the best way. Or at least, it felt easy until he found out I'm a resort guest. Obviously he's thrown, and I know we can't continue to carry on the way we have been. He has a professional image to uphold and I'm sure guests wouldn't look too kindly on one of the resort owners fraternizing with their daughters.

But why can't we just be discreet? Why not take full advantage of just a *little more time*? He's the one who said we should enjoy "right now," and I have every intention of doing that. Unless "right now" meant while we were eating together last night, and nothing beyond that. I definitely didn't get the sense that he wanted to come up to my hotel room when we parted ways at the resort elevators. In fact, he ran away so fast that I barely had time to say goodnight. What if he's just not into me anymore?

Ugh. I'm driving myself crazy thinking about him. I need a distraction. A Sebastian distraction.

After grabbing coffee and a bagel from the lobby coffee shop, I take a long walk on the beach and call Brooke. She's so excited to tell me all about her new job, which is going great, that I barely get a word in edgewise. Thankfully. By the time we hang up, I'm in a much better mood.

Hours later, I walk out of the resort's spa, freshly

massaged and sugar-scrubbed and just a smidge early for dinner with my parents. I thought the spa at Espadrilles was great, but the one at this resort is even better. My hot stone massage wasn't in a private room, but on a private *balcony* that I had all to myself, so I could watch the ocean waves while my back and shoulders were rubbed into a state of blissful relaxation. I also got a 24-karat gold leaf facial, and my skin is glowing.

Back in my room, I change into a flouncy blue dress with a ruffled hem and do my makeup. Then I sit down and compose a list on a sheet of cream hotel paper. It's my top ten picks for the draft. I'm going to slip it into my dad's pocket and not mention it. He can be the one to decide whether or not to consider my choices when the time comes. I can't think of any other way to get through to him.

I go down to the restaurant to meet my parents. I'm a little early, so I decide to hang out in the bar while I'm waiting for them to arrive.

I have no problem finding a stool at the bar. The place is virtually empty save for two couples at a corner table. The ambient music consists of orchestral covers of pop songs, which I enjoy listening to as the sound floats from strategically placed hidden speakers. I'm glad it's not busy. I'm feeling incredibly zen after my massage, and I'd like to stay that way for as long as possible.

A pretty bartender with unruly auburn curls and warm brown eyes greets me with a friendly smile. I bet she earns a lot of tips with that smile. She makes me feel at ease immediately.

"Welcome in. Before I take your order, can I see some ID?" she asks. "House rules."

"Sure," I say, digging through my clutch for my license. "Here you go."

"Thanks," she says, glancing at it quickly before handing it back. "Sorry to ask, but it's policy. I have to card everybody."

"No worries. I know I look young. I just graduated from college, actually."

She nods, popping the tops off a few bottles of local beer. "Where from?"

"NYU. Stern."

"Wow, congrats! Believe it or not, I went to NYU too. For psychology."

I laugh. "And now you get to do therapy from behind a bar. That's kind of the perfect degree for this job, isn't it?"

"You have no idea how much my academic training comes in handy around here," she says, grinning. "Let me drop these beers off and I'll be right with you."

She delivers the drinks to one of the occupied tables and then comes back.

"So, what can I get you? It's happy hour and our featured special is the Goombay Smash."

"That sounds good. What's in it?"

She grins. "It's three kinds of rum, apricot brandy, and some juice. And yeah, it is good, but I might advise something else if you've got plans tonight."

I arch a brow in amusement. "I'm meeting my parents for dinner in about twenty minutes."

"Yeah. You don't want the Goombay unless you plan on being wasted at that dinner. But you do you! This is a judgment-free zone. I'm happy to make you whatever you want."

I'm about to order a limeade when a tall, dark-haired man slides onto the stool next to me and interrupts.

"That drink sounds like exactly what I need after the day I've had." He flicks his AmEx across the bar and shoots me a wide grin. "And I'll pay for her drink, too. Put it on my tab."

"Oh. Thank you." Taken aback, I force a polite smile in return and then address the bartender again. "I'll have a switcha. Non-alcoholic, please."

"You got it." She gives me a little wink and then moves away to make our drinks.

At my side, the dark-haired man clears his throat and messes with his tie. His cologne is overpowering. It smells expensive and spicy, the kind of scent you can't ignore. I can see him staring at me from the corner of my eye, and though I'd like to pretend I don't notice—or just walk away—my good-girl training is strong, and my manners win out.

Resisting a sigh, I turn to him and play along, giving him the attention he so obviously craves. "Rough day, I take it?"

"You have no idea," he says with another bright-white smile.

Now that I'm looking at him straight on, I realize that he's younger than I thought—maybe late twenties—and extremely handsome. Handsome in the way of an Armani underwear model. Handsome in the way where I wonder if that jawline hasn't had a bit of surgical enhancement. Handsome in the way where he absolutely knows it and is used to getting exactly what he wants from women because of it.

Not only that, but judging by the cut of his suit, the

flashy diamond watch peeking out of his sleeve, and the way he threw his credit card around, he's also filthy rich on top of having the classic "tall, dark, and handsome" trifecta working for him. Not surprising. He wouldn't be at this resort if he wasn't.

Unfortunately for him, not all women appreciate arrogance. But I'll bet he doesn't know that.

"This asshole," he goes on, "pardon my French, but this asshole thought he could screw me in an acquisitions deal. Guess he didn't realize I'm the kind of CEO who reads the fine print on every single contract. Especially when we're talking multimillion-dollar agreements. Which, all of my deals are."

"Wow," I say, nodding along as my eyes start to glaze over. "Sounds intense."

"It is. Some people think I'm too young to basically be running this company on my own, but there's not a single detail I overlook, even though I have an entire legal department whose job it is to go over the jargon for me. That's what makes me so strong in a leadership role. See, I don't just sit in my office all day with my feet up and wait for everyone else to do the work. I'm down there in the trenches right next to them, which is how it should be."

"Of course. How can you be sure they're doing their jobs the right way if you don't look over their shoulder all the time and correct them?" I say seriously, even though I mean it sarcastically.

"Exactly!" he says, thumping a fist on the bar top and looking pleased that I'm apparently on the same page. "You don't just delegate and then walk away and leave the responsibility to someone else."

I have to bite my tongue hard, because walking away and leaving the responsibility to someone else is actually the *definition* of delegation. This guy sounds like a nightmare of a CEO. A micromanager from hell. I feel bad for his employees.

I'm grateful to see the bartender returning with our drinks.

"Here you go," she says. "One Goombay, one switcha."

We thank her and she walks away again, leaving us to our mostly one-sided conversation. I immediately take a long gulp of my limeade, already starting to regret going the non-alcoholic route. Next to me, the man takes a few swallows of his Goombay Smash, seeming unbothered by the amount of booze in it. I can smell the rum from here. It almost covers up the fog of spicy cologne, but not quite.

"Like I was saying," he continues, "there's nothing about my company that I don't know inside and out, top to bottom. A good CEO doesn't just spend his time flying all over the world in his private jet all the time, you know? Although I suppose that's exactly what I'm doing right now. Ha ha!"

"Ha," I reply, subtly checking the time on my phone.

"Anyway, the moral of the story is, you can't expect someone with as much money, power, and experience as I have to miss something like an underhanded clause in a business contract. You know what I'm saying?"

"Yep. Can't believe anyone tried to put one over on you," I reply, hoping I sound impressed enough for him to decide he's finished talking about himself. Clearly he's not going to stop yammering at me until he's 100% certain that

I realize how incredibly rich and powerful he is. I know his type.

He thrusts out a hand at me. His fingers are long and delicate, a thick gold ring on his pinkie.

"Sorry. I'm Mason Sharp, but I'm sure you guessed that." His piercing blue eyes drill into me, a look of concentration on his face, and it takes a second for me to understand that he's trying to smolder.

I shake lightly, but he almost crushes my hand in his iron grip, and I can't hold back a wince.

"Of course," I say as I try to rub the feeling back into my hand, even though I have no idea who the hell he is. I'll definitely remember the name, though. I can't wait to call Brooke later and tell her all about this ass hat.

Over his shoulder, I spot my parents walking into the dining area of the restaurant, and I swear I've never been so relieved to see their faces before.

"Gosh. Look at the time," I say, sliding off my stool as quickly as I can. "If you'll excuse me, Mr. Sharp, I have a dinner to get to. Thanks for the drink."

He grins and raises his glass at me in some kind of farewell toast. "It's a small island," he says with a shit-eating grin. "I'm sure I'll run into you again."

"We'll just have to see."

I wave at my dad as I walk toward the table, and he stands and pulls out my chair for me with a smile. It only takes a second for me to subtly tuck the folded list of my draft picks into his jacket pocket, and he doesn't even notice. He looks relaxed for once, and I'm happy to see that the island is having a therapeutic effect. My mother glances up at me and then quickly back down to her menu.

"You look lovely," my father says. "Blue is your color, Blair."

"Thanks. How was your day? Did you and Mom get out to the beach at all?"

"We golfed," Mom says, and now I realize why Dad looks so good. "Who is that young man you were speaking to at the bar? He looks very nice."

"Oh, nobody," I say breezily. "Just a guy. Have you two checked out the spa yet?"

We make pleasant small talk while studying our menus, but I'm acutely aware of my mother shooting furtive glances over to the bar. Mason is still there, and I start to wonder if Mom is trying to check him out for herself, which almost makes me laugh out loud. Not that he isn't objectively attractive, physically speaking. But she has no idea how off-putting he is.

The waiter takes our orders and brings our salads. The conversation dries up, and I find myself staring out the windows at the beach beyond, the unreal cerulean waters, the palms swaying in the breeze.

"Remember that time we spent the summer in Montauk, when the brownstone was being renovated?" I say, still looking out at the waves. A smile plays on my lips. "And when we had to go back to Manhattan, Sophie said she wasn't coming because she was going to live with the mermaids?

"And Mom, you told her she could stay but only if she got permission to live underwater from the mermaids, so she wrote a letter and threw it in the ocean, and then you 'found' her reply letter the next day and gave it to her at breakfast and it said there wasn't room in the mermaid castle for her but that she could ask again the next year, only we didn't go back, Sophie and I went to camp upstate instead..."

"What's wrong, Victoria?" My dad asks this with genuine concern.

I snap out of the memory and look over at my mom, who's looking at me with an aggrieved look on her face, as if she caught me chewing with my mouth open or I just threw my salad on the floor.

"What?" I say.

She looks down at her plate and her lower lip starts to wobble. "Please, Blair. Must you?"

"Must I what?" I challenge, attitude creeping into my voice. Because I think I get it now. I mentioned Sophie, and we're on *vacation*. Not that any time is a good time to talk about my dead sister, but apparently, saying her name while we're on a family holiday is especially uncouth.

Mom flashes me another injured look and clears her throat. Or tries to. It sounds more like a pained squeak, and my stomach clenches. She wants to pretend Sophie doesn't exist, as usual.

Dad gets the hint. He pats my hand and tactfully changes the subject. "Did you notice that Ted Polansky is here at the resort, Blair? What are the chances of that?"

"His ERA just dropped below two-point-five," I say, willing to let the Sophie thing drop. "Not that his Fielding Independent Pitching number is anything to scoff at, but that's pretty incredib—"

"He's very handsome," Mom interrupts, sniffing as she pulls herself together.

"So what?" I say. "I'm more interested in his stats than what he looks like. Dad?"

He just shrugs helplessly as Mom continues, effectively hijacking the conversation.

"You should try to get to know him while we're here," she adds. "You're still single, after all."

"Mom."

I look over at Dad for help, but he's giving all his attention to his salad now. Mom keeps babbling, off on a tangent about the benefits of dating a professional athlete, and I let out a sigh. As I nod along, stuck listening to her antiquated dating advice, all I can do is pray that this dinner is over soon. I'm probably going to need a drink or two to recover from it. Unless...

I wonder what Sebastian is up to tonight.

14

BLAIR

There's a knock at my door and my pulse skyrockets.

I don't even glance through the peephole. I know exactly who it is. I'm the one who texted him. Three simple words: *I need you*. When he responded asking where I was, I sent him my room number.

Pulling open the door, I breathe in Sebastian's scent and fist the front of his dress shirt as I pull him into the room. Our lips clash. I push the door closed behind him and wrap my free arm around his waist, hungrily grinding my hips against his.

"I wasn't sure you'd come," I pant in between kisses.

"I can't stay away from you," he replies, kissing me harder and driving me back against the bed.

Peeling off his blazer, I throw it across the room, and it lands...somewhere. My fingers eagerly tug at the buttons of his shirt, but he grips my wrists and halts my attempt at getting him naked. His eyes sweep over mine with a look of concern.

"Something's wrong. Tell me what happened."

He asks like he's ready to take someone out on my behalf. It only makes me hotter for him.

"You met my parents. Need I say more?"

I try to keep my tone joking, but he doesn't laugh.

I don't want him to feel sorry for me. I don't want him to be anything but deep inside me, making me forget about the horrible dinner I just left and the creeper at the bar, and everything else that's been shitty over the past couple of days.

"Don't worry about it," I tell him dismissively. "Just let me take your clothes off."

"Blair..."

Sebastian works his jaw, still holding my wrists. Dark intensity flares in his green eyes. Sexual tension sparks in the air. I can tell he's at war with himself, and the last thing I want is for him to walk out. Things have been off between us ever since he found out who my parents are and realized I was a guest at his resort. I need to remind him how good we are together. The other stuff doesn't matter.

I don't wait for him to finish whatever he's trying to say. I'm not going to let him reject me. Taking a step back, I ease my wrists away from him and reach for the hem of my dress. Then I slowly pull it up and over my head, wriggling my body enticingly in the process. Dropping the dress to the floor, I stand there in front of him in my white lace bra and thong. I feel vulnerable and exposed.

Sebastian doesn't move. He's frozen in place as he sucks in a breath, his eyes roving my body. It's like I've cast a spell on him. At least, that's what I hope. I've never tried to seduce anyone before.

Moving backwards into the room, leading him closer to

the bed, I unhook my bra next and let it slide off, feeling my nipples perk in the air conditioning. Then I hesitantly slide a hand down the front of my underwear, letting out a soft gasp as my middle finger grazes my tingling clit.

When I look up at him again, I know I've got him.

With a growl, he drops to his knees and hooks his thumbs through the waistband of my panties. As he works them down my legs, he kisses the rise of my hipbones and my lower belly. His tongue flicks the sensitive skin of my inner leg and runs higher, along the crease of my thigh. Closing my eyes, I welcome the sweet haze his touch brings and savor each lick and kiss as he removes my final layer.

The slide of lace. The warmth of his lips and the rough scrape of his stubble against my skin. Molten desire floods between my legs. God, what this man does to me.

Digging my hands into his hair, I try to urge him up while I kick the thong away from my ankles. But he won't rise. He resists with a quiet groan, then nips alongside my knee. Giving in, I enjoy the growing weakness in my knees, the heat pooling in my lower belly. When he pushes me back onto the bed, I don't resist. Scooting back, I reach for him again, but he doesn't get on the bed with me.

Instead, he positions my ass so it's almost falling off the mattress and then pushes my thighs wide apart as he sinks to the floor again with his head between my legs. I'm so wet that the air feels ice cold against my lower lips. It only makes me want him to slide into me and warm me up even more.

I can't stop from squirming as I reach for him again. "I need you. Now. You don't have to—"

"Relax, Sunshine," he says, and I shiver as he teases me. "Let me make you feel better."

Oh, there's the promise I wanted. Lowering my arms, I go limp against the soft linens and anticipate all the ways he's going to make good on his word. His breath heats my mound as he takes his time massaging my inner thighs, moving closer and closer to my pussy. I'm breathless by the time he presses those perfect lips to my slit.

His tongue darts inside of me. Jolting from the shock of pleasure, I dig my fingers into his hair and hold on tight as he feasts on me. While he licks and sucks and works me into a frenzy, his hands cup and knead my breasts, thumbs stroking my nipples until they tingle. My body is a mess of sensation.

"I want you to fuck me again," I moan as I start to feel an orgasm approaching.

He just keeps on lapping and nibbling, teasing my clit until I'm rocking myself against his mouth faster and harder and I don't know up from down.

"Please." I'm getting desperate now. "Sebastian, please."

But he's not giving in to my begging.

He continues sucking my clit as he slips a finger inside me, then two, pumping in time with my thrusts. In my mind, I flash back to the last time we had sex, the last time he was filling me with his cock, groaning in my ear, hitting that hot spot deep inside me, giving me more, more, more, and the memory is enough to make me shatter. I cry out as I come, clenching around his fingers, whimpering his name. The waves roll through me fast and deep, and he doesn't stop fingering me until the contractions subside. Only then does he climb onto the bed beside me, rolling onto his side to watch me catch my breath.

Satisfied but still needy, I reach for his belt, ready for more.

He gently pushes my hands away again. "No."

Disappointment washes over me. "Why? Did I do something wrong?"

"No. You're perfect."

I don't get it. He knows that I want him, and I know he still wants me too. He just proved that, despite his willpower last night, or whatever his standoffish behavior was.

He lets out a sigh and adds, "It's not appropriate, Blair. I'm sure you can understand that."

"Fine," I say, trying to sound cool and detached instead of dejected. "Can you at least stay, though? Just for a little while?"

"I can do that."

I burrow under the covers beside him, not because I'm self-conscious about being naked, but because I don't want to remind him that us being together is inappropriate. When he turns onto his back, I rest my head on his chest and take a deep breath. The sound of his heart beating soothes me.

"This is nice," I whisper. "You feel nice."

"Hm," is all I get as a reply, but I swear I detect a hint of wistfulness.

After a moment, he adjusts himself so he can put his arm around my bare shoulder, and I snuggle even closer next to him. We just lie like that for a while, the room getting darker as the sun dips below the horizon.

"What happened with your parents earlier?" he asks quietly. "Or do you not want to say?"

I hesitate. The only person I discuss the whole Sophie thing with is Brooke, and that's because Brooke and I have been friends for so long. I've told her the story in bits and pieces over the years, not all at once. But Sebastian isn't asking to be nosy, and he's not trying to push me into sharing my grief with platitudes about how I'll feel better if I talk about it, he's asking to be kind. And that melts me.

"We were at dinner, and I broke the 'Don't Talk About Sophie' rule," I say quietly. "Sophie's my older sister. *Was.* She died six years ago, when I was in tenth grade. She would have been graduating from our private high school that year, but...she got pregnant, and my parents didn't think she should keep it. They thought having a baby so young would ruin her life. So my sister ran away."

"Where did she go?"

"California. She was a beach girl. She always loved summertime the best. And she craved palm trees, I don't know why. We were born and raised in...in a big city, but she dreamed of living in a place where people weren't caught up in the hustle and bustle. She talked about learning how to surf one day, doing the whole zen thing, riding waves. I really hope she got to paddle out at least once while she was in California.

"She died out there. Complications from the pregnancy. I got one postcard from her and then I never heard from her again. It was one of her roommates in Venice Beach who finally got ahold of us with the news. When my parents told me what happened, I refused to believe it. I thought maybe they were trying to...I don't know, scare me out of running away, too. It wasn't until her roommate sent us a box of Sophie's things that I finally stopped thinking she was going to come back someday."

"I'm so sorry," Sebastian says softly, rubbing slow circles over my shoulder.

"Yeah," I say, my voice cracking with emotion. My eyes are filling with tears, but for once it actually does feel better to talk about her. About what happened. How unfair it was. "The baby didn't make it, either. My sister just wanted to have a good life, a simple life. And look what she got."

The tears are falling now, silently, but I can't stop them.

"My dad became a total workaholic, started sleeping at the office just to avoid being at home. My mom turned into a zombie. She could barely go through the motions, and it was like she was in a whole other world. She basically stopped talking to me for almost a year. I was the one who got sent to therapy, but my parents probably needed it more than I did. Now we act like a family as best we can, but God forbid I say my sister's name. I hate that. I hate having to pretend she never existed."

"You've been through a lot," Sebastian says. "All of you. That kind of loss changes a person. I guess I can understand why your parents seem so overprotective."

I nod. "They think if they keep me in a bubble that I won't turn out like Sophie. That I'll be safe. But you can't control someone's life like that. And you can't control when people die."

"No, you can't."

"I looked up to her so much," I tell him between sniffles. "I was a goody two-shoes, but she was always a rebel. Our dress code at school said we had to wear tights with our skirts, so she wore fishnet stockings. We weren't allowed to dye our hair unnatural colors either, so she just dyed the hair underneath the top layer of brown so the teachers wouldn't see it at school. It was hot pink. Mom freaked out when she realized. But Sophie didn't give a shit what anybody thought, she did things her own way."

"Sounds pretty punk," he says, handing me a handful of tissues from the box on the nightstand.

"I guess so. But she was kind. To everyone. She had a soft spot for outcasts and nerds. Like me."

"You could never be a nerd."

"Shows how much you know the real me," I joke. "I miss her every day. Every single day."

He goes silent, and when I tilt my head to look over at him, I see that his eyes are closed.

"You okay?"

"Yeah," he says. "It's just...I know what it's like. To lose someone. Someone your whole life revolves around, who you thought would always be there. And I know how it is when you want to keep the memories alive, even though it hurts to relive them. Years go by, and it never stops hurting."

"It doesn't," I agree.

I suddenly think back to the first day we met, how I saw him staring out at the ocean with that melancholy look on his face. I'd bet anything he was thinking of the person he lost. I wonder if it was a girlfriend, a sibling, a parent. But I don't ask. I don't pry. It feels intrusive. He'll share when he's ready.

Propping myself up on my elbow, I kiss his cheek, feather-light. Then again. Then closer to his mouth. So gently. He turns his head and kisses me back, just as soft. Then he brushes his lips against my jaw, my chin, my eyelids.

Tears slip down my cheek, but Sebastian doesn't stop kissing me. Despite the ache in my chest, there's a lightness there that I haven't felt in a very long time.

Soon we're kissing more deeply, tongues touching briefly, but still ever so carefully, as if we can kiss each other's pain away.

I wonder if maybe we can.

15

BLAIR

I saw a completely different side of Sebastian last night. *Good* different.

I'd fully expected a vigorous round of mattress calisthenics when he showed up to my room looking as hot and bothered as I was, but what I got instead was...maybe even better? No. Definitely better. I don't mean the oral sex, either. I mean our conversation afterward. I haven't felt so seen, so understood on a soul level, since Sophie died.

Plenty of people have felt sorry for me, of course, and promised me that time would heal my wounds, compared their own grief over a death to what I was going through with the assurance that it would get better—which it barely has, to be honest—but no one else has just sat beside me in my grief and held me while I let it flow through me. Sebastian wasn't offering sympathy, but empathy. He knows what it's like.

Even still, I can't stop obsessing over the game of hot and cold that he keeps playing. I know he's trying to be professional and not cross any lines with a guest, but the lines have clearly already been crossed. We've already had plenty of sex. Why can't we keep having more? And how can he possibly justify eating me out last night while refusing to go any further? That still counts as "sex with a guest."

Men are so confusing.

Not that I didn't enjoy every second of what we did. But I have less than a week left on the island, and I can't help thinking that he and I should be taking advantage of every opportunity we have to be together. I know I sound naïve, but what we have is special. I truly believe that. Especially after last night, when we bonded the way we did. I've never been so vulnerable with a guy before, and he doesn't seem like the type of person who lets his guard down around people, either.

And yet, once again, I start to second-guess myself. What if I'm wrong about Sebastian? What if he's been playing me this whole time? Or what if he hasn't been, but I'm overly romanticizing the whole situationship? I keep telling myself I'm fine with this fling being temporary, but deep down I can't help wishing that there was some way we could keep seeing each other. Even if it's only a few times a year.

That's not how summer flings work, Blair, I silently scold myself. *You're in denial. You know you're going to have to let him go. The sooner, the better.*

Strolling barefoot on the beach, I turn my face to the sky and let out a groan of frustration. There's no avoiding the fact that Sebastian and I are going to be parting ways soon. Permanently. So it's not even like I have a choice in the matter—I *will* let him go. I absolutely will.

Just not today.

The sun has just come up and there's hardly anyone else out this early in the day. I'm grateful to be alone out here so I can mope in peace. As I walk near the water's edge, I realize the tides must have come in strong last night, because there are tons of unbroken seashells washed up on the beach in a rainbow of colors, and the gulls seem to be having good luck pecking their breakfast from the damp sand.

Kicking up a pretty pink-and-white striped shell, I bend to retrieve it and quickly spot more. My mood lightens as I comb my fingers through the sand and pluck out a small, perfect sand dollar and then a zebra periwinkle. The lap of the waves soothes me, and I move close enough to the water so the surf tickles my toes as the sun warms the back of my neck. This is what I love. This peace and feeling of just being in the moment. These moments will be sparse once I return home, so I let myself wander, following where the trail of pastel-colored shells takes me.

"Hello there," a voice says. A male voice. With a British accent.

I look up to see a guy about my age standing a few feet away. He's wearing a fitted polo shirt, khaki shorts, and boating shoes, with an expensive watch flashing on his wrist. I take in his curly dark hair, his eyes that crinkle with his smile, and his long, lean runner's body. He's very nice looking. He's also got some noticeably cute dimples.

"Hi," I say back, straightening to stand.

"Looks like I'm not the only shell seeker on the beach today," he says. "Those are some nice sand dollars you've got there. I've only found scallops and olive snails so far."

"You show me yours, I'll show you mine," I joke.

He holds out his cupped hand to display what he's found. The snail shells are in perfect shape, a variety of colors and patterns in reds, purples, greens, and oranges.

"Impressive," I say, letting out a low whistle. "Here, take one of my sand dollars."

I give it to him, and he smiles.

"I'll have to trade you something, then. It's only fair. I actually came out here hoping to find an abandoned conch what with the high tide last night, but all I've seen are these little ones. I've been a treasure hunter since I was a lad. Sea glass is my favorite. Here, take this green bit."

"Thanks," I say, pocketing it. "Are you a guest at the Quattuor Club? This is a private beach, but don't worry, I won't tell on you."

"I am a guest, so don't worry about ending up an accessory to a crime," he teases. He thrusts a hand in my direction. "Alec."

I accept his hand for a quick shake. "I'm Blair. Nice to meet you."

"Pleasure's all mine," he says, and it seems like he really means it. "To be honest, this beach is nice, but it can't compare to Balstay Island. Have you heard of it?"

"I haven't."

"It's a pristine, uninhabited little place about an hour south of here. The shelling is excellent. I was going to take a trip there today on my yacht. Would you care to join me? We can picnic on the island, and you can hunt for shells to your heart's content."

I laugh. "Seriously? You want to take me on your yacht? You don't even know me."

"I never pass up an opportunity to take a beautiful woman out, especially on a luxury watercraft."

Geez. All the sex I've been having with Sebastian lately must really have me glowing.

"That's a nice offer," I tell him. "But I already have plans today."

Or I will, if I hear from Sebastian.

"So cancel them," he says, turning on the charm with those dimples. "We don't have to go to Balstay, either. We can go anywhere. Or I can hire us a private snorkeling instructor if you like."

"I'm good. Really. But thank you."

"Let's have an adventure. This is a once-in-a-lifetime opportunity. I promise you won't regret it."

"You are very persistent," I say, shaking my head. "Is that a British thing?"

"It's a me thing," he says. "You could say I'm used to getting what I want. But don't hold it against me—I work bloody hard for what I've got. Come on, Blair. Let me give you the perfect day in paradise. I won't take no for an answer."

Part of me is waffling. He's hot, he seems fun and nice, and I definitely wouldn't mind going on a boat trip. But on the other hand, he's acting entitled, which is a huge turn-off, and I also don't know him at all. Plus, my phone probably won't get service out on the ocean, and nobody will know where I am.

And obviously, he's not Sebastian. That's the main issue. I'm not giving up one second of possible Sebastian time, boat or no boat.

"I appreciate the invite," I say, backing up a few steps.

"But I really do have to get going."

"Blair—"

I look back toward the resort, and that's when I spot a familiar figure on the beach. Dark blond hair curling out from underneath a black, blue, and red Miami Marlins baseball hat, broad shoulders, that cleft chin. It's Ted Polansky.

Hallelujah.

Waving eagerly, I sidestep Alec, who spins to follow my line of sight.

"Ted! Ted, over here."

Ted's entire face lights up when he sees me flagging him down, and I can't help feeling a little guilty, because I fully intend to use him for my own benefit. He wanders over and I lunge toward him, eagerly taking his arm. I need to make something up fast, so I hope Ted gets the hint and plays along.

"Hey, Blair—"

Interrupting him before he blows my cover, I blurt, "Hey, you! I'm so sorry—I know I was supposed to meet you in the lobby so we could go shopping for Junkanoo outfits, but I totally lost track of time out here. I'm so glad you found me! This is Alec. I just met him while I was looking for shells."

Ted's eyes shift to Alec and then back to me, a flicker of understanding on his face.

"Nice to meet you, Alex," Ted says, extending a hand.

"It's *Alec*," Alec says curtly.

They exchange a manly shake, but Alec looks a bit pouty.

"Well," he says, still pouting as he glances between me

and Ted, "I suppose you two had better get to it, then. Cheers."

With that, he spins on his heel and stalks away.

"How rude," I huff, loosening my grip on Ted's arm. "Thanks for the rescue. I owe you one."

Ted smiles, catching my hand in his and pulling me closer. "You could make it up to me by joining me for breakfast."

And...there it is. Another unwanted advance, not five minutes after the first. Not that Ted isn't a catch. He's a genuinely nice guy, and normally I'd jump at the chance to talk baseball with him again, especially if an order of eggs benedict is involved. But the only man I'm interested in right now is Sebastian. There isn't even the smallest blip of interest inside me for anyone else.

Which is a problem, because I can't figure out what Sebastian wants. I could be saving myself for him for the entire remainder of this vacation, and it might be all for nothing.

Still. It's a risk I'm willing to take. Even one last kiss would be worth it.

Meanwhile, I don't want to lead Ted on.

"I'm so sorry, Ted, but I have a full day planned with my parents. I'd invite you along, but we're supposed to be having family time together. I hope you understand."

His crestfallen look brings on another twinge of guilt, but he gracefully accepts my rejection and I head back to the resort alone. I can't shake my unease, though.

Why do men have to behave like that? Like just because they feel an attraction to me, they automatically expect me to reciprocate. Nobody gets to have a claim on me just because we had one pleasant conversation. I'm my own woman. That's my mantra.

Hopefully it will start to have an effect if I repeat it enough times.

16

BLAIR

A PEDICURIST HANDS me a swatch of nail polish choices in sad shades of pale pink and mauve. My mother coos as if they are the prettiest colors she's ever seen. Too bad she's choosing a color for me.

We're supposed to be having a relaxing afternoon getting mani-pedis together, but it's impossible to relax in my contoured, body conforming spa chair when she insists on sitting right at the edge of hers with her calves planted stiffly against the footrest. It took five minutes for the other pedicurist to convince my mother to put her feet in the foot bath, and Mom's been eyeing it warily ever since, as if she's worried something unsanitary might materialize in the water.

Not that I don't appreciate the effort she's making. When it comes to self-care, my mom is woefully out of practice. Ever since Sophie died, Mom has barely tended to her own needs, never mind anything so frivolous as a spa day. I thought it was a good sign that she agreed to do this with me, but now I'm not so sure. If anything, she seems more tense now than she was when we first walked in.

Taking the color swatch from me, my mother considers each option.

"This one." She points to a shade that's easily a mixture of mud and arterial blood. "It's much more neutral than that garish red you've got on, and you can get your toes to match. How about that?"

I know how to play along. I've been playing along for years, haven't I?

"I'm sure it will look great. Thanks, Mom."

To my complete surprise, she finally sits back and sinks into her chair just as her pedicurist comes back over to take Mom's feet out of the water. Maybe she's finally loosening up. I sure hope so.

Shifting in my chair, I reach for my bag on a side table and fish out my phone. Feeling very much like I'm doing something naughty, I check my email and then pull up my text thread with Sebastian. I know this is a bad idea. But I can't stop myself. Between the dueling bachelors on the beach this morning and the stressful spa date I'm having with my mom, I could use something fun to look forward to later.

> Are you free after work?

I type out, and then pause. I don't want him to ignore me because he thinks I'm just trying to get him in bed again. I delete the message and try again.

How's your day going? Still breaking in that new trainee?

I hit send. It sounds neutral enough. And I genuinely care about how his day is going. It's not like the only reason I'm reaching out is because I'm hoping he'll want to hook up.

Not that I'm *not* hoping for that. But I'd be okay with just talking again.

When he doesn't respond, I look over at Mom again and try to strategize. Part of the reason I suggested the mani-pedis to begin with was because I was hoping to talk to her about my future role at the Tisdale Corporation. Not in a specific way—I need Dad for that—but in a more general sense.

I need her to be on my side, supporting me, so she can help persuade my dad to stop clamming up and changing the subject every time I mention the whole job thing. I'm starting to worry that he's got nothing better in store for me than some kind of mailroom position.

"So, um. Have you and Dad been enjoying the island, or are you ready to get back home?" I ask, trying to approach the topic as casually and slowly as possible so she doesn't immediately cut me off.

"Oh, I think it's been good to get away," she says. "We haven't taken a family vacation since...well. It's been a long time."

That surprises me. It's the closest she's come to mentioning Sophie in months.

"Good. I'm glad," I say, patting her hand. "Dad seems like he's in a better mood, too. Must be all that golfing."

She sighs. "I'll bet it is. I think it's boring, honestly, but he loves it. Leave it to a man to get excited about whacking a tiny ball into a tiny hole eighteen times in a row."

We both laugh.

"I've only gone a few times, but the course is very nice," she adds. "Lots of palm trees and tropical plants. You can't forget you're in the Bahamas, even when you're in a sand trap."

"Maybe I'll join him one morning."

"He'd love that."

The two pedicurists get to work exfoliating our feet and calves with a fragrant lemon scrub. For a few minutes, I settle back with my eyes closed and let my mind go blank. Then my phone buzzes in my lap, and my pulse jumps when I see it's a text from Sebastian.

> You have no idea. She was supposed to arrange limousine transportation from the airport for one of our VIPs, and guess what mode of conveyance picked him up?

A smile twitches at the corner of my mouth.

> A clown car? A pedicab? A camel?

> A party bus, complete with a stripper pole inside. It was an unfortunate mix-up. The VIP was not amused.

I can't suppress my laugh.

Sounds like a majorly missed opportunity to me.

When I peek over at Mom, I find her staring up at the ceiling, eyes wide open, like she can't stand to let her guard down enough to enjoy having lotion massaged into her feet.

Tucking my phone against my hip, I ask, "So, um...has Dad mentioned anything about my job?"

"Not really," she says noncommittally.

"Oh. I mean, I'm sure he's planning to onboard me as soon as we get back to New York, it's just...whenever I try to bring it up, he gets all fussy about how we're on vacation and we're not supposed to be thinking about work. Even though I've caught him checking emails on his phone."

She turns to me with an assessing gaze. "You know, Blair, I've been in your shoes. Don't forget, I used to be in the corporate world, too. I've been hungry to climb the ladder and prove myself. So I understand what you're going through. How eager you are to make your way in the world."

"Really?"

"Of course. But I also want what's best for you, and I can tell you that being a high-powered executive with a corner office and two secretaries just isn't what it's made out to be. I spent years of my life practically living at work. I barely made time for anything else, not sleep or proper nutrition or friends or hobbies. In hindsight, I realized how miserable I was, but at the time I didn't even know it."

I nod. I've heard this before.

"Yeah, but then you met Dad when you were thirty-two and you got married and had So—had a family. And you slowed down. In a good way. And then you and Dad formed the Tisdale Corporation and you figured out how to have work-life balance. Right?"

Another text comes in, and I glance down and tilt my phone just enough to read Sebastian's message.

> How about you? How's your day going so far?

"Right," Mom is saying. "But I never should have gotten in so deep in the first place. I almost missed out on everything good in life. Just because you do excellent work and you love your job, it doesn't mean you have to work yourself into the ground. No matter how much you believe in the mission of the company you work for, it can't be the thing that gives your life meaning."

"I get it. But—"

"I don't want you to end up like I almost did."

"I won't," I insist. "I'll still live my life. I just want to get started on my career path now, while I'm still young, that way I have plenty of time to learn and grow and figure things out as I go along."

Mom doesn't reply. Our feet are getting rinsed now and massaged again. I feel like we're bonding, like she's starting to come around. At the very least, she knows where I'm coming from.

"Do you think you could talk to him later?" I ask. "Warm him up a little for me? I still have no idea which department he's thinking of placing me in, and—"

"Oh, sweetie," she interrupts. "A young, beautiful girl like yourself shouldn't be so focused on getting cooped up in an office the second you get back home when we're on this gorgeous island."

This conversation is rapidly going south. "I'd like to start thinking about my next move, Mom. That's the responsible thing to do. So I can be prepared for what's coming next."

"The talk with your father can wait. He's not going anywhere."

I stifle a groan of frustration and attempt to text Sebastian back with one hand.

> Could be better.

I tap out, not wanting to go into the details. Although I wonder if hearing about the Brit and the Marlins pitcher competing for my attention this morning would make Sebastian jealous.

Which could work in my favor...

"And did my eyes deceive me, or did I spot that handsome Ted Polansky escorting you along the beach this morning?" Mom says.

I turn my phone facedown, a flicker of panic going through me even though I know she can't see my screen from where she's sitting. "What? How did you—were you spying on me, Mom?"

What if it had been Sebastian on the beach with me this morning? Or worse—what if she already knows that I've been seeing him?

But no. That can't be right. If my mom had any inkling about my fling with Sebastian, she would have said something. Still, my heart is pounding at the possibility of

getting caught, because it's not just me who'd face consequences. Sebastian could lose his job. We need to be careful. Paranoid, even. There are eyes everywhere, and my
mom is apparently watching me like a hawk.

"Don't be so melodramatic, Blair. I was having breakfast with your father on our balcony, and I said, that looks
just like Blair down there, and who is that young gentleman
with her? Of course your father recognized the team colors
on his hat right away..."

Her voice fades into the background as my phone
vibrates with another text from Sebastian.

> I could make it better...

His message sends a hot twinge straight between my
legs.

What better way to take my mind off of everything
than to let Sebastian screw it out of me? Or whatever else
he has in mind to perk me up. I'm not picky.

I reply with a single word:

> Yes.

Mom's still going on and on about putting myself out
there and being open to meeting new people. I've heard
this speech before. Next, she'll be recounting all the relationships she'd had by the time she was my age and tsking
over the fact that I'm wasting my prime reproductive years,
doomed to bear children in my mid-thirties just like her—as
if that's a bad thing. Who knows if I even want to have
kids?

Are you free around 5?

Sebastian texts back.

That could be arranged.

I respond cheekily.

"Blair, are you listening to me?"

"Hmm?"

I look over at her, slipping my phone back into my bag before she catches me texting and gets suspicious. She's holding up another swatch of nail polish colors. All of these are bright and cheery, the kind of sea greens and deep turquoises and neon oranges that perfectly complement an island vacation. Quite a stark contrast to the color she picked out for me before.

"I really like this cotton candy pink, but maybe it's too young for me. What do you think?" She hesitates and then adds, "We could get matching polish?"

My heart squeezes a little in my chest. Sophie loved pink. Even after she turned into a rebel. Mom knows this more than anybody, thanks to the hair dyeing incident. This feels like a truce, maybe.

"That pink would look great on you, Mom," I tell her. "Let's definitely get matching polish."

The line between her brows disappears, and she reaches over to take my hand in hers.

"I love you."

"Love you too, Mom."

I guess this spa date wasn't such a bad idea after all.

181

17

SEBASTIAN

I CHECK my watch for what must be the fiftieth time and then nod at Lord Alec Bingham-Cavendish.

"...because the sub-elite just cannot comprehend the demands incumbent upon philanthropists," he's saying loftily. "Not that I want to be pitied, mind you. But with millions of pounds in investment and property income pouring into the Bingham-Cavendish trust each year, I see it as my duty to reallocate some of those resources to the lower classes."

"Of course," I respond. "Why not help make the world a better place?"

"Precisely. Hence the founding of my grant-giving foundation, ABC, which are my initials..."

The man has been bragging about his charity work for the last twenty minutes straight. My eyes glazed over nineteen minutes ago. When I screened him as a potential match for the Tisdales a few months ago, I thought the philanthropy he engages in spoke well of his character. Not only that, but when we initially spoke on the phone, I got the impression that Lord Alec was a kind, generous person with the means to give his partner a good life, the kind of life where she'd never want for anything. Now that I've gotten to know him better, I'm starting to wonder if he could ever love anybody more than himself.

We're at the marina, loitering beside the slip where my yacht, the *Nina Simone*, is docked. Alec has the use of the vessel while he's on the island, as he's a sailing enthusiast, which is why his first date with Blair was supposed to be a yachting excursion. Unfortunately, that date never happened.

"Where is she? It's almost five now. We've got to get under way if we want to catch low tide at the caves," Alec says as he smooths his palms over the lapels of his linen blazer and checks his breath.

"I'm sure she'll be here any second," I reassure him, keeping an eye on the far end of the dock so that I can disappear before she notices I'm here.

As soon as I see Blair, I'm going to hide. Once Alec makes contact with her, I'll send a quick text to Blair telling her that I can't see her again. I'll reject her in no uncertain terms, leaving Alec to comfort her with a yacht trip to the famous James Bond Grotto. There, they'll snorkel and swim as the sun goes down in a sea cave filled with exotic fish, colorful coral, and a series of underwater tunnels. Afterward, they'll get back on the yacht and enjoy a candlelit dinner, prepared by one of the resort's chefs.

If that doesn't scream "magical first date," I don't know what does. I pulled out all the stops.

And yes, putting together meet-ups like this is part of my job here at the resort, but I've arranged this very special date between Blair and Alec Bingham-Cavendish for multiple, very pressing reasons.

First, it will serve as a do-over for the disastrous meet-cute I'd organized between Blair and Alec on the beach the other morning, which apparently went to hell when Ted Polansky—the baseball bachelor—showed up and cock-blocked Lord Bingham-Cavendish.

From what Alec told me during our debriefing, he was just about to whisk Blair off for a day out on the yacht when Ted stole Blair away. Alec required some calming down after that, but managing high-maintenance clients is under my purview, so I handled it. But he's been impatient to "properly interview" his potential fiancée ever since, and while I'm put off by his use of the term "interview," it's also part of my job to ensure that each match gets a solid intro-duction to the bachelorette, hence this second attempt to get sparks flying between him and Blair.

Secondly, this date with Alec will help keep Blair away from me, and me away from her. Which has become an increasingly urgent matter given our inability to keep our hands off each other.

Every second I spend with Blair Tisdale is another second I spend playing with fire. It's time for this thing between us to end. For good.

Obviously I should have broken it off sooner, but I never expected it to last so long. I assumed it would be nothing more than another one-and-done fling. A night (or two) of pleasure. Instead, the woman has somehow infil-trated my thoughts on a daily basis, to the point of distraction.

I can't even jerk off without images of her O-face

appearing in my mind. Her flushed cheeks, her heavy-lidded eyes gazing up at me, those kiss-swollen lips. Not to mention the unbidden flashes of her perfect tits bouncing beneath me, the curve of her hips under my hands, that round ass shaking as I pound into her from behind. A little shudder goes through me here on the dock, even as I try—and fail—to banish the memories. This is exactly the problem with seeing her. I can't focus.

Regardless, it's high time to let her go. If I keep sneaking around with her, my business partners are going to find out what I'm doing, and then the only question will be how ugly the consequences are. It's not just about me losing my job and tainting my name. If word of this affair got out, it would ruin the agency's reputation as well as my partners'. The Quattuor Group would be destroyed. We'd all be ruined. All because I couldn't keep my dick in my pants. I can't let that happen.

Becker, Nate, and Theo will be arriving on the island soon, so the clock is ticking. Fortunately, by the time Blair gets back to the resort with Alec tonight, my business partners will already be here, and the threat of their watchful eyes will keep me from sneaking off to see Blair again. At least, that's the plan.

I hate myself for lying to her to trick her into coming to the marina, and I hate even more that our little fuckfest is over, but I have no other choice.

Ideally, between Lord Alec and Ted Polansky and Mason Sharp, Blair will soon be too distracted by eligible men to even remember my name. I don't like the idea of her getting passed around amongst them like a tray of goddamn hors d'oeuvres, but that's not my business, is it?

My business is to make matches. There's no reason for me to feel conflicted about it. She's nothing to me but a piece of ass.

I feel a buzz in my pocket and slip out my phone just enough to read the message on the screen. It's from Blair. Shit.

> Sorry I'm running late- almost there.

Knowing Lord Alec is already impatient, I'm about to ask for more details on his 'ABC' charity—just to keep him distracted for a few more minutes—when his phone rings obnoxiously loudly. I recognize the ringtone, *Rule Britannia*, immediately. How patriotic.

"Lord Bingham-Cavendish," he answers, turning his back to me.

"Mr. Argos?" a voice calls from the deck of my boat. "It's after five."

I wave at the captain, who I hired to pilot the yacht tonight so that Lord Alec could give his full attention to Blair.

"Just another few minutes," I tell him, glancing at Alec, who is now pacing down the dock on his phone call.

The captain gives me a salute and heads back to the bridge.

When I turn around, Alec is standing there with a pained expression on his face.

"Sorry, mate, but I've got to reschedule," he says.

"What? Is it a family emergency, or—"

"One of my new properties in Knightsbridge has hit some red tape with building control, so I've got to get hold of the Secretary of State to fix it before the entire project gets cancelled."

"Can't it wait until tomorrow? It's after ten p.m. in the UK."

He nods. "Which is exactly why I've got to get hold of him now on his home number, so he can handle the issue first thing in the morning. I'll have to raincheck with Blair. You'll let me know once you've made the arrangements. Whatever you think is best. Ta."

With that, he walks away, already dialing on his phone.

For a moment I just stand there, stunned. Here's a guy who paid a quarter of a million dollars to retain the agency's services, and he just turned his back on his potential future wife to make an after-hours business call? Is his real estate empire really more important than the woman he might be spending the rest of his life with? Maybe she'd be nothing but a trophy to him, something to take out and show off at his discretion. In which case...maybe he's not good enough for Blair anyway.

The sound of footsteps on the dock has me turning around, and although I absolutely expected to see Blair walking toward me, I wasn't prepared for the sight of her in a body-hugging white dress, long blond hair tossing in the breeze, bombshell red lips curved up in a wicked smile. She looks good enough to eat. No, better. Damn Lord Alec and his real estate problems.

"Hey," she says. "I was Zooming with Brooke and I lost track of time."

"You're perfectly on time," I say without thinking.

"I assume you're taking me out on your boat," she says.

"That's why you wanted me to meet you at the marina, right?"

"Absolutely," I hear myself say, even as I silently remind myself that I need to dump her right here and now like I intended to.

"Nice boat. I love Nina Simone, by the way," she says, pointing at the name on the side of my yacht. "Didn't realize you were a jazz fan."

"I could say the same about you. Though Nina's more of a blues and folk musician."

"Strongly disagree," she says. "She transcended genre. Though obviously her training at Juilliard was in classical, so if anything, she's a classical musician. Despite the 'High Priestess of Soul' moniker."

"Favorite album," I challenge.

"*Wild is the Wind.*"

"Ooh. Nice choice. But *Sings the Blues* is perennial."

"Both sixties albums," she points out. "You can't go wrong with sixties Nina."

"Fair point."

"Mr. Argos!" It's the captain again.

I look up at him. "Captain Conway."

"You don't want to miss the low tide," he says.

"Low tide?" Blair asks.

"I—" I hesitate, and then press on. There's no backpedaling now. "Did you want to go to the James Bond Grotto?"

She laughs. "You mean the famous cave where all the tourists and celebrities go? Not really. But I'd love a yacht ride, if you're offering."

I don't even hesitate. I just lead her onto the yacht, her warm body pressed against mine.

My pulse is racing. Everything about this is wrong. The whole point of this date was to wash my hands of Blair and pass her off to Lord Alec, not spend another evening with her. But I'm on an adrenaline high, lust in my veins, intoxicated by the scent of her perfume, heady and sweet and reminiscent of all the illicit sex we've had. I tell myself I'll keep my hands away from her, that this is the opportunity I need to break things off, to let her down gently and get her in the mindset of wanting a rebound...but I know it's a lie. The tension between us is already singing.

Once I tell the captain there's been a change of plans, and that we'll merely be traveling in a lazy circle, I lead her to the bar on the sun deck. Nina Simone's voice spills from the hidden speakers, and Blair lets out a squeal of delight.

"Wine? Cocktail? Bougie lemonade?" I offer.

"I'm more interested in seeing what's below decks," she says, the barest smile tugging her full lips.

My cock jumps to attention as tingles race down my spine. It's like she's already touching me, her nails raking down my back, her hungry mouth trailing down my abs. It's almost hard to breathe as equal amounts of desire and apprehension work through me. I can't do this again. I have to quit her. I have to stop. My business partners are arriving tonight, for fuck's sake.

But I'm addicted.

"I'll take you on the grand tour, then," I say, sealing my fate.

She's on me the moment we step into the master cabin. Her arms loop around my neck and she crushes her lips to mine, already wrapping one long leg around my waist. I drive her back against the door, and it closes with a bang. Reaching behind her, I click the lock, then lift her up onto my hips.

"We shouldn't...be doing...this..." I mutter between kisses, even as I wrap my hand around her breast and squeeze. She's a guest at my hotel, she's barely old enough to drink, and she's a bachelorette.

"I know," she pants, pushing me away.

"We can stop," I tell her, trying to catch my breath.

"We can definitely stop," she agrees, dropping to her knees. But I don't stop her at all.

Blair quickly works my belt and opens my pants. As she does, I notice she's wearing the souvenir bracelet I bought her. Part of me sees it for the warning sign it might be, but the other part of me—the more assertive part—ignores the bracelet, focusing on the fact that I'm rock hard and aching for the sweet oblivion of her mouth. She looks up at me with those big blue eyes, licks her lips, and frees my cock.

"I've missed this," she says.

I groan deep in my throat. Batting her eyelashes, she takes me in her mouth and slides me deep.

"Mmm," she moans.

"Fuck."

Palming the door, I give in and absorb the pleasure. Her mouth is hot and wet as she bobs back and forth, pulling me in more deeply each time. Fisting her hair, I guide her mouth and watch as she sucks me off. The tip of my cock slips down her throat. She swallows, her throat clenching wet and tight around me, and I almost lose it.

"Jesus, Blair."

She grins with my dick in her mouth and it's the naughtiest thing—she knows exactly what she's doing to me and I fucking love it. In fact, I'm going to come if she doesn't stop, and I don't want that. Not so fast.

Forcing myself away from her, I pick her up and carry her over to the bed.

"Take that dress off."

Her eyes flash and she pulls her lower lip between her teeth. Kneeling on the bed, she lifts the dress over her head and throws it across the room. Her breasts spill over the cups of her white demi bra. Cupping them with both hands, I swallow hard as the full mounds perfectly conform to my palms, her nipples peaking hard against my skin.

"Look at these perfect tits."

Dipping my head, I take one nipple between my lips and suck it through the fabric of her bra until her chest heaves, fingers digging into my hair. Reaching behind her, I unfasten the bra and whisk it away. Then I return to her nipples, sucking and toying and teasing each one in turn until she's clawing at my shirt in desperation.

"Take me, Sebastian," she says, her voice a throaty growl. "I'm ready to fuck."

"God, I love it when you talk like that."

"You're a dirty old man," she teases.

"The dirtiest."

I step out of my pants and boxer briefs as she takes off my shirt, and then I push her back on the bed and soak up the sight of her lying there in her white lace panties, chest heaving with every lust-filled breath, pupils blown wide with desire. She's fucking perfect. A fantasy come to life.

It takes me less than two seconds to rip her panties off

and shove her legs apart. Burying my face between her thighs, I grip her hips and dig my fingers into her flesh as I lave her clit with my tongue. Her sharp gasps and frantic moans urge me on. I can tell she's getting close. My cock throbs against the mattress as she thrashes beneath me, riding my tongue faster and faster. Any second now.

"Sebastian," she pants. "Yes. Fuck, yes. *Yes*."

Her taste floods my mouth, her thighs clamping tight around my head as she comes, grinding her pussy against my lips, my teeth, my tongue. I can barely hold myself back from climbing on top of her to fuck her while she's still orgasming. But I manage to keep myself in check.

When I pull away, I look out the window and see the sun setting into the ocean, streaming gold and orange and hot pink.

"Look," I tell her, pointing.

She turns onto her side. "It's beautiful. Like a painting."

"Don't look away," I say as I fish a condom out of the nightstand drawer and roll it on.

I curl up behind her on the bed, spooning her, slipping my cock between her thighs. We both watch the sunset as she reaches down and guides me inside her. I start to pump into her, right hand tucked around her body to stroke her clit, left hand cupping her breast. Fuck, she feels good.

She meets me thrust for thrust, her ass pushing back against me, moans spilling from her lips. Groaning, I pick up the pace until I'm slamming into her. Hard, deep, fast, losing myself in the liquid glide, the sound of our bodies slapping together, the jiggle of her tit in my hand.

"Oooh," she whispers, her voice pitching higher. "Yeah, yeah, yeah."

"Yeah," I answer back. "That's it. That's my girl. Watch that sunset. Don't close your eyes."

Her moans change, getting wild and harsh.

"I'm coming again," she gasps. "Sebastian."

"Fuck."

Exploding into her, my eyes on the view out the window, I shiver with each jerk of my cock, with the feel of her pussy contracting around me, with each shared moan.

My phone rings from the pocket of my discarded pants on the floor and I vaguely remember I'm supposed to be somewhere right now. It doesn't matter, though. I needed this. Blair's naked, satiated body tangled with mine, my cock still spurting into her, my mind blissfully empty. I'm exactly where I'm supposed to be.

18

BLAIR

> Good morning! Your father and I are having breakfast with Ted Polansky in an hour. You should join us, sweetheart.

GROANING, I fling an arm over my eyes and shove my phone under the pillow. It's not even 8 a.m. This is not how I wanted to wake up today.

Last night was so perfect. The yacht, the sunset, the sex (obviously), the amazing steak and scallops that Sebastian's personal chef had prepared for us on the boat. I couldn't stop thinking about the date after I got back to my room last night, so I tried to watch TV to distract myself and ended up marathoning way too many episodes of *Bridgerton*. Honestly, I'm still on cloud nine.

Or at least, I was until I got hit with this Ted breakfast invite before I'd even cracked open both of my eyes. I know I should respond to Mom's text, but I don't have a legitimate excuse to say no. And I'm definitely not going. The last thing I want to do on my remaining days of vacation is sit through an uncomfortable meal where my mother will no doubt try to play matchmaker for me and Ted. Not that he'd need much encouragement from her. Considering the way he acted on the beach the other day when he helped me escape from that British guy, it seems pretty clear that Ted is into me.

Which is flattering. And under normal circumstances, I'd probably be interested in getting to know the guy better. He isn't hard on the eyes, and we had a great time talking baseball the first time we met at the beach bar. But these aren't normal circumstances.

Right now, the only man I want to spend my time with is Sebastian.

My phone buzzes again.

> Should we pick you up from your room on our way to the restaurant?

Dear God, no. Anything but that.

Frantically, I scan my suite, as if I can find a place to hide from my parents. Instead, I spot the room service menu on the desk across the room. *Hallelujah.* There's my excuse. I rush over to grab it and flip it open, quickly zeroing in on what sounds like the perfect vacation breakfast.

After I dial room service to order the Fire Engine—a spicy beef and veggie hash served over buttery grits—with fried sweet plantains and starfruit salad, I grab my cell and text my mom back.

> Would love to join, but already ordered room service. Maybe next time?

I set my phone down and go into the luxurious marble bathroom to take a shower. Room service said my food would be here in about thirty to forty minutes, so I have time to get ready for the day.

Sighing under the relaxing pulse of the hot water, I glance down at my wrist and smile at the coin bracelet that Sebastian bought me. Every time I look at it, I feel a burst of butterflies in my stomach like some lovesick teenager. Not that I actually love the guy. I barely know him. I just really, really like him. And there's nothing wrong with that. I can really, really like the person I'm having a summer fling with, can't I? Or am I already in too deep?

My heart sinks. Even more proof that I've crossed a line.

I finish my shower, then jump out and throw on the plush hotel bathrobe so I can dial Brooke for help. If anyone has answers to all these pesky questions I've been asking myself, it's my best friend.

"Pick up, pick up, pick up," I chant as I walk over to pull open the balcony doors, breathing in the fresh ocean breeze that caresses my face.

"Hey!" she says breathlessly. "I just got out of the subway. Everything okay?"

"No, everything is definitely not okay," I admit, sinking into one of the lounge chairs on the balcony. "How much time do you have?"

"Enough for you to tell me what's going on," she says. "But if you need more time than I can give you on my walk to work, I'll sneak into the meditation lounge in an hour and call you back."

I laugh. "Wow, meditation lounge? Bougie. Sounds like the new job's working out great."

"It *is* great. And I'd love to talk about how great it is. Right now, though, I need to hear all the details of your not-okayness. So spill."

It only takes a few minutes to give her the rundown on what I've been up to with Sebastian. When I tell her the part about him being one of the resort's owners, she lets out a gasp.

"Scandal!" she teases. "So wait, is he like...in his forties or fifties? Blair! You naughty girl."

"No. He has to be in his early to mid thirties. He's not, like, my dad's age."

"Still. Older men are hot. I bet he really knows what he's doing in bed. I'm jealous."

My face goes hot. "I'm not going to deny it. Definitely way better than any of the guys I dated at Stern. And his tongue. Jesus, Brooke, you have no idea."

A shiver goes through me at the memory.

She cackles. "Okay, okay, so...let me just recap. Super-hot older guy with fire bedroom skills is pleasuring you at every free moment, including on his freaking yacht. You enjoy each other's company, you're using condoms, and both of you are aware that it's a temp situation. Please tell me what I'm missing here, because I do not see a problem with anything you just told me. Is he married?"

"No! Or at least, I don't think so. He doesn't wear a ring or have a tan line for one."

"Okay, then what is it?"

Taking a deep breath, I say, "I think I like him too much."

It takes a moment for Brooke to respond. "Are you joking right now?"

"You know what I mean! I'm afraid I'll get emotionally attached. Actually, that's a lie. It's too late. I'm already attached. Why do I have to live in New York? Ugh."

"Blair, you don't *have* to live in New York. You could probably move to the island and work remotely. I mean, your parents own the company. Lots of people work from home these days."

I mull it over for half a second, shaking my head. "First of all, I don't even know if seeing me more long-term is something he'd be interested in. It's probably not what he wants."

"Can't hurt to ask."

"Okay, but secondly, I'm not going to just give up my entire life to live on an island so I can screw some hot guy until we get bored of each other. I'm excited to start working at the Tisdale Corp. and I know that being in the actual, physical office is crucial to my success. And thirdly, Sebastian said he was here for work, but just because he co-owns a resort here, it doesn't mean he lives here year-round."

"Well, wherever he lives, you can still try to do the long-distance thing. It could work. At least, for as long as you both can make it work."

"I've thought about that," I admit. "But again, I don't think that's what he wants."

"Why don't you just *ask* him what he wants instead of trying to guess?" she says pointedly. "Maybe he's having the same exact thoughts you are."

"Well. It's just..." I hesitate, standing up to pace the

balcony, and then push on. "The thing is, he's very hot and cold. Half the time he acts like he doesn't want to sleep with me, or he stops before we go too far. The other half of the time, he's a total beast and I probably couldn't keep him off me if I tried."

Brooke laughs. "Damn, girl. Classy problems."

"I know. But still, it's like he's constantly holding back. Isn't that a red flag? Maybe he's not that into me."

"Blair, please. That date he arranged last night tells me everything I need to know about his interest level. It required a lot of effort and planning, and it was romantic as hell. He wants you."

"I know he 'wants' me, but I can't tell if there's more to it than just the sex we're having and the fact that we seem to enjoy each other's company. Maybe that's all it is and I'm just...imagining that there could be more to it because I like him too much."

"I'm sure he's just fighting his attraction to you because it's inappropriate—you're a guest at his hotel, and there's the age gap. Plus, you both know that this thing you've got going has an expiration date. So here's my advice: Either talk to the guy and find out if this could turn into more than just a fling or spend the rest of your life regretting the fact that you didn't have the balls to ask," Brooke says. "Your choice. I know what I'd do in your position."

"Yeah," I say, sighing. "You're probably right."

"We both know I'm right," she shoots back. "I just got to the office. Are you good now?"

"I'm good. Thanks for talking."

"Always. Call me if you need to and I'll see you soon, okay? Love you."

"Love you. Bye."

I hang up just in time to hear the chime of the doorbell going off inside the suite. It must be my room service. And I'm still in a bathrobe with wet hair.

"You're a mess, Blair," I scold myself as I tighten the robe and go to the door.

After the food cart has been rolled into the room and I've signed off on the bill, I take my plate and my cup of coffee out to the balcony so I can enjoy my breakfast in the open air. As I eat, I think about what my best friend said.

Brooke is right. I should just talk to Sebastian and see how he feels about meeting up again in the future. But I wouldn't call that a long-distance relationship. The term implies a level of commitment that I doubt we're ready for. It hasn't even been two weeks yet. This thing is casual, and I like it that way.

Besides, having a relationship isn't my first priority. My career is. Learning how to run the baseball team is. Sebastian would just be the cherry on top. Would he want to be my cherry? I wouldn't mind being his...

My phone buzzes from my pocket and I set my coffee cup down and pull out my cell, pulse racing in anticipation. It's not Sebastian, though. It's my mom. Again.

> Ted looks exceptionally handsome this morning. I'll send you a photo.

I start texting back, *You don't have to—*

But it's too late. A picture of Ted comes through. He's sitting next to my dad, smiling right into my mother's camera, and I wonder if she told them she was taking a picture to send to me. Ted's eyes sparkle and his dark blond hair flops adorably over one eye. He's wearing a polo shirt, and this might be the first time I've seen him without his Marlins hat. He is handsome, but it doesn't do anything for me.

> Very nice. Hope you're all having fun.

It's obvious that my mom is not-so-subtly trying to set me up with Ted. Ever since she got here, she's gone out of her way to mention him at every opportunity. It's either something about his good looks, or his multi-million-dollar contract, or what a genuinely nice guy he is. She even casually mentioned that he'd probably make a great father one day. I can't believe she thinks her efforts might actually pay off.

Another horrifying thought strikes me. Who knows what she's telling Ted over breakfast right now? If she's campaigning as hard with him as she has been with me, he could end up getting all kinds of wrong ideas about me. I'm definitely not looking for a husband, despite my mom's wishes.

The thing I care most about right now is getting my career started. Forging a path for myself, chasing my dreams, accomplishing my goals. That's what I want to focus on. If I can include Sebastian in there somewhere, even better. But mainly, I'm more than ready to step into the world as a self-sufficient adult. I don't need my mother hovering over my shoulder, trying to plan out a life for me just because she thinks I'll be happy, healthy, and safe with a trophy husband and a nice house and a fat bank account. Security isn't the be-all, end-all for me.

I want more.

I worked damn hard to earn my degree, and I love what I studied. I'm eager to step out on my own now. I'll never be satisfied or fulfilled living a purely domestic life. My mom is just going to have to find a way to accept that.

After I finish my breakfast, I go back into the room and trade my bathrobe for a bathing suit and sheer coverup dress. Then I put on a little makeup, grab my sunscreen, and dig around in my suitcase looking for a book to take down to the beach. I figure I can get an hour or two of lounging in before my parents hunt me down. At first, I pull out a women's fiction novel. It's the perfect vacation book, about three generations of a quirky New England family who come together for one final summer at their lakefront cabin. But I'm in the mood for something else. Something...empowering.

I set the novel aside and grab a non-fiction book on women in leadership roles instead. One of my professors at NYU recommended it to me. It's exactly what I want to read. It is *my* vacation, after all.

As I take the elevator down to the first floor, a smile tugs at my lips. Because after twenty-two years, I've finally hit my rebellion-against-my-parents stage.

And now it's time to do things my way.

19

SEBASTIAN

STEPPING into the lobby this morning was like entering a different world. With the start of the Junkanoo festival tomorrow, an influx of new guests has infiltrated every available space in the resort, including the café, bars, and restaurants. Not to mention the private beach and the pools. All great for business, of course, but it means an end to the relative quiet that I had enjoyed last week when I only had a handful of guests to manage. This is officially the start of our high season.

Even worse, my partners are here for the next forty-eight hours. My stress is through the roof.

I'm at one of the pools with Becker, Theo, Nate, and Nate's baby sister Eliza, who just graduated from her heinously expensive private high school on the Upper West Side. We're supposed to be having a business chat while Eliza enjoys the pool, but we're not getting much accomplished with all the guests milling around and Nate pacing around in circles while he blabs away on some private call.

Not that I'm surprised at our lack of productivity. We all know the real reason my partners flew here is to enjoy the Junkanoo, as they do every year. Calling this a business trip is just an excuse to get a tax write-off for their mini vacation. Meanwhile, I'm the only one of us who actually has to work. I'm the one running the resort, after all.

People-watching behind my sunglasses, I recognize married couples that I've arranged in prior years, unmarried couples I've worked with who are enjoying long- and short-term situationships, past and present clients and their families. It's no wonder we're so booked. Once a client has retained our services, they're officially a member of the resort, so they're eligible to book a stay depending on availability. And people love to come back, year after year. Who wouldn't? We provide a peerless luxury experience that transports our guests to a haven of indulgence. Violinists to play for you and your partner while you dine on your private balcony. Horseback rides on the beach at dawn or dusk. Twenty-four-hour car service, room service, spa service. Your wish is our command.

Not only that, but the happy matches we've made have resulted in the kind of brand loyalty that money can't buy. And yet...the clear evidence of all those happy matches doesn't sit well with me today. Because when I think about Blair, I can't ignore the pang of guilt in my gut. As long as I keep fucking her, I'm putting her match—and the entire business—at risk.

But no matter how much I try to keep away from her, I haven't been able to stop myself from sampling the goods, over and over and over again. And she's not just any client, she's a bachelorette. The whole point of her being here, albeit unbeknownst to her, is for her to be matched to someone else.

Maybe it would be forgivable if I'd only been with her once, but I'm in way too deep for that. Sleeping with a woman on deck to be auctioned for marriage is totally taboo, and I can't even get myself off the hook by explaining that it was initially a case of mistaken identity. Because the second I found out that Sunshine was Blair Tisdale, I should have called Becker and told him everything, flown back to NYC and removed myself from the Tisdale match purely due to my conflict of interest. Instead, I've kept the whole affair under wraps.

I know what I'm doing is wrong.

And I still keep doing it.

I glance over at Becker, who is busy ordering all of us a round of drinks from one of the pool bar's cocktail waitresses. Theo eyes me curiously from his lounge chair on Becker's other side. He gets up and moves to sit next to me in Nate's empty chair. I try not to tense up. Theo would have my hide if he found out I was gambling the Tisdale commission by sleeping with their daughter.

I nod as he gives me an inquiring stare. "What's up, Theo?"

"You keeping an eye on all the MILFs from your little corner over here?"

"You're funny."

He raises a brow. "I see one that's exactly your type in the cabana by the towel station."

My stomach drops, and I follow his gaze, expecting to

see Blair with her parents. But instead, it's a woman in her early forties, with dark, silky hair and deep brown eyes. She has the full lips and high cheekbones of a model, and Theo is right—she does look like my type. Or what used to be my type. Not anymore, though. As gorgeous as the woman is, she's just not doing it for me.

"Hot damn," I say, going along with it just for the optics. "Too bad there's a rule about fraternizing with the guests." If only he knew how ironic that comment was, coming from me.

Becker turns to face us and cuts in with a change of subject that I'm grateful for.

"Who is Nate talking to?" He tilts his head in Nate's direction.

"No clue, but he's been on that call for a while now," Theo says.

"Probably sweet talking some new client, if I had to guess," I add. "Must be a heavy hitter if he's blowing off our meeting for the call."

"He did have dinner with one of the Rothschilds last week," Becker muses.

We all watch Nate, as if there are clues to be had based on his facial expressions, which there aren't. At one point, he throws his head back and laughs.

Meanwhile, Eliza paddles around the edge of the pool, following him and splashing his feet and lower legs with water. She's trying to get his attention, but he expertly ignores her, not missing a beat on his phone call. She has a mischievous look on her face, as if she's used to torturing her brother for kicks.

"I'm not sure it was the best idea for Nate to bring his sister," I think out loud. "It looks like she's going to be a distraction, and Nate isn't going to have the time to babysit her."

"Eliza's over eighteen," Becker says, waving me off. "She can take care of herself."

"Trust me, Sebastian, she's not going to be a problem. She came here to party, not hang out with her brother," Theo chimes in.

"Maybe," I say. "But she'd do well to remember he's on the clock. I just hope he prepared her to entertain herself while she's here."

Not that she seemed to have any trouble entertaining herself last night while her big brother was completely oblivious. Her suite is directly next to mine, and while the walls have excellent soundproofing, I had to get out of bed in the middle of the night to close all my windows because she was apparently making good use of her balcony.

"She'll be fine," Becker insists. "There are plenty of things to do on the island."

"Still. We should all keep an eye out for her. She's trouble," I tell them.

"For real? You barely know her," Theo scoffs. "What are you talking about?"

"I heard her with a guy in her room last night. On the balcony, actually. Woke me up out of a dead sleep."

Theo looks horrified. Or repulsed. Or both. Becker's frowning.

"I know," I say. "TMI. And it was the last thing I wanted to wake up to at one in the morning, believe me.

But the real issue is, it's bad for business. Who else would the guy be besides one of the staff, or one of the matches?"

I know I'm being the world's hugest hypocrite here, but I'm trying to gauge their reactions. Because I sure as hell can't casually mention that *I'm* the one who's been fucking one of the matches and then see how they feel about it.

"Did you say anything to Nate?" Theo asks, darting a glance toward him.

"Not yet."

"Well, don't," Theo says. "He'd freaking lose it. Beck? You with me?"

"Absolutely. Not to mention, he'd tear the place apart trying to figure out who put his hands on his baby sister. Let's just keep it under wraps," Becker says. "Meanwhile, Sebastian, why don't you go ahead and have Eliza moved into a suite on another floor? Plausible deniability and all that. The less we know about the whole thing, the better."

"Sure," I say. "I'll make up something about a maintenance issue."

"Good idea," Theo says.

Shaking my head at Becker, I say, "I just can't believe you're giving her a pass."

Does that mean there's a chance I could get one, too?

Becker shrugs. "Like I said, she's eighteen. Don't you remember being that age? I'm sure she's just trying to take advantage of her summer vacation before heading off to college. I'd do the same thing in her shoes. Think about it. Once you're a full-fledged adult, you can't fuck whoever you want anymore. There are consequences."

His statement is sobering. Neither Theo nor I have a

response. Luckily, we don't need one, because the waitress comes back with a tray full of drinks for us.

After Beck takes a gulp of his scotch, he picks up Nate's Negroni and stands with both glasses. "I'm going to take Nate his drink. Doesn't look like that call is ending anytime soon. Why don't we raincheck this meeting until later? I've got a call to prep for myself."

"So do I," Theo says. "I mean, it's month end. I've got bank recs to catch up on."

They both walk off, and I sit for a few minutes with my drink, deeply pondering how fucked I am now that my business partners are all here.

I finally get up and start back toward the hotel when I see Mr. and Mrs. Tisdale waving me over from their table and chairs on the opposite side of the pool. My pulse picks up, but since I have no good excuse for not chatting with them, I put on my client-facing smile and head over to play nice and pretend with all of my being that I'm not messing around with their daughter. The daughter I'm contractually obligated to marry off to one of the three eligible bachelors that The Quattuor Group has vetted.

"Mr. and Mrs. Tisdale. How's the vacation going?" I ask. "Perfect weather for lounging by the pool, isn't it?"

Mrs. Tisdale nods. "It really is. However, we wanted to speak to you about something."

Adrenaline floods my veins at her inscrutable tone. Then Mr. Tisdale settles a heavy hand on my shoulder.

"If there are, uh, any issues with your accommodations, I'd be happy to address them," I say, shifting into customer service mode while praying this has nothing to do with Blair.

"It's about Blair," Papa Tisdale says quietly.

Fuck. Did she say something to them? Is their parental intuition kicking in? Do they know?

Papa Tisdale looks over his shoulder, then glances around the pool area, presumably looking for Blair. Seemingly satisfied that she isn't within earshot, he goes on, "She mentioned to us that she'd met someone here."

My stomach drops. "Really?" I choke out. "Who?"

"She wouldn't say," Mrs. Tisdale sighs. "But my odds are on Ted Polansky. I saw them on the beach the other morning, walking arm in arm. And she's been positively glowing lately."

"Glad to hear it," I say, ignoring the tug in my chest.

Mr. Tisdale smiles broadly. "Your agency did a great job picking him out. Blair's such a huge baseball fan, it's a perfect match. Not that her options aren't still open."

Ted Polansky. Of course. It makes sense. The guy is *nice*. Not to mention financially comfortable, easygoing, family oriented. He can offer Blair all the happiness she deserves.

"And you know what's so funny?" Mrs. Tisdale goes on. "All those diamonds he could afford to buy her, and it's a letter bracelet she's all starry-eyed over! Some cheap souvenir. She barely takes it off."

The two of them exchange smiles, and I make myself join in. But inside, I'm in full-blown panic mode. This is exactly what I was worried about. Blair is clearly way too attached. She cannot, *cannot* be allowed to have feelings for me. A casual fling with no strings attached is one thing, but it can't mean more than that. Blair Tisdale is here at the resort for one reason: to be matched to a suitable bachelor.

I have to salvage this. Fast. Get her to walk away from me so she can get back on track to meet the love of her life and live happily ever after.

But there's only one way I can think of to do it.

In order to save this match, I'll have to break her heart.

20

BLAIR

The air is alive with excitement.

My skin lights with goosebumps as I immerse myself in the Junkanoo. There is color everywhere: magenta, neon green, sunflower yellow, turquoise and cobalt and fiery orange. The performers in the parade are dressed in vibrant costumes of feathers, glitter, wings, and elaborate head-dresses and sparkling chest pieces. Wrists and ankles are adorned with bells that jingle loudly as the dancers show off their routines in time with the music. I'm thrilled to be able to celebrate the island's culture this way, right along-side the locals.

To my absolute surprise and delight, my mother seems to be enjoying herself as well. When I had suggested she join me, she initially hesitated. "Didn't Ted Polansky ask you to accompany him?"

He must've mentioned it when he joined them for breakfast the other morning. "We never made concrete plans," I had told her. "I'd rather go with you. Unless you want to spend all day golfing with Dad again? But you and

I haven't really had a girls' day, just the two of us, in so long."

Her face had brightened immediately. "Of course I'll go with you. I'm sure we'll catch up with Ted somewhere at the festival anyway."

I honestly don't care if we see Ted or not, but I didn't let her know that. Truthfully, I was more excited at the prospect of running into Sebastian during the parade.

Now that I'm here, I can't stop scanning the crowd, hoping to see his face. He's bound to be attending. He can't own a resort that overlooks the main street where the parade route is and not participate.

And when I do spot him, I know he won't be able to miss me. In preparation for the festival, I went to a small local boutique and chose a flirty two-piece outfit. The bright pink halter top matches the polish on my fingers and toes, and the body-hugging canary yellow skirt has three layers of ruffles that sway with every step. I took extra time curling my hair and then spritzed it with smoothing serum, so the long curls flow down my back and bounce when I walk.

The ensemble is a little over the top, but it fits the theme, and it feels good to be another bright spot in the crowd. My mother—in her linen dress and sensible flats—hasn't said a word about my sartorial choices, another pleasant surprise.

She walks easily beside me as we nibble on the conch fritters and sip the switcha we bought from one of the street vendors.

"Gosh, these are good," Mom says, handing the paper carton of fritters back to me.

"See? I told you it was worth trying them," I gloat.

"Too bad they're fried. I'm going to have to do extra Pilates when I get home with all the junk I've been eating."

"It's not junk! Seafood is really healthy, Mom. Even if it is battered and fried. Besides, it's important to partake of the local cuisine when you travel. Here, you have the last one," I tell her. "I want to find us some coconut rum cake next."

She hesitates, glancing around like she's checking to see if anybody's watching before she devours the last fritter. Then she throws the empty container in a trashcan and finishes off the limeade.

"There. Now we're all set for cake," she says. "I mean, it is the local cuisine, right?"

"Totally," I agree.

I'm not sure why she's in such a cavalier mood today, but I'm loving it. She's lived in a bubble of self-denial and moderation ever since my sister's passing, as if punishing herself for not being able to prevent it. But she wasn't always like that. My mom used to eat the cake, drink the extra glass of wine, buy herself flowers on Sunday afternoons. After Sophie died, though, Mom stopped treating herself. She lost her zest for life.

Seeing her indulge now is a joy I didn't know I was missing.

We wander some more, stopping at various booths that have been set up for the festival with local wares. There are wood carvings, woven bags and baskets made of dried palm fronds, guava jam, shell earrings and matching necklaces. We find a table loaded with sparkling Junkanoo headpieces and even a fruit bowl hat that I jokingly try to put on my mother. Of course, she won't have it. So I put it on my own head and do a little twirl, modeling it for her.

"Blair, really. Take that off before someone sees you."

"Mom, someone seeing you is the idea of a hat like this. You can't wear an outlandish headpiece like this and hope to hide from the public. It's very fashionable."

"Fine, then. I'll buy it for you."

"No!" I shriek, laughing.

We find the rum cake I've been searching for, and the seller slices it into bite-sized pieces so we can eat it as we walk. Meanwhile, I never stop looking for Sebastian in the crowd. Where is he? As soon as I spot him, I'm going to make an excuse to my mom so I can run off and disappear with him.

Because it's time for me to confess that this isn't just a vacation romance for me. It's turned into something real, something worth pursuing. I have to know if he feels the same way. If he doesn't, at least I'll know for sure. I don't want to live with the regret of being too chicken to find out if Sebastian and I could have had more than a fling. Brooke's pep talk was exactly what I needed to hear.

And the Junkanoo is exactly the right place to declare myself. The festival, with all its color, pageantry, and vibrant music, and the smell and sound of the ocean nearby, is the perfect romantic setting to tell him I'll do whatever it takes to turn this into a genuine relationship, long distance or not.

Mom pats my arm, looking intently at something up ahead. Then she waves. Oh no.

Ted freaking Polansky *cannot* show up right now and ruin this for me.

But then I see who she's waving at—a man and a woman about her age, looking a little shellshocked and lost on the edge of the crowd.

"You know them?" I ask.

"Your father and I met them at the wine bar. I'm going to say hi. Go find Ted! I'll catch up with you after."

"Have fun, Mom," I say, gently shoving her in the couple's direction. "I'll just do my thing. Call my cell if you need me."

She gives me a nod and sets off in their direction. Taking advantage of my newfound freedom, I browse a few more vendor stands, drop a few dollars in a hat for a band that's playing, and look for an alcohol stand. One of the performers hooks me by the arm and pulls me into a swing. We hop around in three big circles before he spins me twice and sets me back where I was. Heart soaring, I continue on my quest for a drink.

I should text Sebastian and tell him to meet me. Maybe I will, once I have some fortifying alcohol in my system.

A bar on wheels appears up ahead, and I get in line and end up ordering the 'Tutti-frutti Zootie' which comes in an oversized plastic goblet with several swords of fruit in it. A long, fat straw makes it possible to get to the actual alcohol in between bites of maraschino cherries and pineapple wedges. The booze hits almost immediately, and within a few minutes, I feel a pleasant buzz. It helps take the edge off of the anxiety I'm feeling about the possibility of getting rejected by Sebastian Argos.

Moving through the crowd, I get caught up in another impromptu dance with a couple of performers. These ones are a little more exuberant, and my drink sloshes over the sides of the goblet and splashes my feet. Sipping the drink faster to avoid more spillage, I dance my way out of the circle. That's when I see a dark head in the throng of revelers farther down the street.

My pulse goes wild. I would know the slight curl to that dark hair and the set of those shoulders anywhere. I've traced the muscles on that broad back enough times to have his shape imprinted in my memory. Sebastian is here.

I weave my way through the crush of bodies to follow him. As I hurry along, the performers and spectators seem to tighten and swell around me. By the time I maneuver around the wall of people, I've lost him.

Taking out my phone, I decide to send him a text message when I hear someone yell my name. I glance up, heart pounding, only to see Ted Polansky heading straight toward me. My stomach sinks. If I have any chance of catching up with Sebastian, I can't get entangled with Ted right now.

"Blair!" he calls again.

I feel guilty, but I turn away and pretend that I can't hear him. I don't look in his direction, even as he yells for me again. Moving through the crowd, I finish my drink and toss it into a trashcan while searching wildly for Sebastian.

Giving the crowd one last scan, I almost stumble over my wedge sandals. Sebastian!

He's standing next to a brunette woman in her twenties with her hair up in a ponytail, wearing a bright purple bodycon dress that fits her curves like a glove. Even from afar, I can clearly make out her sky-high cheekbones and full lips. She's stunning.

She smiles up at Sebastian in a familiar way, her eyes

lighting up as if they know each other. He says something to her, his hand on her elbow, his body language suggesting that yes, they do know each other. I don't recognize her. Is she local? Another guest at the resort? A girlfriend I don't know about? Part of me wants to turn and run, but instead, I hurry toward him.

As if sensing my laser focus on him, Sebastian turns his head and looks at me. Our eyes meet instinctively and hold. It feels like time stands still. Like this moment is just for us.

My heart pounds in my chest. I try to memorize every last detail of the scene, because I don't want to forget a single part of this perfect night. I'm mere steps away from the man I think I might be in love with, surrounded by light and life and magic, and I'm about to tell him how I feel.

Except...Sebastian isn't smiling back at me. He looks tense, his brow creased.

I raise my hand to wave, but he looks away, lifting a hand to cup the cheek of the woman in the purple dress.

Icy dread hits my gut. I freeze mid-step, so shocked to see him touching her that I can't move. But I see everything.

Sebastian's arm goes around her waist and he pulls her against him, dragging her body up until she's on her toes and they're practically nose to nose. And then he leans in and kisses her. His lips are glued to hers, his eyes closed, and when his jaw flexes, I know with abject certainty that he's plunging his tongue into her mouth.

A wave of nausea almost knocks me off my feet, tears filling my eyes until I can't see anymore.

The euphoric effect of the alcohol has vanished. I feel like I'm turning to stone inside.

"Blair!"

Ted Polansky's voice shocks me from my stupor, and the next thing I know, I'm running into the crowd and away from Sebastian. Away from Ted. Away from everything, as I bolt from the perfect night I didn't want to forget.

Now, all I want to do is forget everything.

21

BLAIR

"Your text last night didn't say why you disappeared so suddenly. I take it you found Ted?"

Rather than responding to my mom, I force a coy smile and grab a blue floral patterned wrap skirt off one of the clothing racks, holding it up for her approval. The last thing I want to talk about is anything that happened last night.

"I knew it," she crows, assuming her presumption is correct.

The triumphant look on her face instantly raises my hackles. She's probably imagining the romantic evening Ted and I had together, plotting wedding colors, picking out baby names. In reality, not only did I not "find" Ted, but I got completely blindsided by the man I actually *did* want to find.

Mom means well, I'm sure, but her attempts at playing cupid on this vacation are really grating on my nerves. Especially when my heart has been aching so badly ever since I saw Sebastian with that woman at the festival. Hence my choice to keep my sunglasses on indoors. I can't let Mom see how puffy my eyes are. She'll immediately start asking questions that I have no interest in answering.

After I left the Junkanoo, I went back to my hotel room, grabbed a bottle of wine from the wet bar in my suite, and drained the entire thing (while crying and texting Brooke) on the balcony. Then I tried to watch a baseball game between the Yankees and the Red Sox, both teams being the Rockets' biggest rivals, but I couldn't stay focused. All night long, I tossed and turned. And at breakfast this morning, I could barely stomach a yogurt parfait.

It's not like me to be this invested in a guy. Men only serve to railroad plans, cause turmoil, and generally be an obstacle to the goals I want to achieve. Honestly, I'm shocked at how much the Sebastian thing has gutted me. We've known each other for less than two weeks, and I never intended to actually fall for him. He was supposed to be a fun vacation hook-up. Nothing more.

Unfortunately, my stupid heart had other plans.

There's no way I could have seen this coming. I knew Sebastian and I had a connection; I knew I was starting to get attached, but I never thought he'd be able to hurt me like this. We were both firmly in favor of casual sex with no strings attached. And then all of a sudden he's making out with another woman in front of me, and I completely fall apart.

I'm just as upset with myself for having this reaction as I am with Sebastian for kissing her. Which isn't even fair. He and I aren't dating. We're not exclusive. Everything about our situation is temporary, and definitely not serious. He didn't do anything wrong. It just *felt* wrong seeing it happen. And it feels even more wrong the more I think about it.

Which is a lot, because I can't stop replaying that kiss I witnessed. In my mind, I watch it happen over and over again. The way he looked at me, the way we locked eyes first—he wanted me to see what he was doing. But why? Did he want to hurt me on purpose? Did he think it was necessary to remind me that he and I aren't committed?

Sure, I don't *know* him know him, but nothing about Sebastian's demeanor or conduct has indicated that he's someone with a mean streak. So what the hell? Has he been an asshole in disguise this entire time? Or was that kiss I saw just...some kind of misunderstanding?

Ha. As if there was anything to be misunderstood about the way he stuck his tongue down her throat. Unless he was purposely trying to make me jealous. Except...is he even the kind of guy who'd play childish games like that? He doesn't seem the type.

Maybe he met her at the festival and it was love at first sight. And it happened so fast, he didn't have time to break things off with me. But then why did he look so unhappy just before he kissed her?

Ugh. This is driving me crazy. I can't keep torturing myself with these questions.

Pulling my phone out of my pocket, I send him a quick text before I can talk myself out of it.

> How's your day going?

There. Just a totally casual, totally chill message. Nothing accusatory or aggressive. Maybe he'll take advantage of my olive branch and write back with an apology. If not, maybe his response will give me some other clues about his behavior last night. Like, *Hey, I've been meaning to tell you, I met someone.* Or *I'm sorry, Blair, but I ran into an ex at the Junkanoo and we decided to get back together.* Any kind of explanation would be better than the horrible radio silence I've been getting.

"What are Ted's dinner plans this evening?" Mom asks, and I realize I've been tuning her out for the last few minutes. "You two have been seeing so much of each other, and he gets along so well with your father. Don't you think Ted would like to join us for—"

"Mom!" I cut her off, exasperated. "I never found Ted last night, and we're not seeing each other, so I'm not going to invite him to a family dinner. You're building this up in your head to be way more than it is. I've barely even talked to the guy. He probably has better things to do anyway."

"Oh, Blair." Her voice is sympathetic, but for all the wrong reasons. I'm sure she thinks I'm pining away for Ted Polansky, too timid to make a move. "I know he's a famous athlete, but trust me, Ted would be over the moon if you reached out to him. He's *very* interested in you. Probably because you two have so much in common. I could invite him to dinner myself, if you'd prefer."

That is the last thing I want, but since I can't have her calling Ted behind my back, I just say, "Please don't. I'll handle it, Mom."

"If you're sure..."

"I'm positive."

I spin away from her and stalk over to another circular rack of blouses and tank tops, flicking through the hangers with irritation. The ritzy shop is brimming with upscale vacation wear, a mix of designer labels and locally made batik and linen pieces. Mom dragged me in here after we had breakfast in town at the café next door. Probably because she's concerned about my non-Ted-friendly wardrobe.

Not that I totally blame her for judging my outfit. I put zero effort into getting ready this morning. My hair is in a messy bun and I'm wearing jean shorts with frayed edges and a slouchy tank top over my bikini.

"Blair? Did you hear me?"

I look over my shoulder. "What?"

She holds up a navy-blue halter top with a peplum waist and white trim. It's actually pretty cute.

"I thought this would go with that skirt you liked," she says.

"You're right. It would."

"Well, go get it. I'll buy you both."

I obediently go fetch the skirt, even though I'm 100% certain that the whole reason Mom wants to buy me this outfit is so that I can wear it to dinner with Ted Polansky.

Following behind her as she continues to browse, I run my fingers over buttons and ruffles and different fabrics as my mind drifts back to Sebastian.

"How about these?" Mom says, holding up another hanger.

"Seriously?"

The pants are wide legged and loose, not unlike Palazzo pants, which I happen to love. But it's the pattern that has my jaw dropping. Deep cobalt and pale aqua bloom in the background, while a navy branch-like design with small orange flowers fills the foreground.

"Wow. It looks like the bottom of the ocean," I say.

"Are they too loud?" She looks down at them again, sheepish. "I thought they looked fun."

"No. They're great. You picked perfect," I tell her.

"They'll match the top, too."

I smile. Retail therapy for the win. "They will. Thanks, Mom."

When she gets in line to pay, I hang back and dig my cell out again. No response from Sebastian. I hesitate and then send him another text, this one more direct.

> Can we talk?

My heart beats double-time while I stare at my screen, silently urging him to reply. Normally when we text, he responds quickly. But not this time. Is he ignoring me? On purpose?

"Here you go," Mom says, handing me the boutique bag.

"Thank you," I say, stuffing my phone back into my pocket.

"Should we shop more, or do you want to go see if your father is done golfing? We can drag him to the beach and try to get him in the water. He hasn't gone for a swim this entire trip yet."

I shake my head. "I'm actually not feeling well." It's not a lie. "I think I'll take a little nap and then meet up with you and Dad at the beach later. Thanks for the wardrobe refresh. I can walk back myself if you want to keep browsing."

"Don't be silly. I'll go with you. Should I call the hotel and have them send a car for us?"

"No. That's okay. I think the air might help."

We go back out to the street, and I peek at my phone every few minutes on our walk back to the resort. Still nothing from Sebastian. My stomach is in knots. The second I get to my room, I'm calling him. Meanwhile, Mom makes small talk, none the wiser that my heart is breaking.

As we enter the lobby and pass the registration desk and the hallway that leads to the management offices, I think about confronting Sebastian in his office. He can ignore my texts, but he'll have to say something to me if I'm standing right in front of him. And if he thinks he's going to get away with lying to me, he'll at least have to look me in the eye to make an attempt.

Once my mom drops me off at my suite, I lock the door behind her. Sitting on the edge of my bed, I dial Sebastian and put the phone on speaker. It rings and rings and rings. But he doesn't pick up.

Fine. Time for plan B, then.

I freshen my makeup and change into one of my sexier sundresses with a plunging neckline. If I'm about to get dumped, I can at least remind him of what he's losing.

Checking my cell phone for the millionth time, I slip it into my pocket and head downstairs. When I step out of the elevator, I don't hesitate. I stride into the lobby, head high, eyes locked on the employee-only hallway, zeroing in on the door at the end with the plaque that reads Management. I'm about five steps away from the hallway when a feminine voice calls out to me.

"Excuse me, miss? In the red dress? Can I help you?"

I turn around, preparing to tell whoever it is that I have an appointment with Mr. Argos, but the words die on my lips when I see who's standing there behind the concierge desk.

It's *her*.

The woman he kissed at the festival last night. Her dark hair curls long and soft over her shoulders, and she's dressed in the hotel employee uniform of head-to-toe black.

As I stalk over to her, my heart stutters. Her name tag reads Daisy. Concierge. *Concierge?* Sebastian is having an affair with an employee?

"Can I help you with something?" she repeats, smiling brightly. "Maybe planning an itinerary?"

Swallowing my anger, I match her perfectly polished smile with one of my own.

"Actually, I'm looking for Sebastian. Is he in his office?"

Her eyes narrow. "Mr. Argos?"

"Yes. That's the one," I say, unable to keep the ice out of my tone.

She hesitates for a split second and then says, "I'm so sorry, but he's not here at the moment."

"Really." I study her face, but I can't read her expression. Is she lying to me? "Can you tell me when he'll be back, then?"

"I can't. He flew off the island this morning."

22

SEBASTIAN

"Sebastian? We weren't expecting you for another few days. What are you doing here?"

"I missed you, too, Becker," I say sarcastically.

Taking a seat at Indigo's most secluded corner booth, I ignore the surprised looks coming from my business partners. Theo's got a pile of financial documents stacked in front of him, pen in hand. Nate looks self-satisfied, as usual. Becker just frowns, studying me intently.

"What did you fuck up?" he prods. "Is it that bad? Wait...are you quitting?"

"Like we could be so lucky," Theo jokes.

"You look tense," Nate tells me, rather unhelpfully.

"I'm not quitting. I just didn't want to miss seeing all your ugly faces at the team meeting," I joke, gesturing to one of the wait staff for a drink.

"That's what FaceTime is for," Theo says.

Had I known my early arrival from the island back to home base would cause such a damn problem, I would have called first. Since when do I have to tell my partners every move I make? Operations at the resort are running smoothly, so there's no reason I need to physically be there every waking moment.

Becker's mouth purses and I realize he's not buying my feigned nonchalance. He's worried I really screwed something up and had to come running home with my tail between my legs.

If only he knew the truth.

A tumbler of much-needed scotch appears in front of me. I nod in thanks to the waiter and then take a hard swallow. When I set the glass back on the table, I look up to find my colleagues all staring at me expectantly. Like they're waiting for the hammer to fall.

"It's nothing. I'm peopled-out and I needed a break if you really must know," I tell them.

Nate nods knowingly. "Junkanoo was too much for you. No surprise there, old man."

Becker still isn't appeased, though. I can tell by the look he's giving me that we'll be discussing my early arrival later. And I'd bet anything he plans to interrogate me until I crack. Unfortunately, I have no ammunition to fend him off with. In all the guilty pleasure of having a torrid affair with one of the matches, I never managed to pry any of Beck's secrets out of Daisy. Assuming she even has any.

I'm fucked.

"If we can get back to the meeting now?" Nate reminds us imperiously, rapping his knuckles on the table. Eagerness shines in his eyes and my interest is piqued. I wonder which big client he's closed in on this time. I'd recognize that smug look anywhere.

"We never left it," Becker says, his tone cool. "Go ahead."

Nate flips a leather portfolio open, then opens his laptop and pulls up a spreadsheet with which we're all very familiar. It's Nate's client list. It includes leads he's currently researching and/or pursuing, clients he's already signed who still have contracts to be fulfilled, and countless others who have worked with us in the past. The sheet is so full of data, it almost looks like static as Nate scrolls down to his most recent entry.

The leads section of the spreadsheet, highlighted in yellow, looks even more dense than usual. We rarely have difficulty finding clients, but I'm surprised to see just how busy we are right now. It just goes to show how indispensable Nate is to our business. I assume he'll be asking Becker to hire him an assistant one of these days. Maybe I can pawn Daisy off on him.

The thought brings a smirk to my lips, but it quickly fades when I realize that I might actually need to get Daisy reassigned within the company. She's been pissed off at me ever since I kissed her last night. There was no confusion on her part, either; she knew exactly what I was doing when I used her to send a message to Blair. The only thing that kept her from reporting me to HR was my promise to never make a pass at her again, and I still feel like a dick about it.

Nate slides the laptop over to Becker as he announces, "I am *this close* to locking down the Barclays. They said they're ready to review one of our standard contracts."

Beck raises his brows, studying the notes in Nate's spreadsheet.

"No shit." I sit straighter in my seat. "The finance Barclays?"

"The same. Their daughter is Piper Lily Barclay, socialite and bona fide smokeshow. She's twenty years old and the sole heir. She's going to *print* money for us."

Theo says exactly what I'm thinking. "Don't count your chickens. When it comes to matchmaking, I'd bet on a wild-card over an established socialite any day. Not all men want a high-profile match, and this girl has social media darling written all over her."

"We'll just have to see then, won't we?" Nate says, his confidence unshaken. "I see a nasty bidding war in her future, though. The good kind of nasty."

That has us all laughing. All of us except for me. Because now I'm wondering how high Blair's auction will go. Polansky has it bad for her, Sir Alec is still hassling me about rescheduling his introductory meet-up, and Mason Sharp, the pharmaceutical CEO, is convinced he made such a good first impression that he's already checking out wedding venues.

"You know I'm right," Nate goes on. "Who doesn't want to marry into generational wealth? If you've already got your own, it means you get to maintain status quo with someone of your ilk. If you're nouveau-riche, you get to legitimize yourself. Become classy by association. In fact, that's who I'd put my bet on. One of these tech guys or electric vehicle makers who's looking for instant prestige."

Nate's got some good points—and if anyone has a clear grasp on human nature, it's him.

Not only that, but no matter how much the Barclay girl goes for, auctioning matches with prominent surnames is always a win-win for us. Our commissions are substantial, and a successful pairing boosts our clout even more, which sends fresh droves of clients our way.

The downside is that the more famous and high-profile these young women are, the more likely they are to elope with some prince charming before their auction date or turn down a marriage proposal when the time comes. The agency never forces anyone into a match, so at that point, all we can do is return the bachelor's auction bid and commence finding them another bachelorette. It's a rare occurrence, however. In all our years doing this, the agency has only had to deal with one elopement, two refusals, and one broken engagement. Each time, I was able to find an even better match for the rejected party.

My mind wanders back to Blair. She texted me several times today, but I haven't responded. I didn't answer her call, either. Not because I'm a coward, but because I have to cut her off once and for all so she can move on with her match. And her life. But the look on her face when she saw me with Daisy last night won't get out of my head.

Why the hell did I let myself get in so deep?

And why do I feel so damn guilty when I know I did the right thing? The necessary thing. By the time I return to the island, she and her parents will be gone—and her auction will be over, too. There's no chance of either one of us ruining things if we're not within a thousand miles of each other.

Fisting my hands, I slide them off the table and into my lap. I regret nothing. I had to leave. Blair was falling for me hard. I had to put a stop to it. She deserves the kind of man who can take care of her, and I'm not going to be the prince charming she runs off with before her auction date.

Her father confided in me during one of our initial interviews that he won't rest until he knows she's happily settled. Her mother feels the same; she's utterly fixated on ensuring her only daughter is safe, provided for, and comfortable for the rest of her life. Now that I know about the daughter they lost, it makes sense why they feel so strongly about finding a match for Blair.

She needs to follow through with the auction and step into her future with her new husband. At the end of the day, she'll realize it's what's best for her, and everyone will be happy. My business will have earned its hefty fee and an impressive commission, and I'll get on with my life.

Most of the men vetted for our auctions are looking to marry into a good business deal and not necessarily for love. They all have money. They're looking to preserve their fortunes and their legacies, maybe make a new family connection that can leverage their business or open new doors. It's a smart move. Not marrying for love, but for mutual benefit.

"...Sebastian? Sebastian? Hey, Argos."

"What?"

Nate shoots me a look. "I asked how it was going with the Tisdales? The clients you were supposed to be working with this week, until you jetted off the island to come here for no reason?"

Asshole. Of course he'd ask about them. Leaning back, I take another sip of scotch to steady myself. The last thing I want to do right now is talk about the Tisdale match.

"Everything is going as planned. I wouldn't have left the island if there were any issues," I lie.

"Glad to hear it," Nate says. "Having the Tisdale girl happily matched is exactly the leverage I'll need to sway the Barclays if I can't get them to commit soon."

While we never divulge the names of our clients, we do share pertinent information about them with potential new clients to spark interest and establish confidence in our track record. Letting them know that the owners of a major sports team have utilized our services to successfully marry off their daughter will go a long way.

"Understood," I say, my guts churning.

"She'll be one of our top earning auctions this season," Becker says. "You should meet with her matches and start ramping up the competition between them. Nothing like a little good-natured rivalry to get those final bids up."

He's brainstorming out loud and I want to throat-punch him. At the same time, I know what he's saying makes sense. I wish I could move her auction date up sooner so I could put this whole thing behind me. Once she's married, she'll be completely off limits and out of my mind for good.

"Let's see the Barclay girl." Theo grabs Nate's laptop and pulls up a photo of Piper Lily Barclay on the web browser, then turns the screen toward us. She's beautiful, obviously, but in a purposeful, calculated way. Sophistication and wealth radiate from her cool gaze, and there's not a single glossy hair out of place on her head. If you ask me, she looks like an ice queen. She can't hold a candle to Blair.

"We should place a bet," Theo says. "Which one will go for more? Barclay or Tisdale?"

Blair's photo pops up next to Piper's and my chest goes

tight. Her smiling eyes and full lips call out to me. I know exactly how that mouth tastes, how the pulse in her throat beats faster when we fuck.

"Cut it out," I growl, closing the laptop. "We're professionals, Theo, not bookies."

"Leave it to Sebastian to ruin the fun," he grumbles.

My partners discuss a few more clients, I give Becker a quick rundown on the next set of matches flying in next week, and then Theo takes over to discuss the financials in detail. Glancing around the club, I fight the urge to bolt. The impulse is so strong that my legs twitch. I don't want to be here.

Tossing back the last dregs of my drink, I stand and clear my throat.

"I have something to take care of. If you'll excuse me."

No one questions me as I leave. I don't have a destination in mind, I just know that I have to get away from this meeting. Coming back early was a mistake, but I couldn't stay on the island and risk partaking in any further indiscretions with Blair.

As soon as I step inside the elevator, I take out my cell and reread her messages. Then I make myself delete them without sending a reply. Hopefully the radio silence will send a clear message—that our fling was just that and nothing more.

But if that's true, why can't I deny the fact that if I were given the chance, I'd do it all over again?

23

BLAIR

I'm face down on my pillow, trying not to scream. My tears have dried and I've moved aggressively into the anger phase of my feelings.

How fucking dare he.

I can't believe he just up and left the island like that. What a coward. I guess he wasn't man enough to face me after I caught him kissing his employee in the street. Ethics of that aside, I'm at least owed a proper goodbye. Even a text message would have been better than the brush off he gave me.

Rolling onto my back, I stare up at the ceiling, still seething.

Well, fuck him. I'm staying right here on the island. I'm not cutting my vacation short to go home early and lick my wounds. Or making up some excuse to my parents so I can chase after Sebastian in—wherever it is that he went.

I could probably go back downstairs and pressure his concierge-slash-mistress into telling me where he ran off to, but no way am I doing that. And who's to say he didn't tell "Daisy" to lie to anyone who asked about him, specifically any women who asked? I wouldn't put it past him. The scumbag.

What kind of name is Daisy, anyway?

And another thing...he ditched her, too. So maybe he really is just a player who figured out that his whole 'sad, broken man with a tragic past' routine was an easy way to get into women's beds.

But even as I think it, I can't totally convince myself it's true. Am I just that naïve?

Actions speak louder than words, I remind myself harshly. *And he ghosted you.*

Maybe I should just confront Daisy. Find out what was going on between them. Tell her that I've been seeing him as well. Lay it all out on the table. Except what good would that do? She's probably just as innocent in all of this as I am, oblivious to Sebastian's manipulations, and I'd only be hurting myself—and her—further by getting into the details of my affair with him.

That's not who I am, and that's not the kind of person that I want to be.

I need to get my chin up and walk away from all of this. Put it behind me as fast as possible. Forget that I was about to put my heart on the line and try to have a real relationship with the guy.

In fact, the more I think about it, the more I realize that I dodged a fucking bullet by catching him in the act with that other woman. If I hadn't seen it with my own eyes, I might still be getting played. Sebastian would have probably enjoyed stringing me along for as long as he could get away with it. And who knows how many other women he has in his back pocket? I don't need to be one more girl in his harem. No thanks.

Getting off my bed, I go outside on the balcony and take a big breath of cool ocean air. Closing my eyes, I relish the feel of the warm sun on my face and begin to relax. Regardless of what Sebastian did, I really do love it here, and I refuse to let my vacation end on a bad note. Maybe I need to finally take a page out of my best friend's book and find someone else to spend my remaining time with.

And guess what? I'm not exactly hard up for male attention these days.

Back in my room, I text my mom to tell her I have a migraine and won't be able to make it to the beach. After tossing a handful of outfits onto the bed, I pick through them, then make another pile of the clothes I've deemed too sexy for the parentally-advised portion of this vacation. From those options, I choose a body-hugging black dress that laces up the front and dig out my highest heels. Then I spend time curling my hair, contouring and highlighting my face, and applying false lashes and pink lip gloss. Gold hoop earrings are the finishing touch. I'm going all out.

I give myself a once-over in the floor length mirror and nod. Brooke would approve. Although, if my mother sees me, I'm dead. Then again, if she sees me like this on Ted Polansky's arm, she'll probably instantly forgive me...after lecturing me about my outfit.

Too bad, Mom. Like it or not, I'm an adult.

Smiling at myself, I fluff my hair a little more, touch up my lip gloss, and grab my bag.

I hold my head high as I clip down the hallway, brimming with confidence. The heels make my legs look a mile long and the outfit leaves little to the imagination. In the elevator, I suppress a grin as a woman nudges her husband for staring too long. Clearly, I'm doing something right.

The big question is, where would I be hanging out on a weeknight if I were a pro baseball player on vacation? A dance club? One of the local bars in town? Enjoying the beach?

Answer: none of the above. Because the Mets-Phillies game is on, and anyone with even an ounce of interest in Major League Baseball is going to be watching it. And where better to do that than the resort's upscale sports bar?

Unlike the townie bars, it won't be full of tourists and noise, plus the wine list is incredible and the menu is even better. They serve everyone's favorite bar foods, but with an island twist. Chicken wings with guava hot sauce, nachos with conch ceviche, lobster quesadillas. Most importantly, flatscreen TVs line every wall, so no matter where you're sitting, you can watch whatever sport you're in the mood for.

The bar is surprisingly full when I stride in. I forgot how many new guests had checked in for the Junkanoo, and it looks like they're here to stay. All eyes turn to me, some briefly, some lingering, but there's only one pair of eyes I care to have on me right now.

Smiling, I work my way through the space, keeping an eye out for Ted. My plan is to grab a seat at the bar, order a glass of wine, and watch the game until he comes to me. Which is exactly what I do, casually twirling my hair as I subtly glance around in search of that Marlins cap.

And then I spot it.

Across the room, Ted sits at a high-top table by the accordion glass doors that are all pulled open to showcase the beach scene just outside. He's talking to another man, whose back is facing me. They're both watching the Mets game on a TV to their left, Ted gesturing to the screen and shaking his head at the runner who just got tagged out while trying to steal. Ha. I knew Ted would be here.

I take a fortifying gulp of wine and then reposition myself on my stool so I'm at a better angle for him to see me. My heart races, but mostly from nerves rather than excitement. Am I really doing this? Trying to lure Ted Polansky over to me just to build up my self-esteem because I got rejected?

Yes. I am definitely doing this. I take another drink of wine to strengthen my resolve.

Ted hasn't noticed me yet, but the man on the stool next to me sure has. He's been clearing his throat for the last couple of minutes trying to get my attention. I steadfastly ignore him while trying not to gag on his pungent cologne, my attention on the TV. He finally stands up. Hopefully he's leaving now.

But instead, he leans onto the bar on one elbow, so close to me now that I can feel his body heat.

"Hey," he says, nudging me in the arm.

Glancing over my shoulder at him, I realize he looks familiar. Blinding white teeth, piercing blue eyes, a jaw that could cut glass, and a reeking stench of entitlement that almost overpowers his cologne.

Narrowing my eyes, I say, "Oh. Aren't you the..."

"Mason Sharp," he reminds me, and I'm almost impressed when he doesn't actually add the phrase *God's gift to women* at the end. "We met at the Cove restaurant."

"Right," I say disinterestedly. "I forgot about that. Well, have a good night."

I return to the game, but Mason doesn't budge.

"My night will be a lot better if you join me for a stroll on the beach. Unless you'd like me to buy you a drink first?"

Is he fucking serious?

When I look back over at Mason, scathing rebuttal on my tongue, I catch sight of Ted and his companion across the room again. Only this time, I recognize the other man who Ted is with. It's my father. Both of them look my way.

My heart skips a beat, and Dad's brows knit as his gaze meets mine. As far as he knows, I'm supposed to be in bed with a migraine right now. Oops.

"I have plans with someone else, actually," I tell Mason. "So no thanks."

He smirks. "If that someone else left you here at the bar all by yourself, I doubt—"

"Blair!" Ted says, appearing behind Mason like an angel in a baseball cap. "There you are."

Mason turns around, probably to say something jack-assy, but whatever it is seems to get stuck in his throat as he tilts his head back to take in Ted's impressive six-foot-four frame.

I grin with self-satisfaction. "Hi, Ted. Perfect timing, as usual."

Sidling up to me, Ted puts a protective arm around my shoulders and nods at Mason.

"Ted Polansky," he introduces himself, extending a hand. "And you are?"

Mason shakes with Ted, looking irritated. "Mason Sharp."

The two of them stare each other down, and I might be flattered at this little love triangle if I didn't find Mason so utterly unappealing in every way.

"Mason was just leaving," I cut in. "Why don't you take his stool, Ted?"

"Cool," he says, nodding as he slides onto the vacant stool beside me. "Catch you later, Mase."

"Bye," I say sweetly to Mason, then smile at Ted. "Did you see Mauricio try to steal third?"

"He's got the speed, but everybody has eyes on him right now. He shouldn't have risked it."

We dive into a breakdown of the first few innings, and the next time I look over my shoulder, there's no sign of Mason Sharp anywhere in the bar.

"Don't worry. He's long gone," Ted tells me. "Though the smell of his cologne might take longer to disappear."

I laugh. "Thanks for rescuing me again. What were you talking to my dad about? Is he trying to lure you onto the Rockets?"

"Of course not," Ted says earnestly. "I came in to watch the game and he was already here at a table, so I joined him. How about you?"

I bat my lashes and put a hand on his forearm. "I was looking for you."

His face lights up. "Really?"

"Really. I thought we could get dinner. Just you and me."

He's practically drooling. Slipping my arm through his, he looks at me with the first flash of desire I've seen in his eyes since meeting him.

"Anything you want, Blair. You just say it and it's yours."

24

BLAIR

TED GETS STOPPED for an autograph the second we step out of the bar and then again by a woman who asks him to sign her chest.

Instead of grabbing his arm in a jealous fit, I step back to give them room. Ted glances at me first, gauging my reaction, but when I gesture at him to go ahead, he takes the proffered Sharpie and signs away.

Once he's done, the woman takes off, giggling with her friend and showing the signature to the rest of her group.

Looping my arm in his again, I lean into him and remind myself that I should try to enjoy this outing. Ted is hot, very attentive, and a genuinely decent guy, not to mention a great ball player. Any woman would be lucky to go on a date with him. The fact that he's not Sebastian is a good thing. I need to give this a fair shot.

"Does that happen a lot, Mr. Star Pitcher?" I tease.

"Getting asked to sign my name on people's bodies?" He shrugs with a grin that's half embarrassed and half prideful. "Kind of, yeah. Now that you mention it, I'm realizing how weird it is."

"People's bodies or women's bodies?"

"Oh. I guess I never thought about it." He pauses. "Women, definitely. Men usually have T-shirts or tickets to sign. Not that women don't give me those things, too—"

"It's fine," I say, giving him a pass before he starts thinking he needs to apologize for it. "All part of the job, right?"

"Right," he agrees, relaxing.

We leave the resort and head into town. Passing by familiar places, I realize this nighttime stroll through the streets doesn't have the same appeal that it did when Sebastian accompanied me. The magic I saw everywhere on the island is gone now, and I wonder for the millionth time if I made a mistake. Everything reminds me of Sebastian.

But as we go a little farther, weaving our way through the evening foot traffic, I begin to ease into being with Ted. He's the first guy I've ever been on a date with who is just as excited to talk about baseball as I am. He's a perfect gentleman as well, which I appreciate. There's a reasonable distance between our bodies, as if he's afraid of encroaching in my space.

And yet...the times we do brush against each other, there are no sparks. I miss the electric energy that Sebastian and I had between us.

The streets are crowded and so are the bars, conversations and laughter spilling out onto the pavement. The remnants of the Junkanoo are still going, and I can hear live calypso music coming from somewhere close by. The weather is perfect. A lot of shops have lanterns and torches lit outside their doors. I guess the magic is still here, I just need to shrug off my heartbreak and open my eyes.

We pass several cafés and restaurants offering local cuisine, but when I ask Ted where we're going, he says he has a favorite spot he wants to take me to. I wonder if it will be as good as Mo's. And then we turn a corner, and he leads me toward a popular American-style chain restaurant—the only one on the island—and opens the door for me.

I look at him with my brows raised. I'm surprised he'd want to eat here, of all places.

He tosses me a sheepish smile as if he's reading my mind.

"Is this okay? I have a shellfish allergy, so I've had a hard time eating around the island because all the local places serve seafood. Plus, no one offers nutritional information, and I can't plan my meals without it. My trainer has me on a pretty strict diet."

"I totally get it," I tell him. "This is great. No worries."

I'd rather be sitting on the back patio at Mo's eating conch fritters and plantains, but I'm not going to tell him that. Absently twirling my letter bracelet as the hostess seats us in a booth, I smile at Ted and then pick up the menu. It's all the usual suspects—potato skins and mozzarella sticks, salads, flatbread pizzas and chicken and steak. Nothing really sparks my interest except the wine list. Maybe I'll just order one of the flatbreads.

Silence stretches between us while Ted studies the menu like it's his job, so I say something to fill the space. "The shrimp scampi flatbread sounds good."

He lowers his menu and shakes his head. "It would be best if you didn't order that. Sorry, I just don't want to risk cross-contamination. Our plates might touch. Plus the fumes have allergens. I'm actually anxious that there's seafood being prepared in the same kitchen, but I'm usually fine here."

"Right. Your allergy. I didn't realize it was so sensitive."

"It is. But don't worry, there's an EpiPen in my back pocket just in case."

The waitress appears, and Ted orders two baked chicken plates with double steamed broccoli as the side, no rice, no butter, and two glasses of ice water with lemon. Great. He ordered an allergy-safe dinner for me too. Setting down my menu, I hope the disappointment doesn't show on my face. Bland, baked chicken is the last thing I would have chosen and there's no way I'm eating vegetables without butter. She looks at me and I force a smile.

"I'll have a glass of the sauvignon blanc, please."

She walks away and Ted looks at me with concern. "Just wine? You really shouldn't skip meals, Blair. You definitely don't need to lose any weight. You're perfect just the way you are."

Aaand now I'm realizing that he didn't order for both of us just now. He was ordering himself *two* helpings. But I don't want to tell him that I assumed one of the dinners was for me, because he's so freaking nice and it will just make him feel bad—and me look dumb—so I just nod and say, "Yeah. Thanks. You're right. I just wasn't all that hungry, but maybe I'll get something small."

He flags down a waitress that wasn't ours and I order a Caesar salad with grilled chicken. Ted seems pleased with my choice. Then our original waitress arrives with my wine and the waters. Surprisingly, the sauv blanc is pretty good.

"Do you want to try it?" I ask Ted, sliding my glass toward him.

"No, I'm good. I don't drink alcohol."

"Ah. That's...very healthy of you."

"Thanks," he says, holding up his ice water. "Cheers."

"Cheers." I take a healthy swallow of my wine and then settle against the back of the booth. "I'm glad we could spend some time together. We haven't really had a chance to get to know each other."

His face lights up. "No time like the present, right? I want to get to know you, too. What do you do in your downtime?"

"Downtime?" I laugh. "I haven't had much of that over the last four years. Business school is no joke. It's been nothing but studying and homework and keeping on top of the markets."

"You must have hobbies," he says. "What do you like to do with your friends?"

"I think my only hobby is scouting all year long for the draft, which I love to talk about with my best friend, but she can't stand it. The only baseball topic she's interested in is her ranking of which players' asses look the best in their uniform pants. Not to objectify you guys or anything."

He throws back his head and laughs. "Guess we're just pieces of meat to the female fans."

"Not *only* the female fans," I point out.

"You're right." That gets him laughing all over again.

"So...how are you feeling about the MLB season so far? Obviously your team's been faring well, although statistically speaking, last year was better all around. There's still time to improve, though."

He nods. "I'm feeling good, personally. My strikeouts are up this season. As for the team, you're definitely not wrong. But we still have time to make up the gap. A few of our best players have been out with injuries, too, so that's been skewing things a little off kilter."

"For sure," I say, warming to the subject. "If it makes you feel any better, the Rockets are off to a bumpy start, too. That's why I was so excited about the draft."

"Your club picked up some bangers," he says.

"I know!" I say, trying to ignore the pang in my chest over the fact that I didn't get to sit beside my father during the draft in an official capacity. "Two of them were in my top ten. Wyatt Ramirez and Derek Rajan. I was really gunning for Ty Jamieson, too, but so was everybody else."

"The kid's got some serious talent," Ted says. "Great picks, by the way."

"Thanks," I say brightly. "It's easy to keep tabs on the stats when you actually love the game."

"I love it, too. Sometimes I still can't believe I get paid to play baseball. How lucky am I?"

Just then, our meals arrive. Well, his meals and my salad. It's not even full size, more like an appetizer portion. It looks great, though, and I dig right in.

"How about you?" I ask. "What do you enjoy doing in the off-season?"

"Working out, PlayStation. I like to cook. And go running with my dog, Arwen. She's a rescue—a shepherd mix."

"Hold up, hold up...did you name your dog after a Lord of the Rings character?"

He actually blushes. "Not just *any* character. The half-elven daughter of Elrond. She's the Evenstar of her people!"

I can't help laughing at him. "Wow, so you're kind of a nerd, too. I didn't see that coming. That's kind of amazing."

We share a smile, and I realize that Ted and I could totally be BFFs if it weren't for the fact that I already have one. Although, speaking of Brooke...maybe I should introduce them. Because Brooke just so happens to have a very deep, dark, secret love for all things Tolkien.

And as much as I'm honestly enjoying myself with Ted right now, there's something very clearly lacking between us: physical chemistry. I can appreciate that he's a catch—he's hot and nice and funny—but I'm definitely not going back to his room when dinner is over.

Instead, I'm going to go back to my suite, order as much conch as I can off the room service menu, and then pack my bags so I can get the hell off this island. My flight back home is tomorrow, and I'm more than ready to go. My future is waiting.

25

SEBASTIAN

"I FORGOT what a delightful asshole you are when you're drunk, Sebastian."

"And I forgot what a delightful asshole you are all the time," I shoot back at Becker. "Oh, no, wait. I didn't."

He just laughs, never one to be affected by an insult or a disrespectful comment.

The East Village party scene pulses all around us as I drain my second glass of scotch, not nearly buzzed enough to enjoy myself. I'd forgotten how much I've grown to dislike the city's special brand of nightlife thanks to spending so much time immersed in the island's laid-back atmosphere.

The music in here is so loud, I can't hear myself think. Beautiful people dressed to the nines are packed on the dance floor like it's rush hour on the subway, arms up, bodies writhing. It's well after midnight, and a weekday, but nobody cares. They're living their best lives. Must be nice. Meanwhile, I'm sitting at the bar next to Becker with a scowl on my face, questioning my choice to meet up with him.

There used to be a time when I was always down to hit up the hottest clubs with my friends, but now the scene just makes me feel irritable and restless. The only reason I agreed to come out was because I didn't want to spend my first night back in the city drinking alone at home. It seemed too pathetic.

"And I'm not drunk," I add. "But I will have another scotch. Bartender! Barmaid! Hey!"

"Easy there, tiger," Becker says, shaking his head as he pulls my arm back. "Her name is Riley. And trust me, you're not going to get her attention by calling her 'barmaid.'"

He pulls a few bills from his wallet and folds them lengthwise, then tucks them between his fingers and holds them in the air. The redheaded bartender must have a sixth sense for cash, because she materializes just seconds later with fresh drinks for both of us. Becker didn't even have to ask.

"Thanks, Riley," Becker says.

"Anything else I can get you?" she asks, sliding the money out of Beck's hand.

"We're good for now," he says.

She nods and walks off to the other end of the bar, where a bachelorette party—evident by the hot pink 'Bride to Be' sash that the woman in the middle is wearing—is screeching for some rosé. Something in my stomach clenches, and I look away and take a drink of my fresh scotch.

"How'd you know her name? You pulled a Nate there," I ask Becker, glancing over.

"She told us when we sat down. Which you probably would have remembered if you weren't a few sheets to the wind already when you walked in here. So what's the story, man?"

"What are you talking about? A man can't have a few drinks after work?"

His eyes narrow. "Don't bullshit me. I know you better than that. Something's up."

"Nothing is up." I lift my glass and take another drink. A long one.

"Then why did you fly home early? And what got up your ass at the meeting today?"

When I don't respond, Becker shakes his head and has a few sips of his own scotch.

"Out with it," he prods. "You've been intolerable since you got back from the island. Something happened while you were there, so what is it?"

I scoff. "Fuck if I'm going to tell you."

"You *are* going to tell me. I have a vested financial interest in the business that we co-own, and I'm not going to have you running off clients with your bad attitude and letting the resort suffer because you can't do your job right now. Tell me what the hell is going on so we can fix it and get you past this."

Tapping my finger against the side of my drink, I consider not tossing back every last drop in the glass, but who am I to waste perfectly good alcohol? I down it all and set the tumbler down with a thunk. The barmaid I barked at earlier—Kaley? Kylie? I can't remember—promptly appears and sets down another round. Becker grabs mine before I can and holds the drink protectively against his chest.

"Give me. The drink." My voice is a barely contained growl.

"Not happening until you talk," he says. "I'm your friend, Sebastian. You know that, right?"

"Dammit, it's a woman!" I blurt before I can stop myself. "Now give me the fucking drink."

He obliges, and I brood as I sip at it. That's when I realize my vision is going hazy at the edges. Maybe I really am as drunk as Becker says. It would explain my loose lips.

"Okay. So now that we've established the source of your discomposure...what happened?"

I shrug. "I don't know. I guess I...fell for someone I can't have." I don't elaborate. There's no amount of alcohol that could incapacitate me to the point where I'd admit who the woman in question is. Becker might be understanding, but that understanding has its limits. Blair Tisdale is still forbidden.

"It happens." Becker takes a breath, seems to consider, and then adds, "Hell, I did it once."

Drinking steadily for the past few hours has done a number on my brain. There's no way I heard Becker admit what I think he just did. He glances at me quickly and then looks away. Suddenly, I wish I hadn't drank so much. I need to sober up. I don't want to be so inebriated when I pry Becker's story out of him that I can't remember the details later.

I grab the glass of water that I haven't touched since we got here and take a few swallows.

"You're a cipher," I tell him. "I wasn't even sure you knew what love is, and now you're telling me there's one that got away?"

Becker grows quiet as he watches the dancing bodies around us. The gorgeous women in their scanty club outfits and the men reeking of cologne and testosterone. The boisterous bachelorette party. The music seems louder all of a sudden, and I lean closer so I don't miss a word from Becker.

"Here's what I know," he says, tracing the rim of his glass. "Power and money trump love every time. And I never want to be on the wrong side of that equation again."

Flashing a grin with no humor in it, he takes a deep drink and then falls broody and silent again.

His confession is a shock to me. Becker has always struck me as the kind of person who gets what he wants, when he wants it. He's got all the wealth and power a person could ever dream of, and I've seen how easily he moves through the world—because people look at him and they see the ruthlessness. I've seen it firsthand myself in our business dealings, and he's never given me reason to think that merciless attitude doesn't also extend beyond his professional life.

It never occurred to me that the guy wasn't born that ruthless, wasn't destined to become the person he is now. So what happened in his past to change him? And who is this mystery woman? And is it possible that Becker will ever get the hell over it and live his life?

I'm one to talk, aren't I? When exactly did I decide that I was destined to be alone forever, as evidenced by the fact that I've self-sabotaged so spectacularly? I'm just as bad as

Becker, building up walls to keep people out. Maybe worse. Because it sounds to me like he got rejected, but Blair never rejected me. I was the one who fucking walked away from what I wanted.

No. I *ran*. I did this to myself.

Focusing on my grief over Rachel and my fear of being emotionally annihilated again has kept me shut down for years. But when I met Blair on the beach that day, something shifted. The light began to peek through the clouds. And ever since then, a part of me has wondered if she could be the sunshine that might help pull me out of my own darkness. Because when I'm with her, I feel...alive again.

I realize Becker's expression has gone stony, and I bet he's hoping like hell that I don't pry into what he just told me. But I've had way too much scotch to mind my own business.

"Maybe you could still get the girl," I tell him.

"There is zero chance of that."

Immediately, I think of Rachel. "She passed away, then?"

Becker slaps his fist on the bar. "Jesus, Sebastian. Drop it. Look, I'm going to assume the woman who broke your heart is still very much alive and breathing and you're here killing your liver instead of doing something about it. So why don't you remedy that?"

He wouldn't be so encouraging if he knew who I'd been fucking on that island, would he?

Raising my glass, I say, "Killing my liver has less repercussions."

"Sounds like you got yourself into a mess."

If he only knew.

The music gets louder and beats more aggressively in my head. The noise and chaos have me on edge, and when a douche in a shiny silver shirt jostles me from behind, it takes Becker's hand on my shoulder to keep me from blowing up and starting something. Shoving his hand off, I stand up and turn toward the exit.

"Where you going?" he asks.

"I need air."

"Then we'll get some air together. Let me close out the tab."

He waves at the bartender and signals for the check, but I don't wait. Instead, I careen through the crowd, zigzagging my way to the door. The second I get outside, I realize it wasn't just the motion of the bodies around me that had me so unsteady on my feet. The ground is tilting. I can barely stay upright.

Staggering a few paces away, I lean against the wood-paneled exterior of the building, giving the bouncer a nod. Beyond him, a red velvet rope holds back a massive line of people waiting to get inside, all of them talking or smoking or staring at their glowing phone screens. I'm about to turn away when I see her. A woman with long, sunny blond hair falling down her slender back, a red dress practically painted onto her perfect body. She's standing in line with a handsome young guy who's built like a linebacker, her arms looped around his thick neck.

My heart starts to pound, my adrenaline roaring. It's her. It's Blair. And she's with another man.

He leans down to kiss her, his hands reaching down to cup her ass, and as she tilts her head to kiss him back my vision goes dark at the edges.

A roar escapes me, and I think I can hear Becker calling my name behind me, but I'm already racing toward her and this piece of shit. How dare he take what's mine? My rage is an inferno.

Before I know what I'm doing, I'm barreling into the velvet rope to rip her away from him, pushing the guy on the chest and driving him backward against the wall.

"The fuck?" he curses, pushing me back.

My fingers loop around Blair's wrist, and as she looks up at me in surprise, I suddenly realize I've made a huge mistake.

"You're not Blair," I say just as something slams into me and drives me onto the sidewalk.

I'm too drunk to act quickly. My brain knows I screwed up, but my fists are already up, and the linebacker is on me in a blink. Before either of us gets an actual punch in, Becker shoves himself between us, yelling at us to be cool as he pushes us both apart.

The bouncer is involved now, walkie in his hand, asking Becker if he should call the cops.

I don't know exactly what happens next. One minute we're on the street, a crowd of onlookers surrounding the ugly scene I've caused, Becker pulling wads of cash out to bribe the bouncer into letting Linebacker and his girlfriend into the club, their first round of drinks courtesy of Beck as well. The next minute we're in a cab that's pulling to a stop outside my apartment building. Then, Becker's got me by the arm as he half-drags me out of the car. I stumble up the front steps with my arm looped around his neck, and he helps me punch in the security code to get the entry doors open.

I try to apologize but he cuts me off.

"Forget it. Just go to bed and sleep it off," he says. "I don't want to see your face again until you're sober."

"Sure, Beck."

"And I'll have breakfast sent over in the morning to help with the hangover, so answer your goddamn door when the delivery guy arrives, yeah?"

I mumble something in response.

Lying in bed with no real memory of walking through the lobby, riding in the elevator, or even unlocking my front door, I look up at the ceiling in the darkness. I made a mistake tonight. Hell, I've made a lot of mistakes lately. I need to start making better decisions.

Maybe I can't have Blair, but if she'll listen, I can at least explain things to her. Explain why I did the things I did. She should at least understand what her parents are planning for her. She should be able to make her own choices. Live her own life. She deserves that, and so much more.

As soon as I'm sober, I'm going to call her and tell her everything.

26

BLAIR

I'VE BEEN CALLING my dad's cell all morning, but he won't pick up. I tried his office line, too, but his admin told me that he's in meetings all day, which I'm not even sure is true. So now I have no choice but to show up in person and surprise him.

I'm waiting outside the apartment building where I've been living for the last three years—one of my parents' properties, of course, although I'm anxious to find my own place soon and move out—and tapping my foot impatiently on the pavement as I wait for the valet to bring my Mercedes up from the underground garage. I'm so stressed out that my hands are shaking as I text Brooke for moral support. This isn't at all how I wanted my first day at work to go.

My plan was to have a conversation with my dad today and finally talk about all the things he didn't want to discuss while we were on vacation, like my position in the company and my official start date and when to meet up with HR to fill out my paperwork. But we just got back from the island yesterday, and he and my mom went straight home to unwind. I figured I'd be able to reach him at 6:30 this morning, when he's usually drinking his coffee over the *Wall Street Journal*, but my call went straight to voicemail, and I've had no luck since then.

But today is Monday, so as far as I'm concerned, it's my first official day with the Tisdale Corp. Surely he should have expected me to want to hit the ground running. I am his daughter, after all.

Not only that, but diving into work is the best remedy I can think of for the broken heart I've been nursing. It's obvious from the lack of communication that Sebastian has walked out of my life for good. Which hurts like hell, but maybe it's the best thing that ever happened to me. Because now I can fully focus on myself, just like I'd intended.

My career is waiting. My future is waiting. And I can't wait to get started.

Even if my father isn't cooperating.

The valet pulls up to the curb with my car and I get behind the wheel and slot myself into rush hour traffic, praying I can make it to the Tisdale Corp offices quickly. It's a three-mile drive but it can take up to forty minutes, and nothing says unprofessional like showing up late for your first day of work.

As I head south on 9th Ave toward Midtown, my phone rings over the car speakers. Expecting it to be my father calling me back, I almost press the button on my steering wheel to pick up the call. But the name that pops up on the dashboard touchscreen makes my blood run cold.

Sebastian.

The name hits me like a kick in the stomach. Gripping

the wheel tightly with both hands, I listen to the sound of the ring as my blood boils. There was a time when I would have fallen all over myself to pick up a call from Sebastian Argos, but not anymore. Fuck that.

I'm not at his beck and call anymore. He ghosted me, he can suffer the consequences. Punching the decline button, I straighten my spine and give myself a pep talk.

I'm ready to take on this job, ready to prove I'm an asset to the team, and I am not backing down. This is my path. I *will* be taken seriously, and I *will* exceed everyone's expectations.

Fired up now, I hit the mic button and tell the Bluetooth to dial my father's number one more time. It rings once and then goes straight to voicemail. Dammit. I hang up before it connects, clenching my jaw in frustration. Why won't he take my calls?

A place in the family business has been promised to me since I started high school. When my father realized that I was serious about working for the Tisdale Corp, serious about learning the ropes of team ownership, he bent over backwards to teach me everything he could about what he does. I want nothing more than to be a part of the company and work my way up. It's what I've dedicated myself to for years already, tirelessly and unapologetically. So I don't understand why, now that the time has come, I can't even get my dad to discuss what my first job will be.

Is it such a low position that he's avoiding telling me? Is he starting me off in the mailroom, or as a personal assistant? If so, I'll go with it. I'll work my ass off and earn myself a promotion ASAP. I'm willing to do whatever it takes to climb the ladder. I've told him that, time and time again.

Maybe I really do have to be standing right in front of him in his office, pouring out my heart, in order to convince him that I'm serious about this. If that's what it takes, I'm in.

I drive into the parking garage and hand my keys to a valet, hustling for the elevator.

It's a long ride up to the thirty-fifth floor. Looking down at myself, I smooth my hands over my pantsuit and pick a few nonexistent pieces of lint from my blazer. My heart is in my throat when the elevator doors slide open. Lifting my chin, I walk straight past the reception desk, breezily informing the admin sitting there that I'm here to see my father and nodding at the few employees I recognize.

I don't miss the shock on their faces as they take in the sight of me in my professional clothing, carrying a leather portfolio. The curious looks only get worse as I march down the hall and enter my father's executive suites. His administrative assistant, Miriam, sits in the foyer behind her massive desk. She looks genuinely surprised to see me, too.

"Blair, good morning."

"Good morning. I need to speak with my father." I nod my head at his closed office door.

She looks apologetic. "He's in a meeting right now—I told you earlier he was all booked up today. I'm so sorry."

"I'll wait," I say, dropping into one of the chairs.

"Well...that's fine, I suppose. Is he expecting you?"

"He definitely should be."

Miriam blinks, as if she's not sure how to respond.

I smile. "It won't take long. I'll just try to catch him for a few minutes once he's finished."

If I were anyone else, she'd be chasing me out of here. But I'm the owner's daughter, so she just nods and goes back to working on her computer. Settling back in the plush leather chair, I cross my legs, exhale, and wait.

I can barely catch the rise and fall of the voices coming from behind my dad's office door. He's clearly talking to another man, one who sounds younger than him, but that's about all I can figure out. I angle my ear toward the door in a vain attempt to make out what they're saying, but it's futile. And Miriam keeps glancing up at me as if to make sure I'm not going to barge my way in, so all I can do is smile innocently at her and pretend to be absorbed in something on my phone.

I'm surprised she hasn't called Dad to let him know I'm here. But I haven't seen her pick up the phone, so he must have explicitly asked not to be interrupted, which only happens when he's meeting with someone extremely important.

My pulse picks up. Are we signing a new player? Did we trade for someone we had our eyes on for months? Did one of our draft picks decide not to take our deal?

The phone on Miriam's desk rings, and she picks it up. A moment later, she says, "I'll be right down to sign for it."

Giving me one last glance, she gets up from her desk and heads out of the foyer. I don't know how long she'll be gone for, but this is the best chance I'm going to get to eavesdrop. Which is hardly even eavesdropping when we're talking about the team here. Plus, the Tisdale Corporation is a family business, and I'm family. Every decision that my dad makes will affect me, too.

I tiptoe across the room and flatten myself against the wall outside Dad's office door, then hold my breath as I strain to hear what's being said. As the second man starts talking again, I realize that his voice is familiar. Really familiar.

"Come on, Ted," Dad cuts him off, and it all clicks into place. "You want to play the game, you've got to ante up. You knew that going into this."

"It's not about the money. This just isn't the competition I signed up for."

It's Ted in there. Ted Polanksy. Of the Marlins. What the hell? Did Dad negotiate a trade for him while we were on vacation and not even mention it to me? Is that why Ted was always hanging around? Was his interest in me some kind of political maneuver to get my dad to make a better offer?

I haven't spoken to Ted since our platonic dinner date. He walked me back to the hotel but didn't see me to my room before heading back to the bar. I felt like we parted on good, if platonic, terms, but if he was planning to join the Rockets, he could have said something, or at least hinted at it.

"So are you saying you're out?" Dad asks. "You can still walk away."

"I don't want to walk away from her," Ted says.

Her? Who is he talking about? I thought this was about the team.

"Then don't," Dad says.

"But look who I'm up against!" Ted rails. "Mason Sharp? That British lord? Just think how many millions they're going to be bidding for Blair, just so they can flaunt her like a trophy. I *know* I'm the right match for her. Why can't you and I just work something out before the auction? A pre-empt."

Holy. Fucking. Shit.

The floor drops out from under my feet as my mind reels with the words I can't quite process.

Bidding for me? The auction? A pre-empt?

"That's not the way it works, Ted," my dad says, sounding rueful. "But if it makes you feel any better, I'm rooting for you to be the high bidder. I know you'll take good care of her, and she deserves only the best."

My jaw drops, and my body starts to tremble, but I'm frozen in place. Frozen in horror, in disbelief.

"Those other guys are on the Forbes list," Ted says. "I can't compete with that."

"Nobody is saying they'll bid their entire fortunes on this auction," Dad says. "They've got their spending limits, too. Look, you need to think of this as more of an investment in your future."

"I do, but—"

"How many good seasons do you have left in you? How long until your stats start to drop? And then what? You retire? Listen. Once you two are married and settled, I'll step down and you can take over. You won't just be bidding for my daughter's hand, Ted, you'll be bidding on ownership of an MLB team. So don't make any choices you'll regret."

A sob sticks in my throat and threatens to spill out, but all I can do is gasp for air. My chest is constricting. I can't breathe. But one thing is certain—someone is going to catch me eavesdropping if I don't get the hell out of here.

27

BLAIR

I HURRY TO THE LOBBY, unsteady on my feet, ignoring Miriam as she passes me with a concerned look on her face. I don't give her a second glance as I bolt for the women's restroom. Once I'm inside, I lock the door and sink onto the padded bench to bury my head in my hands.

This is a nightmare. My entire future is crumbling. My body feels ice cold, my heart still pounding as the ugliest pieces of the conversation I just heard echo in my mind.

Think how many millions they're going to be bidding for Blair...so they can flaunt her like a trophy... You won't just be bidding for her hand...you'll be bidding on ownership of an MLB team.

That island vacation wasn't my graduation gift, after all. The "gift," apparently, was being sold off to the highest bidder in some kind of sick marriage auction. No wonder my dad hasn't wanted to discuss my job at the company. I don't have one. I probably never did if the plan was to marry me off all along.

And there's no way my father acted alone. Mom has a hand in this, too. I'd bet my life on it.

Why would my parents do this to me? How could they possibly think this is ethical? And why the hell would they think that auctioning me off like a piece of antique furniture would even be successful in the end? I'm a living, thinking, independent human being and I did *not* agree to this. I'm not marrying some rich, entitled asshole just because he paid for me.

Maybe the worst part of all is that my parents never saw me as a real person with my own hopes and dreams, nor as a businesswoman with the brains, ambition, and potential to take my place working for the Tisdale Corporation. As far as they're concerned, I'm not worthy of making choices about my own life. I'm nothing more than a commodity to them. A product to be bought and sold. It brings a horrible new meaning to the cliché about "being a team player."

Except that the players on the Rockets who get traded to other teams are afforded a lot more respect than I've been granted. In fact, MLB rules say a player can refuse a trade if they've been playing for the same team for five consecutive years. I've been my parents' daughter for twenty-two, and they didn't even tell me what they were planning. I had no say in this, no right to refuse. If I had, I sure as hell wouldn't have agreed to this auction.

Is this my punishment for being the daughter who lived? Is this their deranged way of protecting me? By selling me to someone who will keep me locked away in a tower?

I think I'm going to be sick.

Forcing myself to take slow, calming breaths, I go to the sink and use wet paper towels to cool the back of my neck. Once the nausea passes, I grab a handful of tissues to dry my tears and go back to the bench, still trying to make sense of it all.

How did I not figure this out sooner?

My mind begins to race with all the minutiae that I thought meant nothing, all the red flags I ignored. The uber exclusive, members-only resort, for one thing—my parents were *so* intent on staying there, even though there were plenty of other options and I had tried to convince them to pick a hotel with more activities and more TripAdvisor reviews. But it makes sense if they had already arranged for these millionaire bachelors to be staying there in order to meet me. And then Mom's obsessive interest in every guy that spoke to me, the way she kept trying to force me to see Ted. Plus, Dad avoiding all my questions about starting my new job.

Meeting the bidders was clearly pre-arranged as well. Ted "found" me at the beach bar, Mason "found" me at the restaurant, and the British guy "found" me on the beach. In hindsight, there's no way any of those meetings were coincidences. Were my parents hoping I would hit it off with one of the bachelors right from the beginning and form a relationship organically, so I'd never find out that they'd orchestrated the whole thing? Well, joke's on them. The only guy I fell for was the resort owner.

Anger rises up in me anew, my fists clenching at my sides. How dare they. And to throw in the baseball team as my dowry, while completely shutting me out of the family business at the same time...I'll never forgive them for this.

I don't know what to do next. Do I confront my parents? Or do I cut them off right here and now, run away from all of this, and start over somewhere else like Sophie did? My older sister had the right idea when she ran away. She just wanted to live her life on her own terms. Now I get it. Now it's my turn.

Luckily, I have a place to go. I'm sure Brooke would let me move in with her until I can find an apartment, and I can hire movers to help me pack up my things as soon as I get home. I won't even tell my parents goodbye. I'll just disappear. That'll throw a nice little wrench in their evil auction plan.

Steeling myself for the looks that I'll probably get when I walk out of here, I blot my wet eyes one last time and then march out of the bathroom. I'm so gutted by the betrayal that I barely make it to the elevators without breaking down again, but I'm going to make it out of this office with my dignity intact if it's the last thing I do. And then I hear rapid footsteps echoing on the tile floor.

I turn around and see Miriam hustling in my direction. *Shit*. I need to come up with an excuse for running out without seeing my father. I don't want to get dragged back into his office when I no longer have anything to say to him.

But before I can tell her I've got a migraine, the elevator doors open behind me.

I have every intention of dashing into the elevator and hitting the Close Doors button, but when I look back, I see

Sebastian Argos stepping out of the car. My jaw falls open. He's in a suit and tie, looking better than any man has a right to, and he's the last person I expected to show up here.

"Sorry I'm late—" he starts to say.

He freezes in place, eyes shifting back and forth between me and Miriam, but it's too late. Because I've already realized that he wasn't talking to me. He was talking to her. My dad's admin.

"The other two are already waiting inside for you, sir," Miriam says, smiling at Sebastian.

They're *waiting* for him?

"What are you doing here?" I seethe, even though my intuition already knows.

Sebastian just stands there looking at me.

"Here to put in an offer, too?" I jeer, my voice cracking.

His composure breaks. "Blair. I don't...I can't..."

He can barely look me in the eye.

"What? Spit it out."

"My job is to accept them," he says.

I thought I couldn't feel more hurt, more betrayed, more furious.

I was wrong.

Sebastian wasn't just working at the resort during the course of my fucked-up courtships. He was *in charge* of the whole thing. He did this to me. Every single thing about the magical week we spent together was a lie. He was playing with me all along.

"You arranged the auction," I say, shock making my voice sound dead and flat.

The guilt in his green eyes tells me everything I need to know, even before he answers, "I...yes."

287

All I can do is shake my head. I have no words.

"Mr. Argos?" Miriam says hesitantly.

The elevator doors open with a chime, and I take one last look at the man who has utterly destroyed me.

"Go," I tell him coldly. "Don't be late for your meeting."

With that, I stalk into the elevator just before the doors glide shut.

As soon as I get back to my car, I break into a million pieces.

28

BLAIR

Once I blot the tears off my face and swipe at my ruined eye makeup, I take a deep breath and put my car in reverse. I just need to get the fuck out of here. Put as much distance as possible between myself and those evil men, as fast as I can. But then I realize I can't even back out of the parking space. Because Sebastian is standing directly behind my car.

I almost laugh at his misplaced confidence that I'm not going to run him over. Considering my state of mind right now, I'm tempted. The laugh dies in my throat as a fresh wave of fury washes over me.

Who the hell does he think he is to block my exit like this? To control my movements, to manipulate me? Oh, but I forgot. That's exactly what he does. It's his fucking job, apparently. To make puppets out of women, to laugh as he pulls their strings.

Unbuckling my seatbelt and pushing my car door open, I leave the engine running as I climb out of the car to seethe at him. "Get the fuck out of the way, Sebastian!"

Instead of doing as I ask, he takes a few steps closer. "Blair—"

"*No.* I'm not talking to you," I cut him off, my voice cold.

He raises his hands in surrender, palms up to face me. "Then let me talk. Please."

It's not that I don't see the anguish on his face. It's that I don't care. Not that his emotions are even real, are they? He's obviously an excellent actor, as evidenced by his past actions, by the way he strung me along even as he plotted behind my back to orchestrate the sale of my body, my life, my free will. I'm done falling for his shit.

"Why should I believe anything you have to say?" I yell, stalking toward him. "You're *selling me.* Get away from me!"

Tears are gathering in my eyes again, the rage a ball of fire in my belly, and I push against his chest as hard as I can, but he doesn't even move. He's as immovable as a marble statue.

"What happened back there?" he asks. "What did your dad tell you?"

"Nobody told me shit. I overheard him talking to Ted fucking Polansky about the auction. The secret's out. So please, if this whole thing is just a big misunderstanding, now's the time to fill me in."

I gaze up at him, silently pleading for him to fix all of this with some kind of explanation, even though I know that's impossible. There's nothing he can say that will make the ugly reality of this situation any different. He opens his mouth and then closes it, shaking his head.

"Leave, then!" I yell, slamming my fist into his pec. "Just fucking leave!"

My temples are throbbing and it hurts like hell, but not nearly as much as the pain in the center of my chest where all the love I felt for him has shattered into a constellation of sharp edges.

"I was trying to tell you—" he starts.

That gets a harsh laugh out of me. "Really? When? When did you try to tell me? Was it when you were fucking me in my hotel room? Or maybe once my parents arrived and you fucked me in your sex slave hotel?"

"Jesus, Blair, it's not—look, this isn't a fast conversation, but it's really not like that. You have it all wrong."

"Do I? Well, maybe I do. I mean, it's not like you made me think there was something real between us, when all along you and my father were planning to literally sell me off to the highest bidder out of a pool of asshole millionaires. Birds of a feather, right?"

He drops his gaze, and I know that everything I've accused him of is true. He's a liar, a trickster, a monster. How did I never see this side of him before? He was so good at letting me see the sides of him he wanted me to that I never even thought to look deeper.

I take a step back toward my car. "Fuck. You. Just tell me one thing."

Vaguely aware that someone is walking across the parking lot, I lower my voice but it's difficult. I don't care if someone overhears and I'm too angry to get a grip on my behavior.

"Were you planning to help my father sell me the

293

entire time we were sleeping together?" I go on. "Yes, or no?"

Sebastian's face is made of stone. He doesn't give away a single thing, including the reassurance I was stupidly hopeful for. Nothing we had was real.

My heart somehow breaks even more.

"So you were. Of course you were," I choke out. "I can't believe I thought we were building something between us. But it was just a game for you! You and my father were planning to sell me off the entire time you and I were sleeping together. Do you fuck all the girls you sell? What is it, a trial run? Were you taking me for a test drive, so you could report back to your buyers? God, you're disgusting."

"That's not how it works, Blair. I've never—can we just go somewhere and talk about this?" His voice is pleading. "There's a reason I wasn't upfront when I realized that I was falling for you."

Falling for me? The words hit me hard, and I hesitate.

Some of the fight goes out of me as all the furious, hot energy that had been driving me these past few minutes dissipates. I want nothing more than to go somewhere with Sebastian, anywhere but here, and let him hold me. Let him explain everything. Let him make it better. But it would just be more lies.

Nausea burns in the pit of my stomach. The flight impulse accelerates through me. I have to get away from him as fast as I can. Before I make more bad decisions.

"No," I say. "We're done."

I know that ending this now is the right thing to do, but

it takes all my strength not to crumple to the ground. I grab the door handle on my car and fling the door open, turning to him one last time.

"I can't believe you did this to me," I whisper. I blink hard, trying to hold back more tears so I can look him in the eye as I tell him, "I never want to see you again. Do you understand? *Never.*"

He jerks back, as if I've hit him. Finally, some indication of real emotion—but all it does is make me hate him more. He doesn't care about me. He's just upset because he's losing his toy.

"Blair. Wait. I—"

Then his phone rings. The sound snaps him to attention, and he fumbles to dig the phone out of his pocket. A flicker of apprehension dances across his face and I know immediately who is calling. It has to be my father. My heart lurches. Does he know that I'm out here having a face-off with Sebastian?

"If you care about me, you won't pick up that call," I say, eyes locked on his.

But it's already too late. Sebastian has already accepted the call. He raises a finger to his lips, giving me the quiet signal.

"Mr. Tisdale, I apologize for my tardiness. I'm still in the building, I just—"

Oh, fuck this.

Enough. Ripping the phone from Sebastian's hand, I lift it against my ear.

"Don't bother with the meeting, Dad. Your secret's out. I know exactly what you're doing. In fact, don't bother trying to speak to me again, either. As far as I'm concerned, you no longer have *any* daughters."

With that, I slam the phone to the concrete, vaguely aware of the sound of shattering glass as I get into my car and peel out. I don't look back to see Sebastian's face one last time.

I don't look back at all.

29

SEBASTIAN

Rachel Renae Allen.

It's been a while since I've knelt before her grave like this, with a bouquet of roses in my hand. Red roses, pink roses, in every shade. Orange blooms like the sunset, some the soft yellow of sunlight, pale purple and peach and bright coral. It wasn't the look of them that made roses her favorite. It was the scent. My eyes sting as I'm enveloped by their familiar smell, the smell that only ever reminds me of her. Earthy, sweet, like ripe fruit or raw honey spooned into green tea. Rachel, Rachel, Rachel. My rose.

I whisper her name as I set the flowers down, gathering a handful of petals to scatter all around. This is my ritual. The most connected I can get. And fuck, does it hurt. The pain is overwhelming every single time. I guess that's why I've been away for so long. God, what a coward I am.

The cemetery is mostly deserted, which is typical for the middle of a workday. It's why I normally come at this time, so I can be alone with her. At first, I would get self-conscious talking to her headstone, figuring anyone who heard me would worry about my state of mind. But then I realized that plenty of people have one-sided conversations out here, and after a few visits, I stopped looking over my shoulder. Talking to her was the only thing that kept me somewhat sane after her death.

Not that I enjoy talking to myself while staring at her name etched into flat, cold marble. I don't like the sound of my own voice echoing in my ears as I pour my heart out to her. The introspection can be overwhelming.

Sometimes I visit without saying much at all, and just sit here in silence, remembering her laugh, replaying the times we were the happiest, the times we fought, the times we held each other on the street, in the middle of a packed bar, at home in bed. But as the years have passed, it has become harder and harder to come out here. Not because I'm finally moving on, but because I'm not.

Or at least I wasn't until I met Blair. With her, I found myself laughing again—really laughing—without even thinking about it. There were moments I saw the world through her eyes, experienced things from her perspective. There were so many tastes, sights, and sounds that Blair perceived as beautiful and exciting and new, and she made me see them that way, too.

The last few weeks, I even started to feel like living my life was possible again. Not sleepwalking through it or forcing myself to power through the days and nights as I have been, but simply...living a good life, a decent life. Existing in the real world. Breathing without lead weights on my chest.

But I don't believe that anymore. The darkness is back. Maybe it never left.

I look down at the bouquet of wilting stargazer lilies that lay at the seam where Rachel's stone meets earth. A pang of guilt goes through me. Her sister must have come by recently to tend the grave while I was out of state. She always brings lilies. I should call and thank her, see how she's doing, but we haven't spoken in the last year or so. Some almost-brother-in-law I turned out to be.

The petals in my hand suddenly flutter, and a few swirl around me. I jerk back, stunned, but quickly feel foolish. There wasn't a breeze when I got here, but now there is. Of course it was just the wind. What else would it be?

I settle on the grass and shake my head, smiling at the headstone. "For a second, I thought you were trying to get my attention."

In my mind's eye, I see her tilting her head as if studying me, knowing there's something on my mind that I'm not being forthcoming about. She never pushed me when I got in a mood. She never had to. The patience in her gaze, the love, the lack of judgment, that's what always dragged it out of me.

"It's been a while since I've visited. Too long. I guess I've had a lot going on," I say quietly. "I don't even know where to start. All I know is that I've made a total fucking mess of things."

The grass is sun-warmed beneath me, and I can hear birds chirping in the trees close by. It's comfortable here, and I start to relax. I hadn't planned on staying. I only meant to stop by for a quick hello to ease my guilt over not having been here in so long, arrange the flowers, and then go back to my apartment. But now that I'm here, it's a relief to be able to talk to Rachel. Although part of me is still apprehensive. I've never talked to her about another woman.

"I know you'd say that everything's going to be okay, but my partners are going to fire me the minute I get back to the office. Or maybe just kill me, since I'm sure the Tisdales have called them by now to ask why I spoke to their daughter about the auction.

"I guess I could say I was trying to smooth things over after Blair overheard her dad discussing her arrangement with one of the matches, but Becker would see right through me. And I don't want to lie. I'm actually shocked nobody's tracked me down yet, given how bad things went down with Blair earlier. Maybe I should just start by telling you about her."

My shoulders drop, and I take a breath. "So. Her name is Blair Tisdale. The day I met her, I was sitting on the beach, on the island. I was thinking about you. I was...lost. And then she was there with me, and she made me laugh, and it was like a ray of sunshine broke through all the dark clouds. Her laugh is a lot like yours, Ray. That's what really made me notice her."

Haltingly, I go over the events of the last few weeks, talking through the details, trying to figure out how it came to this and where it all went wrong. But there was no single, defining moment when I crossed a line. I fell for Blair in the little moments, letting her in almost without realizing it, until the way I felt about her suddenly hit me all at once. And by then, it was too late to stop it from happening.

"I know what you'd say, and yeah, I am an idiot," I muse. "I never should have gotten involved with anyone. I just miss you so much. And something about her, about being with her, made me feel...just...alive again, for the first time in years. I couldn't get enough of it. Of her.

"Now I have to face the consequences. I'm going to lose everything. I guess it's what I deserve."

A pair of hushed voices grow audible behind me. I look over my shoulder. An elderly woman and a little girl approach on the footpath, probably a grandmother with her granddaughter. The girl has a bouquet of bright yellow daffodils clenched tightly in one hand. They step off the path and make their way down a row of stones off to my left.

Turning back to Rachel, I keep my voice low. "I'm sorry. I'm sure you don't want to hear any of this. I just...I don't know what to do."

The wind settles, and I catch the sound of the little girl singing as she and her grandmother stand over a grave, the girl gently placing daffodils along the top edge of the headstone.

"You are my sunshine, my only sunshine..." the girl sings, her voice sweet and clear.

"You make me happy, when skies are gray..." the grandmother joins in.

The back of my neck prickles at the words.

Oh. Fuck.

A lump wells in my throat.

Looking at the headstone, I take another long, deep breath. "I can't let her go," I say, shaking my head. "I can't lose her."

And that's when I realize...it wasn't the business stuff holding me back. Because fuck the business. I can find another job. The Quattuor Group isn't the most important thing in my life.

But I convinced myself that it was. And instead of pursuing a relationship with Blair, I let myself hide behind the fact that I had a conflict of interest, made it my excuse to push her away and break her heart. When the real reason I couldn't give myself to her was because I was afraid of getting hurt again.

Sitting back on my heels, I hang my head and allow the grief to wash over me. Just then, the breeze picks up. A small whirlwind of leaves and detritus spirals beside me and the petals of Rachel's roses fly everywhere. I close my eyes against the gust until it's over. When I look down again, I see a yellow daffodil on the ground beside me. As bright and golden as sunshine.

Picking it up, I look over my shoulder for the grandmother and the little girl, but they're gone.

Hitching a brow, I look at Rachel's headstone again.

"Nice," I say with a smile. "Is this your way of telling me to get her back?"

Silence is my answer, but I already know the truth in my heart. I stand up, leaving the daffodil on top of the headstone.

"Okay, okay. I'll do it. I'll find a way to fix this. Your record of always being right still stands."

30

BLAIR

"Dental clinic manager. That sounds like a respectable job, right?"

"That's one word for it," Brooke says dryly.

Lying on the couch—aka my bed while I'm staying at her place—I hold my phone above my face and scroll through the job listings I've Googled. It's a new phone, a burner, because I turned off my old phone and refuse to power it back on. I have no interest in being contacted by my parents ever again.

"It says you need an associate degree in office management, but I'm sure my BS fulfills that requirement, don't you think?"

Brooke scoffs from her spot at the end of the couch. My feet are propped in her lap while she paints my toenails a deep, broody burgundy.

"You're way overqualified and you don't know anything about teeth. Next?"

"Restaurant manager. Must speak Urdu. How hard is it to learn Urdu? Maybe I can take a class."

"I don't know that the restaurant business is going to be your forte, Blair. You don't know the difference between chapati and focaccia. What else?"

"Oh, here's a good one. Personal trainer for an exclusive men's fitness club. No experience necessary. Willing to prep and instruct the right candidate."

My best friend sighs in disgust. "That sounds like a soft ad for porn. Plus, you barely work out. What are you going to train them in? Excel spreadsheets?"

I suddenly remember the bartender I met at Sebastian's resort, who also went to NYU.

"Maybe I can go to bartending school. Nobody will care who my dad is if I'm just pouring whiskey and beers."

"The money might be good," Brooke says, and I can tell she's trying her best to be supportive even though she sounds doubtful.

Covering my eyes with one hand, I drop the phone and blink back tears. This is hopeless.

It's been almost a week since I found out about my parents' plan to auction me off. In that time, I've basically done nothing but cry, drink way too much wine on Brooke's couch, and send out resumes for positions that align perfectly with my business degree...only to receive nothing but rejections. I can easily imagine what these HR departments are thinking—that this nepo baby isn't a serious candidate.

The few calls I did get were from people who were clearly more interested in getting to my father than in what I could bring to the table as an employee.

"It'll be okay," Brooke says, attempting for the millionth time to console me about my future. "You'll find something.

It's just going to take time. You can stay with me as long as you need to."

"I know, it's just...I'll never be the owner of the Rockets," I say, my voice wobbling. "It was my dream for so long. I always thought after graduation I'd spend the next ten or twenty years learning the ropes so I could take over for my dad. And now...I have no idea what to do."

"Blair, listen to me. You are smart, and strong, and so, so driven. You're going to come out on top of this, trust me."

She pats my leg and I nod, my eyes still squinched shut. I've felt so lost these last few days. My heart hurts and I can't eat or sleep. I'm a mess. Brooke has the patience of a saint, but I'm sure at some point she's going to get tired of me loafing on her couch and watching rom-coms at all hours of the night.

"Are you ready to tell me what really happened on the island?" She moves my right foot out of the way and starts painting the left.

I refill my wine glass while I think of how to respond. I don't want to tell her the full story because it's too humiliating. Who wants to admit that their parents planned to sell them off like a prize horse? Or that the guy they were falling for was part of the whole thing? I can't believe how naïve I was.

"You know the story. The fling with Sebastian ended horribly. Then I came back home and my dad decided not to give me a job, and now I have no plan and no future."

"I still don't get the Sebastian thing. It sounded like it was going so well. Did he just...break things off when you said you wanted to keep seeing him? Because honestly, if that's the case, it's his loss. I know it sucks, but you're better off. You don't want to spend the best years of your life chasing after some player who can never give you what you need. Or at least, what you need besides dick."

I groan. "Really, Brooke?"

We look at each other and laugh. It's the first time I've laughed in days, but it quickly melts into a sob that I manage to keep to myself. At least my willpower is getting better. I hold back tears. I don't overindulge in ice cream... anymore. And I sure as hell don't check my old phone to see if Sebastian has called or texted. My parents are probably going crazy because they can't get a hold of me, but too bad.

Brooke pushes off my other foot and screws the top back onto the polish bottle. Then she fills her own glass and takes a long drink, tilting her head to the side as she stares off into space.

"I still don't understand why your dad had such a huge change of heart. You planned your entire life around that job. He knows that. He encouraged it."

"Yeah. Well. I guess he decided a man was better suited for the position."

It's the closest to the truth that I'm willing to share. I pick up my phone and start job-scrolling again. Brooke leans over to see what I'm looking at and points at the screen.

"There. You can be a preschool teacher in the one-year-old room. Whatever that means. But you love kids. It could be okay temporarily."

"I don't want something temporary. I want something I can put my heart into long-term."

"Sounds like you're talking about a relationship."

"Yeah, except I don't want one of those ever again."

She snorts. "Never say never. Maybe you should just find yourself a sugar daddy and live the sweet life."

"Ha. Right."

I take another sip of wine and lean back against the cushions, but I'm still stuck on what Brooke just suggested. Because she might be on to something. Yes, it *is* a possibility. But I honestly can't imagine I'd be happy sitting around at home all day, living off of someone else's money, with no path of my own. Unless...unless I *don't* just sit around at home all day.

What if I can do what my mom did? Basically wrapping her spouse around her finger to get whatever she wanted. Which, in her case, was never an important role in the family business. But in my case...it's all I've ever wanted.

The fact is, whichever man wins the auction gets me, but they also get the Rockets. Which means that the closest I'd ever get to owning the team would be through this sham of a marriage. But if I could get my husband to give me an active role in the business, I could prove my value and eventually take on more and more responsibilities.

It's a devil's bargain. But maybe it's a bargain I'm willing to make. I wouldn't be the first woman in history to work my charms to get what I want, and what I want is my damn baseball team.

Sitting up straighter, I grab the wine bottle off the table, bring it to my lips, and tip it back. I drink the wine until my throat can't hold anymore and I nearly choke.

"Jesus, Blair. Would you like a little oxygen with your alcohol?"

If only she knew how hard it's been to breathe since Sebastian pulled the rug out from under me.

I hand over the bottle and wipe my mouth with the back of my hand. "I need to go make a call."

I go into the kitchen and grab my old phone off the top of the refrigerator. When I power it on, it buzzes for ten seconds straight with alerts for unread text messages and voicemails. I ignore all of them. Dialing my father's number, I dart down the hallway for some privacy as Brooke stares at me with a 'what the hell is going on?' expression.

My father answers on the second ring, but the voice that comes out of the phone is my mother's. "Blair! Where have you been?"

"We've been worried sick!" my dad chimes in, and I realize they've put me on speakerphone. "Just tell us—"

"I'll do it," I blurt, cutting them off. My pulse races as I lean against the wall and crush the phone against my ear. "I'll do the auction."

SEBASTIAN

THE SHOCK of finding out that Blair agreed to participate in the auction still hasn't worn off.

Mr. Tisdale called me a few days ago to let me know she was in, and then the two of us had a long talk. To say he was unhappy would be a gross understatement. If he'd been able to strangle me through the phone, I'd be dead right now. But in the end, we came to an agreement.

Because the Tisdales signed an NDA, and breaking the terms of nondisclosure would hurt them just as much as it would hurt the Quattuor Group. Nobody wants to get a reputation for plotting to auction off their daughter without her consent, and our business would be irreparably damaged if clients found out that one of the owners slept with a bachelorette. Not to mention the toll that a protracted, costly lawsuit would take on both sides. So Mr. Tisdale and I settled on a truce to avoid mutually assured destruction, and I worked out a deal that even Nate would be proud of.

Though I'm honestly not sure how proud he'll actually

be when I do come clean to my partners and tell them I'm going to be joining the Tisdale auction as a fourth bidder.

The event begins like any other. Adjusting my laptop on the conference table, I pull up the private server that hosts the secure auction site where the bids will soon begin rolling in. Each of my partners have their own laptops lined up as well, so they can watch the bidding on their own screens. The air is thick with anticipation and nervous energy, but today, the majority of the nerves are mine.

Behind us, champagne chills on ice alongside some of the city's very best sushi, express delivered from Kuru-mazushi, and complementary truffles from Kee's. Auction day is normally cause for celebration, but I'm not so sure if anyone else will be celebrating this outcome besides me. The time hasn't been right to tell the others what I plan to do, and I have no idea how they'll react. At this point, however, I'm out of excuses to delay the conversation. It's imminent.

Because once they log on to the auction site, the first thing they'll notice is that there are four bidders today instead of three.

Theo comes to stand next to me and looks half-assed at his laptop, then sips his drink and makes a satisfied sound.

"I can already smell the money with this one."

If this goes my way, it'll be my money scenting his world.

"Didn't we talk about not counting your chickens?" I say.

He scoffs. "Blair Tisdale is hot, loaded, and she comes with a professional baseball team. There will be so many chickens, Sebastian. So. Many. Chickens."

He glances at his laptop again and I steel myself as I wait for him to notice the bidder lineup. But all he does is wink at me and stride away. Taking a deep breath, I clear my throat and call him back.

"Theo, wait." It's now or never. "Nate, Becker, I need a word before this gets started."

My other partners turn away from what they're doing and look at me.

"What's up? Something wrong with the auction?" Theo sets his glass down.

"Not wrong..." I start.

I've struggled with how to deliver the news, but there's simply no good way to drop a bomb like this, so I decided I'd go with my gut and just speak the truth when the time came. Now I wish I'd rehearsed something in advance. I don't even know where to start. The gravity of what I've done has never felt so weighty as it does in this moment.

"So what then?" Nate prods.

I look each of them in the eye and then say, "There's going to be a fourth bidder today."

Becker's gaze snaps to mine. "I didn't authorize a fourth bidder."

"What the fuck? This wasn't in today's meeting notes. How did I miss this?" Theo's flustered as he clicks around on his laptop, Nate leaning over his shoulder to look at the screen.

"Because I just added him," I say.

Becker gives me a cool, knowing stare. "It's a risk. I hope you know what you're doing."

I nod. "I do. And I'm going to cash out my partnership stake. By the end of this evening, I'll no longer have a vested interest in the Quattuor Group. This situation was a violation of our rules, and of the clients' trust."

"And ours," Becker adds.

"Which I apologize for," I tell him sincerely. "I've compromised the business and our reputation. That's why I'm resigning, pending the results of the auction."

Pending, because that's the risk I'm taking—the risk that I might not end up the highest bidder. Someone else could outbid me and take Blair away forever. I wouldn't necessarily have to resign in that case, but only if my partners don't unanimously vote to fire me for this conflict of interest.

And if I do win Blair, it will only be on a technicality. I won't force her to marry me. She can walk away a free woman if she chooses.

"Regardless of how the auction shakes out, I'll do whatever it takes to make this right with all of you," I add. "Professionally and personally."

"Wait." Theo looks back and forth at us like he's watching a tennis match. "The hell is going on? Am I missing something?"

Nate crosses his arms. "I think Sebastian's trying to tell us that he fell for the match."

I shoot Nate a grateful look and nod. "I informed the client that I plan to make the final bid. He was...surprised. But he came around."

What struck me most during that phone call was how Mr. Tisdale didn't seem to care about how Blair would feel. After I told him in no uncertain terms that I loved his daughter, he asked if I'd take care of her, said he had to know for sure that she'd be safe with me. But he said nothing about her happiness. Only her security. As if his own daughter doesn't deserve so much more.

"But you can't—can he even do this?" Theo asks, turning to Becker.

"Doubt I could stop him if I tried," Beck says.

"I mean, can he quit, though?" Theo looks back at me. "I don't want you to quit, man. Nate, do you want him to quit?"

"How—when did this even happen?" Nate says, ignoring the question, but before I can explain, my laptop chimes, signaling that the bidding is about to begin.

I lean forward on the table, adrenaline racing, eyes glued to my screen. My three competitors—Polansky, Bingham-Cavendish, and Sharp—have all logged in and verified their information. I do the same, and my generic gray and white avatar pops up, showing me as a contender.

"What's your plan of attack?" Theo asks.

Unclenching my jaw, I say, "I'm going to bid high and keep on bidding until the clock runs out. And pray no one will try to top my max."

"What about the pitcher?" Nate says "He's not the richest of the three, but you said he was in it to win it. He could snipe you at the last second."

It's true. Polansky's a professional competitor. And I have no idea what he's been up to behind the scenes since he met Blair. What if he signed on for a new sponsorship or accepted a licensing deal for merchandise? If Polansky wanted Blair badly enough, there's no telling how far he'd go to fatten up his bank account in order to clinch the auction win. I've never hated a match before, but I do right now.

"Then I'll just have to bid everything I've got. That's the way these auctions work." I put my fingers over the keyboard, my shoulders tensing. "Blair is mine. I'll do what I need to do."

He nods. "Good luck."

"Here we go," Theo says. "Thirty minutes and counting."

My stomach twists.

"The first bid is up," Nate says.

It's the entitled Brit, of course. He's offered one million even. Not unheard-of for an opening bid, but I didn't think we'd hit the seven-figure mark for another few minutes at least.

The next bid comes in right behind it. Then another, and another. Two million. Three. The minutes tick by, and the money keeps rolling in so fast that I don't have time to think or feel. I can only watch the numbers climb higher and jump in with my own bids whenever the action starts to slow down. There's another extended pause in the bidding when it reaches four and a half million. I enter five.

Blair's life, her future, her happiness, all on the line for five million dollars. Clenching my fists, I sit in front of the computer and watch the timer tick under twenty minutes, my heart thumping as I wait for the other bidders to stand down and leave me the winner.

But then the bids start climbing again. Five and a quarter. Five and a half.

"Fuck."

The countdown on the timer is steadily winding down, but it feels like an eternity until the bidding stops again.

We're at $7,777,777. Someone's hoping they'll get lucky with that bid.

I enter eight.

Becker moves to my side and watches, arms crossed, as we reach the ten-minute mark.

"The Brit just messaged me," he says. "He wants to know when a fourth bidder was authorized."

Nate jumps in. "Tell him to read his contract. We can add vetted bidders at any time, to any match. You got this, Sebastian."

"Five minutes and counting," Theo says. "Keep those fingers ready."

We all stare at the screen as the bidding stalls out at 9.25 million. It's my bid. The ticker shows sixty seconds. Fifty, forty-two. Twenty. Ten.

Shit.

I enter one last high bid, as high as I can go—an astronomical amount that I don't even have in hand, but that I'll find a way to get if I win this thing. I can't let anyone beat me.

Three. Two.

One last final bid comes in right as the clock hits zero, and before I can see the amount, the web page reloads as the bidding software sorts out the winning bid. Fuck.

My pulse is pounding, my ears ringing, a bead of sweat trickling down my back, and then the page shows the final amount—$10,100,100 and eleven fucking cents—but it's nowhere near as high as the unhinged maximum bid I put in. Not by a whole decimal place.

"Holy shit," I say. "I did it."

The auction is over.

Blair's hand was just purchased for over ten million dollars. By me.

I'm barely aware of Theo and Nate thumping me on the back and jostling my shoulders as I unsteadily rise to my feet.

Turning to Becker, I hold out my hand. "Consider my resignation letter submitted."

But Becker won't shake with me. "I don't accept your resignation. If this woman is what it takes to bring you back from the dead, then I'll handle any fallout. Congratulations."

32

BLAIR

ON BROOKE'S ADVICE, I've been binging the latest hit reality show about trophy wives married to big money husbands and the daily struggle of their privileged, glamorous lives.

I'm sure she suggested it to help distract me from my own drama or maybe to cheer me up, but the more I'm sucked into the plights of these women with their cheating husbands, cosmetic surgeries, backstabbing besties, and public meltdowns, the more I feel like I'm getting a glimpse into my own future. The auction should have ended hours ago, but I have yet to hear from my parents regarding who I've been sold to. Not that I give a damn.

I've been packing up my apartment in fits and starts since yesterday, getting stacks of boxes staged for the moving crew who will deliver them to the storage unit I've rented. I'm not sure how soon I'll be expected to move in with my new fiancé, but I don't want any of my things left behind at the place my parents own. I don't want to have any reason to ever come back here. The big furniture is all theirs, so it's staying where it is. At least that's one less thing to stress about.

I'm sweaty and irritable as I flop onto the couch to take a break and resume the episode I paused an hour ago, a bowl of cereal in front of me. There's not much else to eat since I've already cleaned out the kitchen as best I can. I donated all the boxed and canned goods that were unopened, and the dishes have been donated. I'll probably donate half of what's in my closet, too. Why worry about clothes when my new husband can just buy me a brand-new wardrobe?

The thought only darkens my bleak mood. All of this feels so surreal. I still can't believe I actually agreed to be auctioned off. I've probably made the biggest mistake of my life.

Then again, I can still back out. Refuse to go through with the marriage. It'll mean giving up the Rockets, but at least I have the choice. I just...don't know what the right decision is. Maybe I'm still waiting for my heart to decide.

My plan to seduce my future husband into letting me help run the team felt so righteous in the moment, but now it just feels wrong and seedy. I was just so desperate to make sure I could still have the life that I always dreamed of. Once I left Brooke's and came back to my apartment, the confidence that I was doing the right thing quickly dissipated.

Glancing at my old phone, I see that I still don't have a call or text from my parents to tell me who the lucky groom is. I guess they're in no hurry to let me know the high bidder's identity, since all they cared about was washing their hands of me and dumping me off on some rich guy. It hurts that they can't even grant me the courtesy of a text, though. This is *the rest of my life* we're talking about.

I shovel cereal into my mouth and then turn up the volume on *Trophy Wives*. I can barely focus on the show, though. My mind keeps straying to Sebastian. I imagine him watching the bids come in, his pulse racing as the dollars flow. Was he relieved to know I'd be married off to some stranger while he took his cut of the profits and got on with his life? Fuck him.

The callbox by the front door chimes, and I heave a sigh. The wait is over, apparently. My parents have finally arrived to inform me of my fate. I'm about to find out who is going to be taking over my spot as team owner, who I'm expected to legally bind myself to in holy freaking matrimony.

I reluctantly get up and go over to swipe at the touch-screen in the entryway, granting them access into the building. I don't even bother to look at the camera feed, I just flip my middle finger at the screen and then unlock the door, leaving it cracked open so they can waltz right in when they get here.

Back on the couch, I top off my wine glass—because nothing goes better with cereal than red wine...but really. I'm going to need it to get through this conversation—and then take a big gulp, tucking the glass protectively against my body. Mentally, I brace myself for the impact of seeing my parents after they've betrayed me so unforgivably.

I don't intend to speak to them again, at least not outside times of obligation like the holidays, when I'm sure my new husband will want to see them and make nice. Neither Mom nor Dad has tried to explain why they decided to put me into a marriage auction behind my back or why my father would choose to hand over the team to some random millionaire.

And yes, I understand that Sophie's death has left both of them broken and traumatized, but they could have done literally anything else to cope rather than get rid of me like this. They lost one daughter and then turned around and tossed the other one away. It makes no sense.

I hear a slight rap on my doorframe that I don't respond to, then the sound of footsteps, and the door closing. There is only one set of footsteps—heavier—which must be my father's. Wow. My mom didn't even bother to come see me. Maybe she actually feels guilty. It would serve her right.

Popping up on the couch, I pause the show, look over toward the door, and do a double take when I realize it's not my dad standing there.

It's fucking Sebastian.

Why is he here? How did he even get this address? Unless...oh. I get it. He's here to deliver the news about who won. My parents were both too cowardly to do it, so they sent the guy who arranged the auction in the first place. I should have checked the damn camera before buzzing him in.

Turning back around to face the TV, I stare at the frame frozen in place where I paused the television. Sinley has her bright red lips wide open as she yells, pointing at the suspected baby mama who works at the country club where Sinley's husband has been spending far too much of his free time.

"What are you doing here?" My voice is cold and hard.

Sebastian comes around the couch to stand in front of me. "I won."

For a moment, I'm rendered speechless. He seriously came to gloat about how much money my auction made for him? How dare he.

"Really? The offer you accepted was that great? Was it —never mind. I don't even want to know. You can go."

"Blair—"

I hold up a hand to silence him. "Actually, you know what? Go ahead and tell me. What's the price for getting the team *and* the daughter?"

"Just over ten million," he says softly.

I scoff. That's a joke. The team alone would have sold for at least a hundred times that amount.

"Wow," I say, folding my arms as I glare at him. "I guess I'm quite the bargain. Buying the team outright would have cost a few extra zeroes over that purchase price." A sour smile curves my lips. "Sounds like you didn't win, after all. You got taken, big time. Got to hand it to Ted for getting the package deal at a rock bottom price. I guess it's good to know my future baby daddy is frugal and financially savvy."

Picking up the remote, I point it at the flatscreen but don't hit the play button.

Ted bought the team for ten million dollars. I was just some cheap bonus material. I can't believe my father let his beloved baseball team go for so little, but then again, when he signed with Sebastian's company, he knew he might not get the dollar amount he was expecting. That's how auctions go. Knowing my father, he'll have another pet project to work on soon, but sadly for him, he won't have a daughter to auction off as a free gift when he gets bored of it again.

"You can leave now," I say.

Sebastian moves closer, then kneels in front of me so we're eye to eye.

"I guess you didn't hear me when I said you can leave. Bye-bye, Sebastian."

"It was me," he says.

"I know it was you. We already covered this. *You* set the whole thing up, *you* arranged all the damn meet-and-greets, and *you* accepted the auction bids. I fucking get it. Goodbye."

I gesture for him to go and then drain the rest of my wine glass. But he's still there. Crouched on the floor, watching me. Waiting.

"What are you waiting for?" I ask irritably, even as my heart flutters in response to his nearness. As he looks into my eyes, all the memories we made on the island rush me all at once. I push them back with all my willpower, but my rage is gone now.

All I feel is empty. Hollow and numb.

"I won the auction, Blair," he says, measuring his words. "It was me. I was the highest bidder."

The corners of his mouth twitch with the promise of a smile. But I feel nothing.

"Oh," I say.

Looking away from him, I grab the remote and unpause the episode.

My life is in shambles. Nothing he can say is going to change that.

33

BLAIR

"LET'S GO," Sebastian says.

The television turns off, and I whip a glare in his direction.

"Hey! I was watching that!"

Practically lunging off the couch, I thrust out a hand for the remote, but he doesn't hand it over.

"Come with me," he says, and the growl in his voice sends a shiver down my spine.

Crossing my arms over my chest, I level him with a look that would shrivel the testicles of any other man. Though Sebastian doesn't look intimidated in the slightest.

"Let me guess," I say sourly. "You want to go to the stadium and gaze out over the field from the owner's skybox? Maybe gloat some more over the great deal you made? No thanks."

Despite my salty attitude, I feel a sharp pang of grief in the center of my chest. I don't want Sebastian looking out at the field from the skybox. I've always loved sitting up there with my dad, dreaming of the day when I'd be the team owner, and now I can't stand thinking about the fact that the box is now Sebastian's. It'll never be mine.

Meanwhile, Sebastian probably doesn't even care about the Rockets. He just cares about how much money he's going to make off the team.

"We're not going to the stadium," he says. "But we are going to be late if you don't hurry."

"Then I guess I'd better grab my purse. Wouldn't want to make you late," I say sarcastically.

I throw my bag over my shoulder, slip into my shoes, and glower at him.

I'm well aware that I could stand to shower, untangle my hair from its messy bun, and change into clothes that aren't yoga pants and a T-shirt. But I'm not willing to pretty myself up for him. New fiancé or not, if he's going to force me into this, he's going to get me at my worst.

My stomach drops as it hits me full force. *Fiancé.* For all intents and purposes, that's what Sebastian is now.

Swallowing hard and redirecting my thoughts, I motion him toward the front door. Grabbing my keys, I follow him out of the apartment and lock up behind me. He leads the way down the hall, and I make no attempt to walk beside him. I don't want to get too close. No matter how I feel about him right now, being in his orbit always does something to me that I can't control.

Honestly, the last thing I want is to go anywhere with this master manipulator, but it's obvious he's not going to budge until I agree to leave with him. Clearly, he's used to getting exactly what he wants, and since he basically owns me now, I can't exactly throw him out. I just want to get this little field trip over with so I can come back and finish packing. I wonder how long I'll be staying with Brooke before Sebastian expects me to move in with him. Wherever that is. Maybe I'll be on my own there while he works on the island, selling off other ignorant young women. It might not be so bad.

Especially since spending any amount of time with Sebastian will only serve as a reminder of how he snowed me into believing that he genuinely cared, that we had something real.

Tears burn my eyes, but I blink them away. I preferred it when I felt nothing. Seeing Sebastian has cracked me wide open all over again.

"Where are we going?" I ask coldly as we wait for the elevator.

"It's a surprise," he says.

I roll my eyes. "I definitely don't need any more surprises from you."

"That's fair," he says, sounding almost apologetic. "But you'll find out soon enough."

It's growing dark outside as Sebastian leads me to a waiting black Town Car. The driver opens the door for me, and I duck into the backseat. Sebastian slides in beside me but keeps a respectful distance. I keep my gaze out the window, refusing to look in his direction.

The car pulls into the evening traffic. Sebastian and I don't speak, but after a few minutes, I realize that we're heading in the opposite direction of the stadium. Huh. I debate asking again where we're going—I was so sure it was Rockets stadium—but I stick with giving him the silent treatment.

There are a lot of things I want to talk to him about, but

I'm still too angry and hurt to attempt having any meaningful conversation with him right now.

The car turns onto the ramp for I-495 East, and a full hour passes in cold silence. I text Brooke and look for jobs on my phone, wishing I had brought a book with me. I had no idea we'd be taking a road trip. Finally, we exit the highway and I spy the familiar lights of Republic airport. It's not for commercial flights, just business and recreational travel.

Where would we be taking a private jet to?

"I didn't pack," I say, annoyed. "Are you going to tell me where we're going now?"

Whipping Sebastian a look, I realize that I already know the answer.

"To the island," he says, confirming my suspicions.

But why? He already got everything he wanted from me. There's no reason to drag me back to the resort. Unless he expects me to be his plaything now that we're set to be married.

A spark of heat flares in my low belly, and I feel the heat rushing to my cheeks. Despite my undeniable physical reaction, I'm emotionally repulsed by the thought. If Sebastian really thinks he can force me into his bed, he's in for a rude awakening.

The car pulls onto the tarmac and comes to a stop where a sleek Gulfstream jet waits. It must be Sebastian's. He gets out of the car and waits for me to climb out after him, his hand gently pressing against the small of my back as he guides me toward the jet.

Once I'm onboard, I take a window seat, setting my purse on the seat beside me to send a clear message that I don't want Sebastian next to me. He doesn't comment, just takes the seat across the aisle. A flight attendant asks if I want anything to eat or drink, but I politely decline. Not because I couldn't stand something to eat but because I don't want to accept any of Sebastian's "hospitality."

Thankfully, I fall asleep on the short flight. A bumpy landing jars me from my nap, and soon after that I'm groggily following Sebastian from the plane.

It's nighttime, but the starry sky is beautiful, and we're greeted by the blissfully warm, slightly salty island breeze. It washes over me, drumming up bittersweet memories and emotions from the last time I was here. I know the best thing I can do for myself is forget everything that passed between me and Sebastian, but that's easier said than done.

Another car is waiting to drive us to the resort, and once we're there, Sebastian leads me to his suite of rooms. My heart pounds in my chest as my eyes stray to the king size bed that's visible through the open bedroom door. It's the only bed available, of course.

"What now?" I ask, sinking onto the couch.

Sweeping me with a brief gaze, he says, "Why don't you go down to the boutique and pick up whatever you need? I already arranged unlimited credit for you there. I'll order room service now so dinner will be waiting when you get back."

Without saying thank you, I get up and leave the suites.

I'm absolutely exhausted as I go down to the boutique, but just walking through the familiar luxury of the hotel lightens my mood. So I have unlimited credit, huh? Unfortunately, there's one thing Sebastian's money can't buy—a separate room.

There's a handful of guests in the boutique when I enter. None of them pay me any mind as I browse the shop and pick out toiletries, some basic dresses, a pair of leather sandals, and a few other things to get me through. My heart isn't into the shopping, but then I start looking for pajamas to wear to bed tonight, and a smirk curves my lips.

What I end up with is an ankle-length nightgown with a ruffle around the neckline that would make even a conservative granny happy. I also grab a pair of men's pajamas, complete with long pants and a button-up shirt with long sleeves.

Sebastian might have bought me at an auction, stolen my father's baseball team from me, and then dragged me here to his turf, but I'll be damned if I'm going to let him enjoy sharing a bed with me.

34

SEBASTIAN

AFTER BLAIR LEAVES, I order room service and then pour myself a stiff drink. I take it out to the suite's balcony, hoping to get some air and think. To say things have not gone as planned today would be a gross understatement.

It's not that I expected Blair to be thrilled about getting auctioned off, of course, but I thought she'd be relieved to know that I was the winner. That she wouldn't be forced to marry Ted Polansky or the spoiled Brit or that self-obsessed CEO Mason Sharp. Hell, and I figured she'd be excited to come back to the island and get away from her parents. She seemed to love it here when she was visiting. But now...she looks so angry and miserable that I'm doubting this trip was a good idea at all.

Seeing her so despondent at her apartment earlier killed me. I can't imagine what she's going through. Her entire life has been pulled out from under her, and she's been betrayed by the people closest to her—including me. My obligation to serve my clients, her parents, kept me from revealing the truth to her for far too long, but it's a shitty excuse for keeping her in the dark.

I have no idea how I'm going to get her to trust me again. All I do know is, I'm up for the challenge. I'll do anything to make it up to her. I just wish I knew where to start.

Pulling out my phone, I idly refresh my email inboxes and find a resignation from Daisy, sent a few hours ago. It's brief and formal and doesn't explain why she's quitting. But if I had to guess, it's due to my deplorable behavior. Between kissing her at the Junkanoo and acting like a total ass ever since I cut myself off from Blair, I've been a night-mare of a boss. It's not how I usually conduct myself, and I'm ashamed. Daisy deserves so much better.

I email her back to tell her that I reject her resignation, that she has the potential to accomplish great things at the resort, and that I think she's become an asset to the team. I apologize for acting inappropriately toward her both in and out of the office and promise that it won't happen again. The cherry on top is a raise and a paragraph's worth of sincere compliments, which doesn't require a lot of effort since she's improved so much in the short time she's been training as a concierge. I also approve the special project she pitched last week—a pre-set menu of combination excursions for guests that focus on activities meant to invig-orate the mind, body, and soul; for example, a beach yoga class followed by a gourmet lunch, a trip to a museum, and a massage at the resort's spa afterward.

I've just put my phone in my pocket when I hear a doorbell chime inside the suite. Room service must be here. I let the staff in and direct them to arrange the domed dishes on the dining table, then send them on their way just as Blair returns with armloads of shopping bags.

"Let me help you with those," I say, reaching for the bags.

"No thank you," she says, stalking into the bedroom and closing the door behind her.

I give her a few minutes, and then knock on the door. "Blair?"

"I don't want to talk to you," she says through the door.

"Will you at least eat something, then? The food is still hot. You can take a plate into the bedroom if you don't want to sit out here with me."

"I'm not hungry."

I fight the urge to argue with her, to insist that she eat something. She's had enough of other people making decisions for her and forcing her to bend to their will.

"All right. There's plenty out here if you change your mind," I tell her.

I fix myself a plate of the steak and lobster I ordered, but I barely eat it as I sit on the couch and watch the news. I keep the volume low, in case Blair calls out for anything, but soon enough I realize I can hear the sound of the TV in the bedroom. Judging by the laugh track, she's watching sitcom reruns.

Just after midnight, I knock on the door again. There's no response. I crack the door open and see that she's asleep in the bed, the TV still blaring. When I step into the room and whisper her name, she doesn't move. I'm sure she's exhausted, both physically and emotionally. I do my best to not make a sound as I shower and get ready for bed. When I slide under the sheets beside her, I notice she's wearing an old-fashioned nightgown that covers her from neck to ankle.

Message received. Not that I'd touch her without her consent anyway. But I stretch my arm across the bed toward her, just in case she changes her mind in the middle of the night and wants to grab my hand. I want her to know I'm always here for her.

The next morning, I wake up early, only to find Blair's side of the bed empty and cold. At first, I panic. Has she left? Gone back to New York? What if I never see her again?

But when I pad into the living room, my pulse slows. She's sitting out on the balcony with a cup of coffee in her hand, her back facing me. The breeze ruffles her hair as she looks out at the sun rising over the ocean, rays of pink and golden light spilling across the sky.

"You been up a while?" I ask, sliding open the glass doors.

She shrugs in response, but I can see she's fully dressed and that her hair is damp.

"Breakfast?" I try.

She shakes her head no.

Okay. We're not doing this. I've given her enough space.

I go back into the bedroom and brush my teeth, pull on casual clothes, and slip into my shoes. Then I go back out onto the balcony and position myself between Blair and the sunrise. Ignoring the glare she gives me, I grab her hand and gently but firmly pull her to her feet.

"We're taking a walk. Or I'll carry you if I have to. Your choice."

Fully expecting her to fight me, I'm pleasantly surprised when she only huffs in annoyance but allows me to lead her down to the first floor, out of the hotel, and onto the beach.

I take her all the way to the water's edge, where we walk close enough to the breaking waves that the surf almost touches our feet. The resort's private beach is deserted this time of the morning, but seagulls fly overhead, cawing at us amidst the crashing of the waves nearby. Blair pulls her hand away and tucks it into the pocket of her shorts, but I don't press her. She's as skittish as a wild horse right now, and I need her to let her guard down and listen to what I have to say.

As we get closer to the spot I'm taking her to, I begin to second-guess myself. I want her to know the truth, but my gut is clenching with anxiety. This is something I've never shared with anyone else.

We go a little farther and I stop. I run a hand across my mouth and try to catch her eye, but she won't look at me. Damn, she's not making this easy. Not that she should. I deserve every ounce of her anger and distrust.

Shaking my head, I just say it. "This is where I was standing when I got the phone call...telling me that Rachel died in a helicopter crash. She was on her way here. On her way to me."

The words are bitter on my tongue. A flash of memories from that day comes back to me, and for the first time, I don't push them away. Blair frowns, but she still won't meet my gaze.

"We'd been dating for about three years. I'd only proposed a few months before. We were still in the beginning stages of planning our wedding...hadn't even picked out a date yet. She'd just found out that she was pregnant, nine weeks along. I didn't know yet. She was flying here to surprise me. To let me know I wasn't just going to be a husband, but also a father."

Cold gooseflesh rises on my arms. Blair looks over at me, and I don't drop my eyes, even though I can feel the tears threatening. It's difficult to clear the lump in my throat before I can speak again.

"Do you remember where we met? In the palm grove over there?" I point to the spot, not twenty yards away. "I was thinking about Rachel. Thinking about the day I got that call. Thinking about how lost I was, how I'd never be happy again. And then...you walked right up to me, and I didn't know who you were or where you came from, but the second you laughed about that damn cock salad, I was a goner. It was like...the sun finally came out from behind the clouds. You were everything I didn't know I needed."

She blinks hard, like she's trying not to cry, but I can see the tears in her eyes. Taking her hand again, I lead her into the palm grove. She doesn't pull away this time, even when I tug her down to sit in the sand with me. It feels safe here, amongst the narrow trunks and rustling fronds, the play of light and shadow soothing all around us. I take a steadying breath and then tell her the rest.

"This is the truth, Blair. I didn't know you were a client's daughter when I met you. By the time I found out, it was too late. I was already in too deep. I couldn't stay away from you, even though I knew better. I knew I could lose everything if I kept seeing you—my job, my reputation, my business partners, the whole life I've built. That's why I left the island. I didn't trust myself with you. I didn't trust myself not to interfere with the other matches, not to try to stop the auction."

"You left because you're a coward," she interrupts.

"Fine. Fair. But look, once I got back to New York, I realized that I had nothing without you. And all I kept thinking was that you'd end up with nothing, too, if you were forced to marry a stranger who'd treat you like a trophy and steal your dreams just for the fun of owning an MLB team. I couldn't stand by and let that happen. That's why I did the only thing I could think of. I made myself a bidder."

"So you could buy me yourself," she says, eyes still glittering with a mix of anger and pain.

"So I could buy you your freedom," I correct her. "You don't have to marry me, Blair. That's not why I did this. I want you to be able to choose, instead of being forced into something you never signed up for. I want you to be happy."

She looks out at the water again, nodding slowly. I squeeze her hands in mine.

"And I know I ruined all the memories we made here," I tell her. "But I had to make sure you knew the truth. About everything."

Turning back to me, she searches my gaze and then gives me just a hint of a smile. "Maybe we should make some new memories, then."

35

BLAIR

"Hold out your wrist," I tell Sebastian as I turn away from the souvenir stand. "This one's for you."

He holds out his wrist and smiles as I tie the letter bracelet on for him. It's nearly identical to the one he bought for me that night at Mo's, except his has a coin with the letter 'S' stamped on it.

"Now we both have one," I tell him.

"It's perfect," he says.

What a whirlwind week it's been. We've spent countless hours taking long walks on the beach or through the center of town, discussing our lives and our dreams over sunrises and sunsets, sharing quiet meals together, sometimes just enjoying comfortable silences. Not to mention all the make-up sex.

Our blossoming emotional connection has been just as strong as our physical one, though. It's been liberating to talk to someone at length about Sophie and how much I miss her. Sebastian has told me a lot about his late fiancée Rachel as well. Bonding over our grief has managed to lessen our burdens rather than multiply them. And even though we both know the path won't be easy, we've decided that we both want to give this relationship a real chance, no matter how challenging it might be.

"Let me take a picture." Sebastian holds his wrist out and I place mine next to his so our letter bracelets bump against each other. He takes the picture with his phone camera and then shows it to me.

"Think I should make it my new profile picture?" he jokes.

"Definitely," I tell him.

And then, to my surprise, he goes into his social media app and does just that.

Who is this man? Gone is the bitter, misanthropic recluse. This Sebastian is lighthearted and smiles often, and radiates an entirely new, relaxed energy. Something I need to work on myself, but unfortunately I'm still holding a lot of anger and resentment toward my parents for conspiring to auction me off, even if I understand their motivation on a base level. It was their misguided attempt to keep me safe and secure my future. They just couldn't see that I was perfectly capable of doing those things for myself.

Sebastian links our fingers together as we walk through town. Some of the shop owners wave at us as we pass by, now familiar with our almost-daily evening rounds. I'm wearing a ruffled white sundress and bright floral flip-flops. He's in khaki shorts and a striped polo. It's a nice change from my grandma nightgown and his work suits. Even our outfits have become more relaxed and fun.

"What's bothering you today?" Sebastian asks as we get in line at a food stand. "You seem distracted. And tense."

I shrug. "I guess I'm just...struggling with the fact that my parents sold me out. Literally, obviously. I don't know how I'm supposed to get over it. Maybe I can't."

He pulls me against him and gives me a squeeze. "I get it. You have every right to feel like that."

"The thing is, I don't want to be angry at them forever," I admit. "They're still my parents at the end of the day. Dad was always my biggest cheerleader, and Mom and I just started getting close again."

He pauses to order for us, then pays and hands me the container of cracked conch and fries.

"Your cock, my lady."

I laugh and slap him on the arm playfully. We find a bench that overlooks the beach and settle in to share our snack and watch the waves. Sebastian twists the top off a bottle of cola and hands it to me. I take a long gulp, relishing every drop of the sweet, cold, carbonated refreshment.

"You don't have to force yourself to forgive them if you're not ready," he says, picking up the thread of our earlier exchange. "But if you decide you want to leave the door open, it wouldn't hurt to reach out and start a conversation."

"What about you?" I ask in between bites of fried conch. "You never talk about your parents."

"We're not close," he says with a shrug. "There's no animosity or anything, it's just...different lives, I guess. They were older when they had me, and now they're retired. They travel a lot."

It makes me sad to realize that Sebastian is so disconnected from his family. No wonder he's been so lonely and adrift since he lost Rachel. And no wonder his coworkers are like brothers to him.

"I think deep down," I muse, "my parents wanted to lock me in a box to make sure they'd never have to go through the type of pain they went through with my sister again. They thought marrying me off to a man with money and resources would give me a safe and comfortable life where nothing could touch me. But that's not the life I want. All I ever wanted to do was prove to them that I was good enough, for the team, for them. They never even gave me the chance."

Sebastian steals a fry from the container and holds it out so I can take a bite. "Grieving does awful things to people sometimes. It's a brutal process that resists logic," he says gently.

"Sophie would have hated all this grieving bullshit," I say. "She'd want us to be celebrating her and remembering all the best times we had together. In fact, I think the best way to honor her memory is to do something that would have delighted her...and horrified our parents."

I give him a sly grin and his brows lift.

"Before you ask—it's a no. I am not taking you cliff diving. Or skydiving. Or anything else reckless and endangering."

"I'm not talking about cliff diving. I'm thinking something with much higher stakes. Something more...permanent."

He frowns. "You want to get a tattoo?"

I laugh. "Not quite. This island is a little bit like Vegas, right? I mean, with the no waiting period for marriage licenses and ordained ministers scattered throughout the island just waiting to officiate some tourist's dream wedding at the drop of a hat. Or maybe two people who wanted to elope and have a very private, very intimate ceremony?"

We lock eyes. My heart is pounding, and my stomach is full of butterflies. Did I just propose to Sebastian?

"If we were to do that," he says, "then you would need one of these."

With that, he reaches into his pocket and drops to one knee in front of me. Stunned, I cover my mouth in shock as he pulls out a velvet box and opens it, presenting me with a huge, sparkling, oval-cut diamond solitaire set on a rose gold band.

"Did you seriously just have that waiting in your pocket?" I blurt, still hardly believing this.

"Honestly? I've been carrying it around ever since I kidnapped you from your apartment. It never felt like the right time to bust it out until now, though." He laughs and takes one of my hands in his. "Blair Tisdale, I want you to be mine more than anything in the world. But only if you want it, too. Not out of obligation, not because there are debts to settle or scores to even out. I want us to have an incredible life together, because we're made for each other, and I've never been so happy as I have been since I met you. Will you forgive me for my stupid mistakes and be my wife?"

He's barely done speaking before I'm leaping off the bench and wrapping my arms around his neck, sending us both tumbling onto the sand. We're both laughing as I scramble to get a kiss, whispering yes, yes, yes against his lips. Somehow, the ring ends up on my finger and it's the most beautiful thing, besides Sebastian, that I've ever seen.

An hour later, we're standing at the edges of the palm grove where we first met, exchanging our vows. Daisy was more than excited to find us a minister in a hurry, and she's here too, standing in as our witness, a bottle of champagne tucked under her arm. My phone is in her other hand, with Brooke dabbing her happy tears as she watches the wedding on FaceTime. Before I know it, I'm saying I do to the man of my dreams after being engaged for less than an afternoon. I wouldn't have it any other way.

We don't have wedding bands yet, so we exchange our letter bracelets as a sign of our love and commitment. It's cheesy and perfect. A few minutes later, Sebastian and I are sipping champagne under the palms, fingers interlaced, watching the waves crash.

Sebastian has his arm around me like he's never going to let go. Rising up on my tippy toes, I cup my hand over his ear and whisper something to him.

"I'm ready to give you your wedding present now."

He kisses me full and deep before pulling back. "I think I like the sound of that. What is it?"

My cheeks heat at the thoughts going on in my head. "Something we haven't done yet. A *place* you haven't been yet. I've never done this before, but I'm ready give myself to you...in every way possible."

Taking his hand, I move it to my ass as I look up at him, a smirk tugging at the corner of my mouth.

A flicker of understanding crosses his face, and he exhales hard.

"Jesus. You're killing me, Blair."

"Let's go."

A grimace pulls his lips. "Actually...as much as I'm dying to carry you over the threshold of my suite and consummate this marriage in every conceivable position until the sun comes up tomorrow, there's something I need to show you first. The hard copy is in my office, but here, I have it on my phone, too. This is all drawn up and ready for you to sign."

He pulls up a typewritten document on his phone and hands it over. I'm not sure what I'm looking at initially. It's a contract. But I can't possibly be reading what I think I am.

"Is this for real?" I ask warily.

"It's real. The contract states that I'll be transferring all of the ownership stake in the Rockets that I get from your father straight back over to you. Whenever he's ready to step down, it won't be me taking his place. It will be you, Blair. Just like it always should have been."

Handing him back the phone, I say, "I...I don't understand. Why would you do that?"

"No one is taking your dream away from you. Not your father and sure as hell not me. This is what you've worked for, and I'll support you any way that I can."

I can't breathe. As my eyes fill with tears, I launch myself at him and smother him with kisses, laughing and crying all at the same time. Nobody in the entire world could possibly be happier than I am right now, in this moment.

"This is incredible, Sebastian! Thank you, but God, you should have led with this!"

He laughs with me. "Oh no. I needed to make sure you

wanted to marry me for my own bat and balls, not my base-ball team."

"You know, I might just want the grumpy version of you back if you're going to make such terrible jokes," I mock-scold, burying my face in his shoulder.

"Hey," he whispers into my hair, his hands trailing down my back to firmly cup my ass. "I'd like my wedding present now."

36

BLAIR

We stumble into the suite, shedding clothes as we head toward the bedroom. I can't get my hands on his naked body fast enough. I don't think I ever realized until now how long it takes to get a man undressed.

Not just any man. My husband.

Sebastian Argos is my husband.

My heart is full of joy, but it's a new kind of happiness —deep and solid and unshakable—that I've never experienced before. With Sebastian, I feel loved and supported unconditionally, excited at the prospect of the life that we have ahead of us.

"I can't believe I get to spend the rest of my life with you," I say, full of wonder.

Sebastian's smile is broader and more radiant than ever before. Cupping my face between his hands, he draws me in for a heady kiss that takes my breath away. Excitement pumps through my body and I'm almost giddy with anticipation. I'm more than ready to give myself to him, body and soul, once and forever.

His fingers graze my shoulders, slowly taking down the straps of my white sundress until they fall down my arms. Then he carefully unzips my dress, letting the whole thing flutter to a puddle at my feet. I'm naked underneath, a sweet surprise. Sebastian lets out a groan as his eyes rake over me and he pulls me against him and kisses me again, harder.

A needy moan works from my throat, followed by a gasp as his fingers trace each ridge of my spine and then slide back up again. My nipples harden and a pool of warmth hits between my legs. The friction of his clothes against my bare skin feels amazing, but not as good as when I finally get his shirt all the way off and his hot, naked chest presses into mine.

"Mmm," I hum, raking my nails down his back just hard enough to make him shiver.

He pulls away, dropping his lips to my neck while his hands trail over the curve of my ass, squeezing me deliciously. When I grind my hips into his, I can feel the hard bulge of his arousal. Eagerly, I fumble with his belt buckle, then slide his shorts and boxer-briefs down. He helps me by sliding his shoes off and kicking his shorts away from his ankles.

"God, I love your body," I whisper, admiring the sight of him standing naked before me. He's perfection. I trace the hard lines of his pecs, the ridges of his abs, the slants of muscle over his hips. When I drop to my knees and wrap my hand around his big, thick cock, he lets out a groan.

"Not so fast," he says.

He palms the base of my throat and looks down at me, a hungry grin on his lips. Squeezing lightly, he draws me back up to my feet and kisses me again before scooping me up in his arms and laying me down on the mattress. The French doors are open wide, letting in the sun, the cool breeze, and the sound of the ocean lapping the shore.

Rolling onto my back, I lean my head over the edge of the bed and motion him closer. His eyes flash when he realizes what I'm doing. His cock is rigid, bouncing a little as he stands before me. I reach for him and grip him tight, guiding him into my mouth. The angle is tricky at first, but with a few practiced sucks, he slides all the way in, thrusting to the base of my throat with ease.

"Oh, fuck. Fuck, that's good," he groans.

Steadying himself against the bed, he bends his knees slightly to make the angle easier and glides in and out, smooth and steady, like we've done this a million times. His familiar flavor fills my mouth. God, I've missed how he tastes. Gripping his hips, I suck and pull as he finds a rhythm and drives deep into my throat, faster and faster. His hands slide down my chest and cup my breasts. Pleasure bursts through me as he plays with my nipples, teasing them until I can barely stand the sensations another second. Soon both of us are moaning in time with his thrusts.

Without warning, he pulls away from me, breathing hard as he strokes himself. I sit up on my elbows to watch him climb onto the bed. It's so damn erotic to see his hand pump on his dick, up and down, slowly working circles around the tip. I want him now. No more foreplay. No waiting.

I crawl up the bed until I'm straddling him, and then I

lean down to kiss his mouth, his neck, his chest. "I want you inside me."

He pulls my mouth onto his for another searing kiss and then asks, "Where?"

My cheeks flame. "Everywhere, all of it. I want to give you all of me."

"And I want to take it," he says.

There's so much love in his eyes mixed with desire as he wraps his hands around my hips and then drives up into me with one hard thrust. We quickly find a rhythm, both of us panting, and then his hand reclaims my throat, squeezing just tight enough that I feel completely dominated. I gaze down at him, watching him watch me, both of us swept up in the connection we're sharing.

My eyelids flutter with every pump of his cock, the delicious feel of him pushing me to the edge but never letting me fall.

"I'm going to get you nice and wet, and make you come," he growls. "And then I'm going to flip you over and take that pretty little ass, just like you promised me."

"Yes," I groan.

His dirty talk sends me straight into an orgasm. My cunt clamps around his cock and pulses of white-hot pleasure burst through me. A satisfied grunt works from his throat and then he's turning me over just like he promised.

Nerves wash over me as he leans over and grabs some lube from the nightstand drawer. He squirts some into his palm and then settles himself between my thighs again.

I look over my shoulder at him, a shy smile on my lips. "Be gentle."

"Always. Now get on your hands and knees for me. I'm going to get you ready."

I do as he asks, and then he brings his lubed fingertips to my tight hole, sliding them up and down, preparing me to receive him. I let out a sigh and he grabs the lube again, adding more slickness until I'm practically dripping. Behind me, I can hear him stroking himself, grunting softly. The sound of his desire sends a hot pulse of need through me. I'm so focused on how turned on I am in the moment that I'm startled when the tip of his cock nudges between my ass cheeks. I suck in a breath, hold it.

"You have to breathe, Blair. Don't hold your breath. Just try to relax. I'll go easy, I promise."

I exhale, shivering as the tip slides into me just a little. My entire body tenses at first but then I take another deep breath and allow myself to stop clenching. He slides in a little deeper when I do.

"Oh, that's good," I murmur. "Just stay there for a second."

Sebastian waits for me, and then I push myself back into him just a little bit more, tensing up again as I do.

"More," I say, and he pushes deeper until he's inside a little more, and a little more.

I'm panting now, aching for more but still intimidated by his size, stuffed with the deepest pressure I've ever experienced. My brain isn't sure how to process it. But his fingers come around to work my clit, drawing my attention there, and when I start to moan, he begins a slow, careful thrust into my ass, moving in shallow pulses, and all the sensations in my pussy are amplified by a million.

"Oh my God," I whisper.

I push back against him as he pushes into me, the glide of his cock growing smoother. I can feel myself relaxing into it, allowing his dick to stroke longer and deeper. His featherlight touch on my clit gets more aggressive, giving me a jolt of pleasure that shoots through me every time I swing my hips forward. The intensity is unbearable, a mix of sweetness and pain, agony and ecstasy, lifting me higher and higher. I'm completely consumed.

I moan his name over and over again as I crest the wave, my words devolving to harsh, animal moans when I come hard, shattering, my voice deafening my own ears. Sebastian moves faster and his hand slides down to my pussy, his fingers thrusting into me in time with his pumping into my ass.

It's too much, but I love it and I want more, more. He pumps harder, harder, filling me completely, and suddenly I'm coming again, clamping around his fingers, all my muscles going limp as I bury my face in a pillow. His urgent sounds match his pace, and then he explodes deep inside me. He withdraws slowly and then rolls onto his back beside me, gently draping an arm over my back.

"I feel like I'm going to pass out," he utters.

"Is that a bad thing?" I tease, turning onto my side so I can look at him.

"Are you kidding? That was fucking incredible. You are incredible."

I can only smile as he pulls me close for a kiss.

"Happy honeymoon," I tell him.

We lie there in silence for a while, simply enjoying our closeness. He traces his fingertips down my shoulder, over the curve of my waist, my clavicle, my lips.

"Have you given any thought to what you might want to do now? I mean, while your dad is winding things down and getting ready to hand off the team?"

It's a valid question but takes me a little by surprise. The truth is, I have thought about it. But my idea is still in the planning stages, hardly more than a dream. But who better to share my dreams with than my new husband?

"Actually, I was thinking of something. I don't want to shock my dad with our agreement about the team just yet, but I would like to show him that I'm more ambitious and a lot more capable than he thinks. He's never given me much of a chance to prove myself, not even after I graduated with honors at the top of my class."

"So what are you thinking?" Sebastian asks.

Looking up at him, I take a breath and then close my eyes and blurt it out all at once. "I'd like to start a charitable foundation for runaways. And I'd like to call it Sophie & Rachel's Treehouse. If you're comfortable with that. I just… I want to honor them, and I want to help young people in impossible situations, and I feel like that's something they both would have loved. Don't you?"

I open my eyes, but I can't read his expression.

He shakes his head, and I start to panic, thinking I've crossed a line.

"Blair, that…that sounds like something Rachel would have loved to be a part of. And your sister, too, from what you've told me. It's a beautiful idea. A brilliant idea."

"Really?"

"Yes, really. Has anyone ever told you how wonderful you are?"

He kisses me and it turns into much more than a quick peck.

"No, why don't you tell me again?"

"You're wonderful."

"I didn't hear you. What was that?"

He chuckles against my lips. "I love you, wife. Did you hear that?"

"Oh, loud and clear. I love you, too."

Grinning, I grab the covers and pull them over our heads as I crawl on top of the man I love and kiss him with everything I have.

I believe we can come up with a few ideas for whiling away the next few hours, and I'm not letting him out of this bed until we enjoy each other again.

And again.

Forever.

EPILOGUE

BLAIR

"Psst. See that woman over there, with the red and blue ribbons in her hair?" I whisper to Sebastian. "She's one of our interns from Columbia. And the guy next to her? He's another one of our interns. I knew there was something going on between them. Aw. Aren't they adorable?"

Sebastian gestures toward them to confirm that they're the couple I'm talking about, but I grab his wrist. "Gah! Don't point!"

"Nobody saw."

"But they could have! Let the kids enjoy their privacy."

He laughs. "There's nothing private about going to a baseball game with forty thousand other fans in the stadium."

"Still! I don't want to burst their romantic little bubble."

We watch as Kaya throws popcorn at Ben and he tries to catch the kernels in his mouth.

"Okay. They are kind of cute," Sebastian admits.

"See? I think we need to revisit the company rule about

not fraternizing with colleagues. Peer romances should be acceptable, just not anything between superiors and subordinates. I'll go over the language when I get back to the office and type up an amendment for you to sign off on."

He pulls me against him and kisses the top of my head. "That's my wife, the hopeless romantic."

"I wouldn't say that," I counter. "I just enjoy a bit of juicy gossip from time to time."

"Is that so?"

Before I can respond, the crack of the bat against the ball cuts through the air and the stadium erupts in a roar. I raise my fist and let out a whoop of excitement along with the crowd. Sebastian and I could have sat in the owner's skybox, but it's more fun to watch the game out here in the stands where we can really experience the energy of all the fans. I look longingly at Sebastian's beer, the outside of the plastic cup dripping beads of condensation under the hot sun.

"Finish it," he says, passing it to me and starting to stand. "I'll go get us another round."

"We can share it," I tell him, hooking a finger through his belt loop and tugging him back down to his seat. "Let's get through this inning first."

I take a gulp, let out an audible "Ahhh," and then pass the cup back to Sebastian. Then I scan the immediate crowd. We're up top where all the elite spectators sit, and there's always plenty of good people-watching to be had. But then my jaw drops and I smack Sebastian on the arm again.

"Look, there's Mr. Barclay, a few rows ahead!" I hiss. "I don't think I've ever seen him at a game before."

Sebastian follows my gaze with zero subtlety, but Mr. Barclay isn't looking our way. In fact, he looks uncomfortable and like he doesn't want to be here. I wonder why he came. Probably to grease the wheels of some investor clients, if I had to guess.

Leaning closer to my husband, I whisper, "I heard his business is in hot water right now. His family are clients of the matchmaking agency, right? Does that affect your bottom line?"

Sebastian quickly kisses me to stop that line of conversation, probably so no one overhears, and I sink into the kiss, wanting more. I always want more. His hand cups my cheek, then slides around to the back of my head where he gathers a fistful of hair. A soft moan escapes me.

"Let's focus on more important topics," Sebastian says in between kisses.

"Like what?"

"Like whether you'd like to give me a private tour of the owner's box?" He lowers his voice even more. "And whether or not you're wearing panties."

"Are those two things even related?" I tease, already out of my seat.

"God, I hope so," he says.

"We'd better go find out, then." I grab his hand and tug him to his feet, a grin playing at my lips. "I have a feeling the Rockets aren't the only ones who'll be hitting a home run this inning."

Coming up next in the Agency Series, Cruel Offer.

She was a gift I didn't want.
But now I want to keep her forever.

If you haven't met my Bellanti Brothers and need something to tide you over while you wait for the next standalone book in the Agency Series, dive into Dante Bellanti's story...

Broken Bride: The Complete Series

I was sold to him to settle a debt... but Dante Bellanti never settles.

My father was always a gambling man.
Unfortunately, he never could pick winners.
When the wolves closed in, he chose himself, like always.

He traded his freedom... for mine.

He forced me to marry.
Now Dante Bellanti owns my body.
I'm just another possession for a man who already has too much.
So I won't let him have my heart.

But you know what they say about gambling.

The house always wins.

And I'm at the mercy of the Bellantis...

All three books of the Broken Bride Series in one bundle.

PAIGE PRESS

Paige Press isn't just Laurelin Paige anymore...

Laurelin Paige has expanded her publishing company to bring readers even more hot romances.

Sign up for our newsletter to get the latest news about our releases and receive a free book from one of our amazing authors:

Laurelin Paige
Stella Gray
CD Reiss
Jenna Scott
Raven Jayne
JD Hawkins
Poppy Dunne
Lia Hunt
Sadie Black

ALSO BY STELLA GRAY

The Zoric Series

Arranged Series

The Deal

The Secret

The Choice

The Arranged Series: Books 1-3

Convenience Series

The Sham

The Contract

The Ruin

The Convenience Series: Books 1-3

Charade Series

The Lie

The Act

The Truth

The Charade Series: Books 1-3

The Bellanti Brothers

Unwilling Bride: A Bellanti Brothers Novella

Dante - Broken Series

Broken Bride

Broken Vow

Broken Trust

Broken Bride: The Complete Series

Marco - Forbidden Series

Forbidden Bride

Forbidden War

Forbidden Love

Forbidden Bride: The Complete Series

Armani - Captive Series

Captive Bride

Captive Rival

Captive Heart

Captive Bride: The Complete Series

The Agency Series

Secret Offer:

A Standalone Forbidden Romance

Cruel Offer:

A Standalone Fake Relationship Romance

(Coming April 2024)

ABOUT THE AUTHOR

Stella Gray has always had her head in the clouds and has been writing since she was in high school. A contemporary romance author, she loves dark romances with morally gray men. When she's not writing, she's either in the kitchen testing out a new baking recipe or spending time in the great outdoors.

Made in the USA
Las Vegas, NV
14 April 2024

88664881R00229